BOUNDARY BORN

By Melissa F. Olson

Boundary Magic series

Boundary Crossed
Boundary Lines

Scarlett Bernard novels

Dead Spots
Trail of Dead
Hunter's Trail

Short Fiction

Sell-By Date: An Old World Short Story
Bloodsick: An Old World Tale
Malediction: An Old World Story

Also by Melissa

The Big Keep: a Lena Dane Mystery
Nightshades

BOUNDARY BORN

BOUNDARY MAGIC, BOOK 3

MELISSA F. OLSON

This is a work of fiction. Names, characters, organizations, places, events, and incidents are either products of the author's imagination or are used fictitiously.

Text copyright © 2016 Melissa F. Olson
All rights reserved.

No part of this book may be reproduced, or stored in a retrieval system, or transmitted in any form or by any means, electronic, mechanical, photocopying, recording, or otherwise, without express written permission of the publisher.

Published by 47North, Seattle

www.apub.com

Amazon, the Amazon logo, and 47North are trademarks of Amazon.com, Inc., or its affiliates.

ISBN-13: 9781503936164
ISBN-10: 1503936163

Cover design by Jason Blackburn

Printed in the United States of America

The story you're about to read was partially inspired by something my dad would say when I was growing up, and I left home overnight: "Remember who you are, and where you came from."
This book's for you, Dad. I never forgot.

Chapter 1

"Come on, Lily," I urged. "You can hit me harder than that."

My best friend glowered at me, the light boxing gloves looking absurdly large on her slim wrists, but she tried again, poking her right fist into the palm I held up for her. When I worked with her brother Simon, I put on defensive gloves to protect my wrists, but it wasn't really necessary with Lily. She may have been a fairly powerful witch, but her physical interests leaned toward yoga and Pilates, not violence.

Violence was more my thing.

We were in the basement of my little cabin just outside Boulder, Colorado, which I'd turned into a reasonably sophisticated home gym. It was after nine on a Tuesday in May, but Lily was a night owl and I was pretty much nocturnal these days. That's what happens when your boyfriend and your boss are both vampires.

"That was an okay jab," I said, trying to sound encouraging. "But if you really want to hurt someone, you've got to get your shoulder behind it." I turned around so I was lined up next to her, demonstrating with my own right arm. "See how I'm putting the whole weight of my body behind the punch?"

I resumed my previous position, and she made another flailing attempt at my hands. "Better," I lied. "Why don't you go work on the heavy bag for a while?"

Lily trudged to the corner and began smacking the heavy bag I'd attached to the exposed rafter, looking tired and frustrated but determined. Behind her, my eye caught a flicker of smoky light, but I forced myself to look away. Ghosts fade over time, and this one was so ancient it was no more than a little flare of death magic. I was actually lucky that this was the only part of my house that seemed to be haunted.

Or at least that's what I kept telling myself.

While Lily beat ineffectively on the heavy bag, I picked up a jump rope from a weight bench and began skipping rope, calling out occasional words of encouragement that had little effect on Lily's form. Lily had an inherent grace thanks to childhood ballet and lots of yoga, but that grace didn't seem to translate to coordination. I tried not to wince as I watched her throw weak punch after weak punch.

The previous fall, Lily's life had been threatened—by her own older sister, of all people—and she'd had to use combat magic to escape. Lily had done everything right, but the whole experience of using powerful apex magic to hurt someone had really scared her. Moreover, Morgan had gotten into her little sister's head. Her taunts about Lily's flightiness and naiveté to the real world had created wormy little holes in my friend's self-confidence.

I hadn't understood how much it was bothering her until a few weeks after Morgan's banishment, when Lily turned up on my doorstep and begged me for lessons in physical defense: shooting, fighting, the whole deal. Teaching Lily seemed only fair—she and her brother had been giving me magic lessons since I'd first found out I was a witch back in September.

Despite five months of training, Lily hadn't made much progress, but then, I knew that this wasn't really about being able to handle herself. It was about *feeling* like she could handle herself.

After a few minutes, Lily paused, panting, and turned to glare at me. "I'm sweating like Ted Striker, and you're not even breathing hard," she grumbled.

I managed to laugh without letting it break my rhythm. I mostly preferred older movies, while Lily watched all the new stuff, but we'd found common ground in our love of *Airplane!*

I put down the jump rope, taking pity on her. "Speaking of movies, how about we stretch and then go upstairs?" I suggested. "I got more of that popcorn you like." Lily and Simon's magic lessons had petered out recently—there was only so much they could teach me, a boundary witch—so the siblings had taken it upon themselves to start teaching me the *history* of magic instead. For Simon, this involved lectures and the occasional assigned reading. Whenever it looked like my attention was wandering, he would bark at me to use my magic, trying to improve my reflexes.

For Lily, though, it meant watching her favorite movies that contained witchcraft so she could critique them for accuracy. I strongly suspected the whole thing was a ploy to eat popcorn and trash movie witches.

Lily's face broke out in a broad grin. "I really think you're gonna like tonight's pick," she said, unstrapping her gloves.

"As long as it's not fucking *Suspiria* again," I warned, not really kidding.

"Hey, it was just a little gore," Lily protested. She hesitated for a moment, rubbing her hands where the tape had been. "Any word from John?"

"No."

A month ago, I'd finally gotten up the nerve to tell my brother-in-law about the Old World.

It was probably the hardest conversation of my life. I'd had to explain that his only daughter was a null, a coveted asset in the supernatural world, which would put her in danger for more or less her entire life. Nulls negate all the supernatural power in a given area, which makes them terribly useful to vampires, witches, and werewolves, for a number of different reasons that range from innocent to atrocious. Theoretically, Charlie would now be protected until adulthood, thanks to my deal with the state's cardinal vampire, Maven, but there would always be some risk. She would always be vulnerable.

John had not taken this news well. In fact, when I finally convinced him that I wasn't schizophrenic, he had pretty much thrown me out of his house. Since then, he hadn't returned any of my calls or texts, and he'd stopped going out with his work friends on Fridays, which was my usual night to babysit. When we were in the same room at a family function he treated me with polite cordiality, but that was it.

I wasn't used to going more than a few days without serious Charlie time, so the last month had been hard.

"He decided to take Charlie and my parents on a last-minute trip to Disney World for Charlie's birthday," I reported. "They left yesterday morning."

"What's Clara doing while they're out of town?" Lily said curiously. Clara was Charlie's vampire bodyguard.

"Oh, she went along. Maven flew a coffin down to Orlando and had a human contact pick her up," I reported. "She's mostly guarding a closed hotel room door, but she checks in with me every night so I know Charlie's okay."

Lily searched my face, sensing my trepidation. "When are they coming back?"

"I don't know."

Lily reached out and gave my shoulder a quick squeeze. She knew me well enough to know that part of me hoped John would never come back to Boulder. He could just . . . I don't know, buy a condo in Orlando and stay there forever. Charlie would be out of reach for Maven and all the other Old World creatures who might want a piece of Charlie.

It was a nice fantasy, but even if John never came back to Boulder, Charlie would still be a null. Eventually, some other supernatural creature would figure out what she could do for them, and I wouldn't be there to protect her.

"You look tired, Lex," Lily ventured. "Have you—"

She was interrupted by a loud, hollow *thunk* from the other side of the basement. Lily paused, giving me a questioning look. "Was that the boiler or something?"

"No . . ." I squinted at the dim light across the room. There were only a couple of bare lightbulbs down here, and they were all over by the gym equipment. It hadn't really sounded like a boiler, more like someone gently tossing a baseball into the window well farthest from us. But the nearest neighbors were half a mile away.

I shrugged it off, figuring a stray rock or clump of dirt had been knocked down, bumping into the glass. Or maybe it was starting to hail. "Anyway, I'm fine," I started, but then the *thunk* sounded again. And again, louder this time. Lily and I had just enough time to exchange a concerned glance before we heard the glass shatter inward and a small, dark blur streaked into the basement, across the concrete floor. Right at us.

I sprinted three steps to a nearby chair and leaped onto it, managing to keep my balance after a wobble. "Lily!" I yelped, but my friend had already jumped onto the weight bench, looking rather comically like a fifties housewife hiding from a mouse. Except this intruder was a lot bigger than a mouse.

"Where did it go?" she called. We were both turning now, scanning the room, but the creature was nearly the same color as the concrete floor. There was a moment of stillness, and then a furious chittering sounded from right beneath Lily's weight bench. She froze. "What is it?" she hissed. "A squirrel?"

"Too big." I squinted, trying to make out the furry shape. It was the size of a small dog, but the body wasn't right. It shifted, letting out a sort of furious, strangled hiss, and for just a second I could make out its full silhouette. "Fox, I think. Gray fox." I tried to remember my aunt Violet's many nature-walk lectures. There was something unique about gray foxes, something important . . .

"They can climb!" I shouted to Lily. But the warning came too late—the fox was already scrabbling up the metal crossbars of the weight bench where Lily still stood. "Lily, run!"

She looked around for a second, panicked, and then reached *up*, stretching on her tiptoes to get both hands around the rafter beams. Kicking her legs, she swung back and forth for a moment. The fox had reached the top of the bench and began swiping furiously at her ankles, letting out a high-pitched, rhythmic bark. In the full light of the gym area, I could see its wild, frantic eyes—and the line of white foam clinging to its lips. *Rabies*, I thought, fear wrenching my stomach sideways. I looked around, but all my weapons were locked away upstairs.

Lily had gotten her legs up and managed to jam her feet and ankles into the tiny space between the rafter beam and the ceiling. The fox snarled—my God, could foxes even make that sound?—and went up on its hind legs, clawing at the air where Lily had been. It turned in a frenzied circle, and then its feverish eyes fixed on me. It hissed, spattering the weight bench with foamy saliva. Shit. I needed a better, higher place to go, but there was only a small metal stand for kettlebells, the weight bench, the chair, and a treadmill, none of which seemed all that great for defense against a rabid animal. I could run for the steps, but the fox would be able to climb those just as well as I could, and if it got through the door, it could infect all my rescue animals.

"What's happening?" Lily shouted, unable to see. Her voice was strained. She looked like she was crouched on all fours, but upside down. Only her ankles were actually being secured by the rafters, which meant she was holding the rest of her body up there. I probably would have fallen by now. Maybe I had underestimated those yoga muscles.

I looked back down, but the fox had vanished. "It's—" I started to say, but I was interrupted by a crash. The fox had managed to tip over the weight bench, which clanged down on the concrete, sending hand weights and water bottles skittering across the floor. My dogs had started barking in a frantic chorus on the other side of the basement door, and were scratching at the knob hard enough for me to shoot a worried look at the steps.

"*Lex!*" Lily wailed, now dangling over nothing but a concrete floor. The fox was nowhere in sight.

"Quiet, please," I ordered. I listened, turning my head back and forth for the sound of movement. There was a bit of rustling, but it wasn't loud enough for me to pinpoint. "Can you throw something at it?" I called out to Lily, referring to the combat magic she'd used against Morgan.

"Not if I can't see it. And not upside down." She made a small grunt of exhaustion in the back of her throat, and I realized she wasn't going to be hanging on much longer anyway. The fall wasn't high enough to hurt her, but if she dropped down, there'd be nothing protecting her from this thing. If I could just *see* it—

I heard a *tremendous* hiss that seemed to come from an inch behind my head. Acting on pure reflex, I dropped and rolled sideways as fast as I could, just as the fox sprang at me. Its body, rigid with rage and madness, went sailing over me like we were playing a demented game of leapfrog, its legs scrabbling for purchase. Even out of the corner of my eye I could see the flash of its exposed teeth as it snarled.

I popped up and raced across the basement, away from the stairs, heading straight for the washing machine. I jumped on top of it, hearing the small thud of the fox hitting the side of the machine below me, but not as far below me as I would have liked. It could *jump.*

It pulled back and leaped again, tiny claws scrabbling impotently. It came close, but I was pretty sure it couldn't jump high enough to get on top of the machine. It hissed and barked with frustration, and a wave of stench rolled over me: the smell of old death. I almost gagged. My dogs had rolled around in dead animals, and I'd smelled repugnant things in Iraq, but this was different. What the hell had this thing been eating?

I looked around for something heavy that I could use to stun or kill it, but I was distracted by the screeching of its claws on the washing machine and the mad, high-pitched noise exploding out of its throat, drowning out the muted barking from upstairs. The fox had to realize I was out of reach, but it was like it couldn't stop itself from pursuing me anyway. I was awed by the intensity of its desire to kill me.

Then the fox suddenly paused, going still, and as I looked at it one word popped into my brain: *unnatural*. Then its head turned away and I realized what the fox was looking at. Only ten feet behind it, Lily had dropped to the ground.

"Lily, run!" I cried, and my friend took a few halting steps toward the stairs. Her legs must have been numb, though, because she stumbled over one of the water bottles and went sprawling onto the floor.

With unbelievable speed, the fox shot toward Lily.

Chapter 2

I didn't think; I just jumped down and banged on the side of the washing machine. "Here, here!" I yelled, and the fox paused for a moment, looking over its shoulder at me in confusion. Then it looked back at Lily, who was struggling to stand on numb feet. I could practically see the fox reach the obvious conclusion: of the two of us, she was the easier target.

I grabbed the nearest thing at hand—a small bottle of stain remover—and hurled it at the fox, managing to clip its left back leg. It turned its head for long enough to send me a perfunctory hiss, but immediately turned to creep toward Lily. She limped backward, but not fast enough. I started toward them, and like a dog being chased by its owner, the fox sped up.

When it was less than a foot from Lily, I panicked, and my instincts took over completely. I dropped to my knees and reached for my magic.

It took less than half a second—*thank you, Simon*—to drop into my boundary mindset, the trancelike state that lets me see the spark of living creatures. When I opened my eyes, it was like staring at the world through thermal-imaging goggles. Lily's life force was brightest—a huge, humanoid blue glow. The little fox's essence was much, much smaller, the size of a matchbox, and it should have been blue as well, but there was something wrong with it. The color was swirling with black, which I'd never seen before. *What the hell?*

No time. I reached out a hand and visualized the tattoos on my wrist sprouting into long, snaking extensions of my fingers. My phantom fingers encircled the fox, tightening around its essence. Then, as my real fingers curled back toward my body, the invisible fingers pulled the life spark of the fox away, separating it from its physical body.

I'd done this with animals before, but for a moment the fox seemed almost to resist me, which was a first. I pulled harder, and the spark of swirling light came away in my fingers, immediately turning a sickly, yellowish-brown color, the color of death.

But it was still swirling with black.

I could absorb death magic into myself for a power boost, but I instinctively knew I didn't want that blackness anywhere near me. Gritting my teeth with concentration, I allowed the vaporous color to dissolve through my ghostly fingers until it was gone. Then I blinked away the mindset and climbed to my feet.

Well, that was the idea, anyway. I'd forgotten how much playing with death essences affects me. As I tried to stand, the surge of power hit me, and I stumbled, pausing to savor the dark sweetness of boundary magic. *Mine, mine, mine* pumped my thoughts, and I felt a great burst of exhilaration and greed. *More.* I wanted to do it again, but this time—

"Lex?" Lily's voice was tentative, a little weak, almost . . . afraid. Of me?

I shook my head violently, clearing the fog of death magic from my mind. When I looked at Lily, she was standing near the fox's corpse, staring at me with concern and, yes, a little fear. My insides twisted with guilt. "Sorry," I mumbled. "Haven't done that in a while. Caught me off-guard."

"It's okay." Lily's eyes dropped to the small body at her feet. "You drained him?"

I nodded. Lily hadn't actually seen me do this before, but she knew about the time I'd accidentally sucked the life out of all the fish in a small pond during a magic lesson with Simon. "Well, good," she said shakily. "I'm glad it still worked with the tattoos."

Right. Lily had created the griffin tattoos on my forearms as a way to help me focus my magic. "I didn't even consider that it might not," I admitted. "I just sort of reached."

She nodded. "We gotta tell Simon the training's paying off." She squatted down to get a closer look at the fox, rubbing her ankles with one hand. "Oof. I don't know what that position would be called—"

"Upside-downward facing dog?" I suggested.

She barked out a laugh. "Yes. Change approved. Anyway, I'm gonna feel it tomorrow." She leaned forward, peering at the fox's corpse, until her closeness started to make me nervous.

"Don't touch it, Lil."

"I won't. We're thinking rabies, right? Should we, like, call someone? Animal control?"

It was such a normal, nonmagical question that it took me a moment to process it. Something had to have infected the fox, and if there were animals running around with rabies, informing animal control would be the right thing to do. Then again . . . "Do you want to explain how we killed it?"

"Uh, good point. I guess we better call Simon, anyway."

I checked my watch. Nine-thirty. "He'll probably be, um . . . working."

Lily snorted and went to the steps to get her phone out of her bag.

Leaving the fox corpse where it was, I began straightening the furniture while Lily talked to her brother. When he wasn't doing stuff for the witch clan, Simon worked as an evolutionary biologist at the university. This wouldn't be the first time I'd called on him for biology help. Nearly six months earlier, an ancient snakelike creature called the Unktehila (or the sandworm, if we're being informal) started eating people in Boulder, and Simon was a huge part of figuring out what it was and how to kill it. Afterward, he had asked my boss Maven if he could study the remains as part of his ongoing research into Old World biology.

Maven had done him one better. She'd set him up with a small basement apartment in one of the buildings she owned, and refitted it into a sort of makeshift laboratory, although Simon actually lived there as well. I hadn't spent much time at the basement lab, but last I'd checked it was a pretty depressing place: concrete floors, blank white walls, no TV or music to distract from the hum of equipment. Plus many chunks of dead snake monster. Lily referred to it as the Basement of Dr. Moreau.

After a short exchange, Lily stuffed the phone in her pocket and reported, "He said it sounds like an average case of rabies, and you shouldn't touch the saliva without gloves."

I blinked. "That's it? He doesn't want to come look at it?"

She rolled her eyes. "He also asked me to remind you that he is not a veterinary pathologist and he hasn't dissected anything but the sandworm and its pellets since grad school."

"So he was testy."

She held up her fingers with the thumb and index half an inch apart. "Little bit."

I frowned, but this wasn't the time to discuss Simon's ongoing withdrawal from the world. "Should we bury it?" Lily asked me, looking at the fox's corpse again.

"I have a better idea. It's just . . . grosser." I went to a shelf above the washing machine and grabbed a couple of rags, positioning them over my hands like makeshift oven mitts. Moving toward the fox, I stepped over it until I had one foot on either side of its head. Then I bent down, held the head carefully with the rags, and tilted it backward. "Plug your ears, Lily," I advised. She clapped her hands over her ears, and I twisted until the fox's neck snapped with a sickening crunch.

Even though her ears were covered, Lily jumped, cursing. "*Why?*"

I straightened, tossing the rags on top of the body and wiping my hands on my gym shorts. It wouldn't exactly cleanse me of dead fox germs, but it was a psychological thing. "Now I can call my cousin, the vet, and he can test it for rabies," I explained. "If he asks, it ran into the washer and its neck snapped."

"Oh. Good call."

"Of course," I said with exaggerated regret, "this probably means we'll have to put off the movie." I shook my head. "So sad."

She tossed a water bottle at my face, but I caught it easily. As I unscrewed the top and took a gulp, I headed for my own phone, which I'd left on the bottom step. I called Jake, who was characteristically cool about the idea of getting a rabies-infected fox corpse delivered to his house at ten o'clock on a weeknight. I could have left it until the next morning, but I just didn't trust my rescue animals to stay away from the body.

And, okay, I just wanted to be rid of the thing.

I hung up with Jake, but before I could put the phone back down, it buzzed in my hand. New text. I frowned down at the screen.

"Is it your undead boyfriend?" Lily said brightly. She made a fake kissy sound. "Tell him I said hi."

I made a face at her. Sometimes I missed the days when Lily and Quinn couldn't stand each other. "No, it's from Maven," I replied. "She wants me to come in right away." Maven kept her communications brief and friendly, but there was no mistaking her text for anything but a command. I looked at the dead fox, then at my friend. "So, Lily," I began. "I need a favor."

She wrinkled her nose at me. "Ewww, really?"

I found an old cardboard box for Lily, who held it as far away from her body as she could. "Rabid fox in a box," she grumbled. "I swear this is the beginning of a twisted Dr. Seuss book."

While she took the fox-box out to her car to keep it away from my animals, I ran upstairs to throw on jeans and a T-shirt. I also strapped a shredder stake to my arm with two doubled-up athletic headbands. Months ago, I'd nearly died for lack of a shredder. I no longer left the house without one. This meant that I wore long sleeves all the time, but that was fine by me. When summer came, it might be a different story, though.

Lily had returned and was waiting for me at the front door, twirling her keys around one finger. Despite her earlier complaints, she seemed pleased to be doing something useful, which probably had a lot to do with her inability to master the art of punching people.

I was just flicking off the lights to leave when I realized my skin was tingling. I paused and held up my arm, examining one of my tattoos. Was it pulsing? Or was something wrong with my eyes? "Lil . . ."

I felt, rather than saw, her turn and look me over. "You killed the fox," she said, understanding. "You have to ground the magic, Lex."

Oh. Right. Witches are made to channel, not possess. If I didn't expel the death magic, I could end up "magic-drunk," which was not nearly as fun as it sounded. Unfortunately, I only knew two trades witch spells, and one of them involved throwing people backward. "Hang on." Stumbling a little, I made it back down the basement stairs and planted my palms flat on the floor so the tips of my tattoos touched the cold concrete. I mumbled the spell Simon had taught me for cleaning a space.

"Good," Lily said approvingly, as the grime, fur, and fox saliva vanished from the floor. "The tattoos help with your control."

"Yeah, thanks to you."

I gave Lily Jake's address, waved goodbye, and climbed into my own ten-year-old Outback, steeling myself for a nighttime drive into Boulder. Since I'd unblocked my ability to see ghosts, being behind the wheel after dark had gotten . . . complicated. A lot of people die in car accidents each year, and their deaths are so sudden and traumatic that they often leave behind remnants, spiritual snapshots of the dead. Driving *through* translucent figures of people was unnerving as hell, so these days I rarely drove anywhere after dark unless my job or my family required it. I had developed a few routes that bypassed as many ghosts as possible for when I needed to go somewhere alone at night, but I still had to mentally brace myself every time. *They're not real people,* I would tell myself. *They're just psychic echoes.*

It sort of helped.

I tried to distract myself by figuring out why Maven had called me in on a Tuesday. I had fallen into the habit of dropping in at Magic Beans, Maven's twenty-four-hour coffee shop, on Sunday and Thursday nights to see if she had any daytime errands for me. A summons tonight meant some sort of Old World emergency, which was bad.

On the other hand, if there *was* a problem, Quinn would be there—we did this job together—and I was looking forward to seeing him. In theory, we'd been dating for six months now, but the first few months of that had been spent dealing with the aftermath of the Unktehila's rampage. It hadn't just killed people in Boulder; it had also attacked a spa in Indian Springs, leaving behind a lot of evidence and plenty of witnesses. Before confronting the creature, we'd arranged for a vampire to wait at the main exit of the spa to catch the people who were stampeding out of the building. She had used vampire mind control—"pressing minds"—to convince them nothing had happened. But a few people slipped the net, including a very sweet and unfortunately photogenic young mother and her toddler, whom the Unktehila had briefly cornered. The young woman was already on the nightly news screaming "giant snake monster" while the rest of us were still off dealing with the bloodshed.

I had to admire the way Maven had handled the whole thing. The official story she'd cooked up was great: some of the natural chemicals used in the spa went bad and were circulated in the air, causing temporary (but harmless) hallucinogenic effects. Several spa clients panicked and stampeded, causing a great deal of damage to the building's interior.

Maven also sent vampires to work their magic on the authorities, getting them to stay out of the spa building while a "team of specialists" safely aired it out and checked for any people left in the building. The police were so busy calming witnesses, dealing with reporters, and handling the minor injuries caused by the public panic that most of them never did much to investigate the chemical story. Those who *did* follow up were pressed to stop.

The Grizzly Springs and Spa couldn't survive the blitz of negative publicity that followed. I'd felt a little sorry for the spa's owners, an older couple who reminded me of my own ex-hippie parents. But Maven, who has money the way other people have skin cells, quietly made them a very generous offer for the property, which of course they took.

Although everything appeared to be tied up with a neat bow, Quinn and I had been kept busy making sure the frayed ends of the official story held together. It wasn't enough to just buy the property and shut it down. Stampeding, hallucinating spa guests could explain a great deal of damage, but they definitely couldn't explain the snake-monster-sized holes in the walls and the pool floor. And as it turned out, the building couldn't simply be demolished because of the fragile underground tunnels that ran beneath it. So Maven had to renovate the whole place, which meant pressing the minds of a number of construction workers on a regular basis. Pressing minds was Quinn's department, but I had to hang around during the daytime to make sure it was working, which meant he and I were on opposite schedules for months.

And then there was the problem of the Unktehila's body. Vampires and werewolves returned to regular human corpses after death, which made body disposal fairly simple. But the Unktehila was something else, an ancient being fused with magic in a way that was intricately tied to its biology. After its death, it had stayed exactly what it was: a fifty-foot snakeoid creature with a diameter of more than six feet. Quinn and I had spent a very messy, very disgusting week sneaking it out of the building in pieces. A *lot* of pieces.

After months of this around-the-clock work, plus the holidays and a two-month stint as interim store manager at the Flatiron Depot while Big Scott had knee surgery, things had *finally* begun to settle down for me. I was really hoping that whatever Maven was bringing me into now would be minor. An errand, maybe. Yeah, an errand would be nice.

Chapter 3

Magic Beans takes up a funny little building on Pearl Street, right in the heart of busy downtown Boulder. There are plenty of coffee shops in the area, but Magic Beans is notorious for two things: being open all night and its weird layout. Instead of one huge room, it's made up of many small ones connected together, like a rat maze with doors. This gives the patrons privacy and lets Maven conduct business without being overheard, but it's a pain in the ass from a security standpoint. Then again, I'd seen Maven in action, and if anyone could handle a security risk, it was her. Vampires don't spend much time worrying about thieves or vandals.

When I arrived, the building was crowded with intense-looking university students, many of whom wore pajama pants and looked like they had gone without a shower for even longer than usual. Although they were all holding still, they managed to seem frenzied, their faces hidden behind books and laptop screens. Everyone in Boulder has a rough idea of the university's rhythms, and I remembered that finals started next week.

I followed the arrows spray-painted on the concrete floor, which wound a neon path through the rooms to the front counter. I didn't recognize the college-aged kid behind the register—Maven must have hired a new guy—but when I asked for Maven he jerked his thumb toward her office without looking up from the open textbook in front of him.

The door to Maven's tiny office was attached to the largest room, in the back of the building, which had a raised stage for open-mic nights and even small concerts. I gritted my teeth as I marched back there, doing my best to ignore the three ghosts that resided in the auditorium room. I was getting better at pushing the remnants to the back of my mind, but I felt a little guilty about it, like when you compartmentalize all the homeless people asking you for change.

Maven's door was open a crack, so I stepped inside. "Hey, Lex," came Quinn's familiar voice. He was seated in one of the visitor chairs in front of Maven's desk, which was at the back of the room. Quinn was tall and handsome in a beat-around craggy way, and like most vampires he usually wore an implacable expression. Maven herself was perched on her office chair, which she'd lowered so her legs wouldn't dangle. She was a small woman who appeared to be eighteen or nineteen, with a shock of awkwardly cut orange hair and perpetually mismatched clothes that she wore in layers and layers, along with additional coatings of costume jewelry and a pair of hideous clear-framed glasses. It was an excellent disguise, but if you looked close, you could see that she was so beautiful it often took my breath away.

Tonight she was wearing her usual homeless-pioneer getup, but her face was harder than I'd seen it in a long time, and she seemed to radiate fury. My heart sank. No, I wasn't there for an errand.

Impatiently, she motioned for me to close the door, and I dropped into the other visitor chair with a nod at each of them. I was pretty sure Maven knew about my relationship with Quinn, but we kept it professional in her presence.

"Thanks for coming," she said, but her voice was stony. A thrill of fear ran through me. "We have a situation in Denver that needs your attention. Both of you." She opened a laptop in front of her and spun it around to face us. The screen was taken up by a number of thumbnail photos. I leaned forward. Headshots, maybe fifty or so. At first glance, I didn't recognize any of the faces. "Quinn, you remember the Denver vampires."

Quinn and I exchanged a glance. Our first case together—the investigation of Charlie's kidnapping—had sent us to Denver. We ended up killing the only vampire I met there.

"Tonight I received a call from Ford, the senior dominus in the city," she continued. "Apparently several of his villani have been poisoned with belladonna."

Vampires do not typically gasp, in my experience, but Quinn's eyes widened nearly as much as they had the first time he was in Charlie's presence. Maven pointed to several of the photos, and when I squinted I could see little names typed beneath the faces: Louis, Phillip, and Lara.

"I'm sorry, I don't understand," I said, as calmly as I could. "Don't they sell belladonna all over the place?"

Two pairs of cold vampire eyes focused on me. "Simon must have told you that magic bonds with certain plants," Quinn said finally.

"Yeah . . ."

"Belladonna is one of them, and it's poisonous to vampires," he explained. "They spent centuries cross-breeding it until it was no longer tied to magic, but every now and then the original strain pops up somewhere. Like a controlled substance."

I noticed that Quinn still used the word "they" when talking about vampires, where most of the others I knew would have said "we." "But what does it actually do to them?" I asked.

"The older two have been paralyzed for several weeks now," Maven said, her words clipped. "Ford hadn't been checking in with them, so he wasn't aware of the problem until a third, Louis, died from the poison. Louis had listed him as a reference on an apartment application, and the landlord called when he found the body." Her eyes looked like they might start shooting sparks at any second. "Louis was young. He couldn't fight it."

I winced, but not from the news. As a boundary witch, I have a special attraction to vampires and vice versa. Most of the time this meant that Maven, who was ancient and powerful, sort of pulled at my attention. Today, though, she was so angry that looking at her was like tumbling into a very deep hole. I couldn't tell if she was upset because Ford had neglected his vampires, or because of the belladonna. Or both.

"The other two, will they survive?" Quinn asked her.

She nodded, the rage subsiding a little. "If they haven't died by now, they should wake eventually. But it could be weeks, months, even longer, depending on the potency of the strain they received. Meanwhile, they have to be cared for, hidden, and fed."

Vampires didn't eat or drink anything other than blood, as far as I could tell. Which raised another question. "How did they ingest the poison in the first place?" I asked.

Quinn answered for me. "There were no injection marks on their bodies, and it's really difficult to get a vampire to hold still for a shot anyway," he explained. "Someone must have watched them, learned their favorite donors, and slipped it into the donors' food. That's one of the reasons why we're discouraged from using the same humans over and over," he said, with a sidelong glance at Maven. I got the impression that this was a Colorado-specific rule.

"Okay, so there's a person who has it in for the Denver vampires, and they gave a rare, ancient strain of belladonna to the humans that are, um, repeat donors. Obviously it's someone with Old World knowledge, but is there any way to tell what species?"

Maven's eyes narrowed. "Historically speaking," she said, her voice suddenly cold, "belladonna and the other herbs are witch tools."

Oh, shit. Tensions between witches and vampires were already high, thanks to Morgan Pellar's attempted coup. Now Maven wanted me wedged right between them again. I glanced at Quinn, but he was keeping his eyes fixed on Maven, like a hound awaiting a command.

"I want you both in Denver tonight," she declared. "We know about three of the humans who were likely poisoned. Quinn, you'll talk to them. Press them, find out if they were willing participants or victims. Lex, I want you to speak to Nellie."

I suppressed a groan. This night just kept getting better. Nellie was a boundary witch like me, only she was dead. The ghosts of boundary witches are, apparently, quite sentient, and Nellie haunted the Denver brothel where she'd died. The last time I was there she'd given me information on ley lines in exchange for a working television, but I hadn't had time to visit her during the past six months.

Okay, to be honest, I hadn't *wanted* to visit her. Boundary magic was intimidating under the best circumstances, and Nellie claimed I was the most powerful boundary witch she'd ever seen. That scared the crap out of me. I was already struggling to adjust to seeing ghosts everywhere I went. The last thing I wanted was to add more to my plate.

"Of course, but, um . . . why?"

"We need perspective from a witch who cannot be involved in the poisonings, and since you're the only person in Colorado who can see her, I think Nellie's a safe bet," Maven said curtly. "I also happen to know she's had experience with belladonna. I want you to ask her if there's a way to wake up my vampires."

"She'll want something in exchange." Nellie was nothing if not enterprising.

Maven just waved a hand. "As long as it's just money, give her anything. Quinn has a company credit card."

I almost chortled. Here we were, talking witch spells and vampire poisoning, and *Quinn had a company credit card*. I managed to swallow the laughter. "Yes, ma'am," I said instead.

"In the meantime, I'll get the word out. No vampire in Colorado drinks from a human they've used before." She cut her eyes at Quinn, and then looked back at me. Oh, yeah, she knew we were dating.

Quinn just nodded. I bit my lip. There were going to be a lot of vampires out hunting that night.

Chapter 4

Nellie's former brothel had once been a lovely Victorian house in downtown Denver, on the edge of what became the red-light district in the nineteenth century. But after Nellie died and the brothel shut down, every attempt to open a new business there or renovate the building back into a home had failed. There were too many strange noises, creepy sightings, and cold spots, all of which had earned it a prominent spot on all the "Haunted Denver" lists.

Decades had passed since the last failed attempt to transform the building, but the city had developed around the ancient eyesore, and it was now only a couple of blocks away from Coors Field, sandwiched stubbornly between a trendy club and a sports bar.

All of my previous visits had been during the day, when the area was deserted, but this time I had to slip down the alley between the club and the brothel, avoiding stumbling twenty-somethings with high heels and blowout hair. I made an effort not to wrinkle my nose as I squeezed past two girls vomiting against the club building. When I was twenty-four, I was driving Humvees through the desert at night, not puking in stilettos.

I hadn't bothered to replace the lock I'd broken on the brothel door—with nothing to steal and Nellie's creepy presence, no one came in here—so I just pushed the door open and fished a camping lantern out of my bag, keeping it away from the boarded-up windows. The strong white light only seemed to make the shadows longer, putting an unnerving emphasis on the grime and spider webs. I swallowed and ordered myself not to get creeped out.

Then, inches from my ear, a female voice exploded. "*Finally!*"

I jumped, whirling around to see Nellie Evans right behind me.

The last time I'd seen her, Nellie had looked bright and vivid, even though it was the middle of the day. But I'd later learned that her strong presence was a side effect of Morgan Pellar's spell to boost the area ley lines. This time, there was no mistaking Nellie for anything but ghost. She was slightly faded, and there was a wrinkle of concentration on her forehead, as if it took just a little effort to keep herself visible, the same way I'd need a little effort to stand on my tiptoes.

If she hadn't been a boundary witch in life, Nellie's ghost would just be a repeating fragment of herself, an afterimage. But Nellie's connection to death kept her sentient. And her personality was very much intact, for better or worse.

"Where have ye been?" she demanded, pouting at me. "I thought you'd 'a been back *months* ago, and me sitting around waiting every day like a damned fool girl with a beau . . ." Her footsteps made no noise on the hardwood floors as she stomped back and forth, shouting at me. The tantrum was a little funny, given her appearance. Nellie was dressed as I'd seen her last: in short-shorts, a polka-dotted tied-off top, and chunky high heels like a thirties pinup girl. She had obviously been pretty once, but she'd lived hard, and it still showed in death. She appeared to be in her midforties, although she'd probably died younger than that.

I waited until Nellie's ranting wore itself out. When she devolved to mumbling under her breath, I said, "Hi, Nellie, how have you been? I see your TV's still working." I nodded toward the television I'd set up in the main entryway.

She glared at me. "Aye, yes, the television. It does work, but it's been stuck on the same damned channel since you plugged it in! Have you heard of these things, *re*-runs?" She pronounced it carefully, like she was trying to speak Chinese. "They show the same programs over and over! And the *children's* shows, argh!" She stomped a silent foot and began to pace again, then slowed and tilted her head to reconsider. "Although that red childish monster, he gives me a good laugh," she allowed. "And the wee monkey who's always creating messes, he reminds me of one of my trollops; she was so clumsy—"

And she was off again. I'd forgotten about Nellie's loopy speech patterns: when she was excited, her diction and vocabulary ran up and down the socioeconomic spectrum and switched back and forth between now and a hundred and fifty years ago. Although I suspected she was always excited. It was like she'd been carefully hoarding decades of conversation for the first person who could see her. "Nellie," I interrupted. "I need your help again."

She'd been at the far end of her pacing, but she whirled back around. "Well, of course you do," she snapped. "You wouldn't-a come back to visit me otherwise, would you? *Would* you?"

I winced. "I was working up to it."

She glared at me, but made a little impatient gesture for me to continue.

"What do you know about belladonna?" I asked.

That brought her up short. For a moment her face was blank. "Why are ye asking *me*?" she said suspiciously. "Dinna your people explain all this?"

I sighed. Sam and I had been adopted by the Luthers when we were babies, so we had grown up firmly outside the Old World, but Nellie seemed to have forgotten. "No, Nellie. I don't know my people, remember?" I didn't mention that I was also trying not to involve the local witch clan this time around. The less Nellie knew about current Old World politics, the less she could use them to manipulate me.

"Ah, yes. Sorry, Lex-girl." Her face relaxed, but in just a second the distrustful look was back. "Did Pale Jennie send you then?"

Pale Jennie was actually Maven, and she had killed Nellie back in the nineteenth century—but in all fairness, only after Nellie had "killed" her first. That's what happens when you try to backstab a friend who's secretly a vampire. "Yes. She asked me to come here and beg for your advice." That wasn't exactly accurate, but Nellie had responded well to flattery before. "She thought you'd know all about belladonna and the other herbs."

Nellie puffed up a little with pride. "I bet she did. Those herbs were one thing I always played close to my chest, even with Jennie. The grist a' magic, my Ma used to call them."

"Is that how you learned how to use them? From your mother?"

"Aye. She grew them in her own garden. That was how Ma was able to feed and clothe my brother and me, selling the seeds to anyone with a grudge against something magical." She scowled. "Colorado weren't so regulated then. We had no vampire tyrant telling us what we could or could not grow on our own property."

"Okay," I said slowly, parsing that for useful information. "So can you tell me if belladonna poisoning has a cure?"

"Aye, I could tell you," Nellie replied, her eyes glinting with greed. "But I'd need something in return, of course."

"What do you want?" Nellie couldn't interact with the physical world, other than creeping people out when she "walked" through them, so there wasn't a lot she could require in terms of material goods.

"I want you to come by here every day and change the channel to something new," she said promptly.

I suppressed the urge to roll my eyes. Of course. "Once a month, for a year. And it won't always be me. Sometimes it'll be a . . . helper." I didn't want to say *vampire* and set her off on another tirade, but I figured Maven could send one of the Denver vampires to do this, at least sometimes.

"Once a week," she negotiated. "For the year, and at least once a month it'll be you."

"Fine," I said, managing not to sound begrudging about it. "But I'm not leaving my watch as collateral for that long. This time you'll have to trust me."

She pursed her lips, but nodded. "All right."

"What's the cure?"

"Ain't no cure," she said, looking infinitely satisfied with herself. "Belladonna is powerful; you have to wait for it to flush through the system. Best you can do is speed that up a little."

"How?"

Her smirk grew even bigger. "Easiest way is to cut the creature's vein, drain out some of the toxic blood, and feed 'em untainted blood. Then wait a day or so and do the same thing all over. A' course, the older they are, the faster they'll heal."

I gave her a skeptical look. That sounded suspiciously like Nellie trying to get me to bleed unconscious vampires to death, and I said so.

Nellie spread her hands, looking innocent. "Believe me or don't. I said I'd tell you whether there was a cure, and I did."

I rolled my eyes. "Fine." I turned on my heel and started for the door.

"Wait!" Nellie appeared right in front of me again, forcing me to stop or walk through her. I'd walked through ghosts before; it wasn't a feeling I enjoyed. Her eyes were calculating. "But I'll tell you something else, Miss Lex, and this one's on me. Jennie, she always had a bee in her bonnet about belladonna. Hated it, worse than Christian missionaries hated opium. Only time I ever seen Jennie get truly furious about something, it involved the grist."

I thought that over for a moment. Could the attacks in Denver be geared toward Maven personally? Like some kind of distraction? That seemed kind of far-fetched. Distracted, I started forward again, but Nellie cried, "Wait! The channel!"

"You didn't negotiate when the year starts," I said sweetly, and left her cursing behind me.

I had every intention of coming back in a week to turn the station; I just wanted to mess with Nellie a little first. So I went outside and called Quinn, figuring he could pick me up in between his interviews. As it turned out, though, he had already finished his last interview and was already on his way to pick me up. I was surprised—he'd had to drive to three separate places and speak to three separate people—but then again, when you were pressing minds, I suppose you didn't have to bother with introductions or small talk. That would save time.

"Did you learn anything?" I asked after climbing into the car.

Quinn shook his head. "As far as they know, none of them were involved."

"What does that mean, as far as they know?"

He gave a little shrug. "One of the women seemed sort of confused, like she'd been pressed before. But that might be the result of Louis pressing her to forget a routine feeding. I can't be sure."

His lips were tight, and I realized he was frustrated. Or was it something else? "Are you okay?"

"I'm just . . ." He shook his head. "Talking to the regulars got to me a little bit."

"How come?"

He was quiet for a moment, collecting his thoughts. I waited him out. We were on Highway 36, about seven miles from Boulder. You could already see the city lights glittering in the distance. Since I was a little kid, this view always felt like home. "Maven doesn't like us to use the term 'human servant,' but that's what these people are," he said finally. "The vampires—*we*—screw up their heads, pressing them into keeping our secrets, never talking about their lives. Some of us even go so far as to make the humans think they're in love. They give up everything on the off chance that—" He cut himself off abruptly, fuming.

"Is that why you won't drink from me?" I asked softly.

Quinn stomped on the brake, driving the seat belt hard into my shoulder. He wrenched the wheel sideways to pull over onto the Davidson Mesa scenic overlook, letting out a sound that was shockingly snarl-like.

Whoa. I stared at him, openmouthed. Quinn was actually *upset*. I so rarely saw him experience visible emotional reactions; I kind of didn't know what to do with it.

"Do you *want* me to drink from you?" he snapped. "See you as food?"

"No, but—"

"You don't get it, Lex! Some of these assholes are using those people like—like drug dealers use junkies for sex." Quinn bunched up his fists in his lap. "It's so twisted, and the vampires feel *nothing* for them, and I would *never*—"

"Slow down," I interrupted. "No, I don't want you to feed from me. Not because I think you don't care about me, or because I think it would make me a whore. Because it's icky." He let out a choked laugh. "But it does sometimes seem like you . . . want to." I blushed despite myself.

He sat quietly for a few minutes, digesting that. "I'm afraid," he said at last, "if I ever start drinking your blood, I won't be able to stop."

"Oh." I could have reminded him that this eventuality had already happened. Months earlier I'd cut open my scalp on a chunk of concrete. Quinn had licked away a few drops of blood, but I'd managed to snap him out of it.

But I knew his fear wasn't rational or intellectual. It was like my nightmares about seeing Charlie killed or kidnapped right in front of me. It didn't matter that I'd won in the past. All that mattered was that I could lose the next time.

I decided to let it drop for now. "So what do we—"

But before I could finish, there was a great, shuddering impact as the pickup truck slammed into the back of the Jeep.

Chapter 5

I couldn't hear.

No, wait, I *could* hear, it's just that everything was drowned out by the ringing.

I shook my head to clear it, but that only made my skull ache. I registered the tendrils of my own hair on my face and finally pulled together that I was upside down, still secured by my seat belt. It was surprisingly dark, though of course the desert was always like that at night. I fumbled at the seat belt latch, but my fingers were clumsy, or maybe it was stuck. The buckles weren't where they were supposed to be, which only furthered my confusion. Had this Humvee been remodeled or something?

I gave up on the seat belt and reached out with my hands, feeling around for my gunner, my driver. Where the hell was the rest of my platoon? The ringing was finally beginning to fade, so I tried calling out their names, listening hard for one of them to reply. But then a hand covered my mouth.

I fought it, my fist beating against the arm that held me in place. Then a voice spoke right next to my ear. "Shh. Lex, honey, it's me. It's Quinn."

I went still, and the whole thing came back to me. I wasn't in Iraq; I was in Maven's tricked-out Jeep, and someone had rammed into us on the scenic overlook, flipping us over. I nodded my head to show that I understood, and he took his hand away.

Quinn was right-side up, having disengaged his seat belt and crouched next to me. Both airbags had gone off, which explained the trickle of blood from my nose. I touched it gingerly. It hurt, but it didn't seem broken. I distantly wondered if Quinn was bothered by the smell of my blood. Then I heard a pop and felt the seat belt loosen, and before I knew it Quinn was helping me down so I didn't fall. I crouched next to him on the roof of the Jeep, silently thanking Maven for getting such an awesome vehicle. Things would have gone very differently in my little sedan.

"Where are they?" I whispered.

"Waiting for us to crawl out."

I shivered. "Are they human?"

"Vampires, I think. Three of them. I only saw one face, but I'm pretty sure he was one of the Denver villani."

I thought quickly—or as quickly as I could, having just had my bell rung. "Weapons?"

"Just a handgun and a shredder. My bag of tricks is in the back; I don't think we can reach it."

"Flares?" The rest of them had the advantage of vampire eyesight, but I couldn't fight if I couldn't see.

Quinn, who had no trouble seeing in the dark, reached for the glove compartment, and thrust a couple of road flares into my hand a moment later. I looked around for a moment, then extended the little legs on one of them and set it on the battered windshield behind me, where it wouldn't start an actual fire. I used the igniter cap to get it started, just like lighting a match. It burst into hissing light.

Having any kind of light was a relief. I could make out Quinn, looking concerned and determined, and the remarkably intact interior of the reinforced Jeep.

"How do you want—" I began, but was interrupted by a long, earsplitting screech that started at the back of the car and traveled slowly toward the front. I froze, listening for footsteps, but I couldn't hear anything over the piercing squeal of metal tearing up metal. They were keying the side of the Jeep, but with something a whole lot bigger than a key.

The sound stopped abruptly, a few inches down the car from my window.

Then a new sound burst into my ear, making me jump backward, bumping into Quinn. "Little pig, little pig, let me come in," sang a male voice, right on the other side of the car door. I felt Quinn press a sidearm into my back, and I slowly took it. I could only make out a blurry circle for a face.

"Not by the hair of go fuck yourself," I yelled back. As fast as I could, I raised the 9 mm and fired two quick bursts at the face.

There was laughing outside the window. Goddamned vampire reflexes. "*This* is the chick everyone's afraid of?" said the same voice. He came strolling around the front of the car, as if baiting me to shoot again. I waited.

"She's not so tough," agreed the other, a woman this time. She had been behind him, and was now standing by my window. The man continued walking his lazy circle around the Jeep, while the woman hovered next to my window. If Quinn was right, there was a third vampire in the darkness somewhere.

They were surrounding us.

I glanced at Quinn, who raised an eyebrow, asking what I wanted to do. He was the investigator, but I was the soldier. He'd defer to me in this situation, but the problem was that all our options were shitty. If we went out, we'd have to climb awkwardly out of the flipped Jeep. Quinn could do it fast enough to attack, but it would take me a few seconds, and he couldn't keep all three of them off me while we were cornered like this. Even if they did let me climb out safely, there wasn't a lot I could do with my magic other than press them, and I couldn't do that without being able to clearly see their eyes.

The woman leaned down to the hole in the bulletproof glass and took a big whiff through her nose. I'd once seen Quinn do something similar. "I can smell your fear, darlin'. And the death in your blood. Mmmm."

I raised the sidearm and shot for the same hole in the window, just on general principle, but she danced back, laughing. "Why don't you come out and play with us?" she called out.

Then it hit me—why hadn't they already killed us? They could have kicked in the Jeep's windows and dragged us out by now, or hell, just tossed in a Molotov cocktail and called it a day. But they were keeping their distance. I looked at Quinn again. I could tell he was thinking the same thing, but he seemed as puzzled as I was.

"We're pretty comfortable right here," I yelled.

"Oh, we don't care about your boyfriend," the woman said through the hole. "We just want you. But if you don't come out, we'll have to come in, and then we won't be *nearly* so nice to Mr. Quinn."

Shit. Quinn read my thoughts and shook his head violently. When I shifted my weight, he actually grabbed my arm. "Don't you dare," he whispered.

Behind him, the male vampire started to kick the safety glass of the driver's side window. He was deliberately slow about it, but he'd still get through the glass in a few seconds. There was no time. I leaned forward and kissed Quinn, taking the hand he'd laid on my elbow and moving it down to my forearm, so he could feel what was under the jacket sleeve. "Take the third," I breathed, hoping the shattering glass would hide the sound.

Quinn's face was tight, but he nodded, trusting me.

Big hands were reaching into the Jeep, swiping toward Quinn in a blur. "Okay!" I shouted. "Leave him alone, I'm coming out!"

The hands receded. "Throw that pistol out first, darlin'," drawled the woman near my window. "We don't want any accidents."

Damn. There went Plan A. I ejected the clip and tossed the sidearm out the open window, hearing it clatter away. "That's a good girl," she purred.

Anger flared inside my head, but I was focused now. I put the clip in my jacket pocket just in case. Then I climbed over Quinn and started to crawl through the open window.

The male vampire was leaning against the Jeep, smirking. I made a show of scraping my back on the window, wincing. I reached up my right hand. "A little help?"

He hesitated for a second, but then gave a tiny shrug. There were three of them, and to him I was one little human. He reached down and took my right hand with his left.

God, I love being left-handed.

I popped up as fast as I'd ever moved in my life, swinging the shredder around to plunge it into his chest. And left it there.

Shredders are spelled to destroy whatever they touch when they're at rest, basically causing a mini-implosion. The idea is to get to the vampire's heart, but I hadn't had the leverage to get it all the way through his breastbone. So instead it destroyed his breastbone. And probably some of the tissue around it.

The vampire dropped to the ground, screaming and clutching at his chest. The female vampire sped around the car toward me, but I'd spent years handling road flares, and I had the cap off and the igniter struck by the time she reached me. She couldn't slow her momentum in time, so she wound up colliding with the flare, which burned my wrist a little. I'd been hoping to actually stab her with the thing, but I settled for setting her clothes and her long blonde braid on fire.

Howling with pain, she ran for the scrubby dirt on the other side of the bicycle path and dropped to the ground, trying to roll herself out. I had to drop the flare, but just as I did, I caught movement out of the corner of my eye and saw the third vampire hurtling toward me. My would-be attacker was abruptly blindsided by Quinn, who burst through the car window like a missile, launching both of them into the darkness. The light wasn't bright enough to make out their fight, but I heard scuffling and snarling. I ran for the discarded gun, picked it up, and snapped the magazine back in, whirling around to point it at the fight.

"It's okay," came Quinn's voice out of the darkness. "He's dead."

I nodded, only then realizing it had gone quiet. I turned the weapon toward the female vampire, but there was nothing left but a skeleton-shaped fire. I relaxed my arm, lowering the sidearm.

Quinn's form morphed out of the darkness. "Your wrist," he said, reaching for me.

I realized I was rubbing it absently with my free hand. "Oh! It's fine." I let him look, but it was barely a first-degree burn. I'd put some salve on it and forget about it.

"Can you get the flashlight?" I asked Quinn. "Let's talk to our survivor."

We converged on the male vamp, who had gone still on the ground, both hands still clutching his chest like he could hold the bones together himself. It had to hurt like hell. Quinn snapped on the flashlight and held it high. The vampire blinked in the sudden light, looking at me with fear.

Good. He should be afraid.

Then I realized he was avoiding my eyes, his gaze darting from my forehead to my chest to Quinn, then back again in a frantic loop. He'd been warned not to look at me. Interesting. "What's your name?" I asked him.

His lips moved, but only a wheezing hiss came out. "The stake must have punctured a lung, maybe both," Quinn observed. "He needs air to talk."

I sighed. "Do you still have baggies in the glove compartment?"

The next few minutes were fairly disgusting, as Quinn had to shove a plastic baggie into the vampire's chest to cover the hole in the lung. I was all for sharing work, but I decided that in this case my best contribution would be holding the flashlight.

Quinn's hands were still actually *in the vamp's chest*, holding the baggie in position, when I asked again, "What's your name?"

"Kraig," he breathed, still avoiding my eyes. "With a K."

I blinked. *That's* what he wanted to use his breath on? "Who sent you after me, Kraig?"

Without moving his arm, he lifted a shaky finger and pointed it toward the back of the car. "Ford."

Quinn and I exchanged a look. So the vampire who'd hung back in the shadows had been the head vampire in Denver. "Is he your dominus?"

"Yes. Yes." His answers were coming fast, as if to show how cooperative he could be.

"How did you find us?"

"Followed the big Jeep," he wheezed. "Figured you'd visit the bloodbags."

Quinn shot him a disgusted look. Kraig was referring to human people. "Why did Ford want you to come after us?" I demanded.

"Don't know."

"What did he want with her?" Quinn asked, jerking his head toward me.

"Don't know."

I moved closer, crouching down next to him. The injured vampire still wouldn't meet my eyes. "You get a choice now, Kraig," I said softly. "Do you want me to press you, so I can see if you're lying, or would you rather we just killed you?"

He agreed to be pressed.

When he finally looked at me, I honed in my focus and called up a connection between us. As soon as I felt it lock into place, I asked him all the same questions again. Unfortunately, Kraig had been telling the truth about not knowing anything. Ford was his dominus—his lord, for lack of a better term—and Ford had said they were to take me alive. That was all Kraig needed to know. He had no idea what Ford was planning to do with me after they took me. He was just a grunt.

I wasn't sure what to do with him after that. The domini-villani relationship is complicated. It's difficult, if not downright impossible, for a lower vampire to resist an order from a dominus, so it was hard to entirely blame Kraig for the attack. I decided to just ask him. "Tell me if you had a choice about capturing me," I commanded.

He paused, examining the question. Vampires can't lie when I press them, but sometimes they need to consider before they can answer. "I could have resisted," he said finally. "I did not."

Quinn stepped away to report all of this to Maven. I held on to my control over Kraig, though I couldn't really ask him any more questions while his lungs were still healing.

In the end, with Maven's blessing, I pressed him to go to Boulder on foot and throw himself on Maven's mercy. I also said he couldn't feed on the way, which would make the trip very painful.

When Kraig had completely disappeared into the darkness, Quinn and I set about cleaning up the mess from the crash. Compared to dealing with thousands of pounds of giant reptile, it really wasn't that difficult. We buried the vampires' remains a few hundred yards away, called the police, and told them Quinn had driven the Jeep and I'd driven the pickup. Quinn pressed them into buying the story, and we called in Quinn's favorite towing company to tow both cars. It was scary how good I was getting at this.

Chapter 6

The tow truck dropped off the Jeep at the same body shop where Maven had commissioned the custom work, and I made a mental note to call them the next morning to arrange service. When we finally got back to Magic Beans, only a couple of hours before dawn, there was no sign of Kraig-with-a-K. When we got back to her office, though, Maven was clearly pissed—but not nearly as upset as she'd been about the belladonna poisoning. An attempted betrayal was something she was used to.

"So," I said, because I needed to make sure I understood what was happening. "We're thinking Ford was going to make a move against you, and he decided to get rid of Quinn and me first?" It wasn't a terrible plan—Quinn was deeply loyal and Maven's best troubleshooter, and I could press vampires.

She sat in her office chair, her small hands steepled in her lap. "Something like that," she said at last. "I don't understand where the belladonna comes in, though."

"Maybe he's the supplier," Quinn suggested. "When you showed signs of interfering with his business, he tried to take you out."

"But then why poison his own people?" I argued.

A different kind of man might have been upset that his girl-friend was contradicting him in front of the boss, but Quinn just shrugged and said, "Because they found out what he was doing, and they needed to be silenced so he could usurp Maven."

"That must be it," Maven said, but her face was still troubled.

I told Maven what Nellie had said about belladonna, and with a sour look she agreed that the whole "flushing with blood" plan was probably Nellie messing with us. I didn't mention what Nellie had told me about Maven's obsession with the herbs. It didn't seem like a great idea to antagonize her when she was already angry.

She sent us home after that, and I was more than a little relieved to leave her presence. Since there were less than two hours until sunrise, Quinn decided to head back to his apartment. He squeezed my hand. "Are we still on for tomorrow night?" he said, his voice low.

Tomorrow night. I stared at him blankly, and he grinned. "Date night, remember? An actual date? No sandworm bits, no blood, no Pellars, much as we love them. Just you and me like regular folks."

I flushed a little. "Right. Date night. A thing which I can totally do. Wait, if we're not hip deep in sandworm viscera, what are we even going to talk about?"

"Boring things," he said solemnly. "Local elections. Gluten allergies. The effects of marijuana legalization on the state economy."

"Oh, so, Boulder things."

"Exactly."

I stood on my tiptoes and gave him a light kiss. "You're on."

I was smiling when I climbed into my car to head home. But something about Ford and the attack still wasn't sitting right. It wasn't until I'd gotten back to the cabin, showered off the road dust, and climbed into bed that I figured out what was bothering me.

Why had they wanted me alive?

In the early morning hours when I finally went to sleep, I dreamed of the desert. Again.

I never used to dream about my last two days in Iraq. Until last fall, I couldn't even remember the events that had culminated in me stumbling out of the desert, covered in sand and dried blood. Oh, I had plenty of nightmares after my discharge, but those were generic, comparatively toothless, and they eventually faded after I took in my rescue animals. But I never dreamed about the worst of it.

Then, six months ago, I learned the reason: my brain had walled off those memories to protect itself from the trauma. A healing witch had inadvertently taken down that wall when she restored my ability to see ghosts. I was aware of the irony: I'd wanted to see ghosts in order to speak to Nellie, and now I couldn't avoid my own personal ghosts. Each night, I thrashed against the blankets and experienced the same horrors all over again. Helplessness. Pain. Violation. Grief. Impotent hatred and fury for the people who had hurt me and killed my friends.

If Quinn was there, he would wake me up, never minding if I hit him or screamed in the process. He would hold me and kiss away my tears, reminding me that I was home, safe. That I had a different life now. And that would help me cope until the next night, when it would happen all over again.

Only one thing ever varied in the dream. Sometimes, when I relived those days, I had my boundary powers, the ones I'd developed and practiced since that night vampires had tried to kidnap Charlie. In this version, as I dragged myself away from the blast that had destroyed our Humvee, I saw the perpetrators closing in and I howled, reaching for my magic. Their life forces flew into my hands, their corpses dropping instantly into the dirt. And I *laughed*.

"No!"

I woke up drenched in cooling sweat, blinking against the morning sunshine. Automatically, I reached for Quinn, but he wasn't there, of course. I curled into myself, bringing my knees to my chin, shaking. Next to me, my dim-witted Yorkie, Dopey, nosed my side, making a little whining noise.

"Sorry, girl," I mumbled, not quite myself yet. "M'fine."

I don't know how long I laid there, staring at the ceiling and trying to collect the person I'd rebuilt after I'd been forced out of the army. The next thing I knew, my phone was vibrating on the nightstand. I reached over and picked it up to see the screen. Jake.

I answered the phone, glancing at the clock on the bedside table. It was almost ten. "Hey, Jake."

"Hey. I got your, um, present." I smiled. Nobody considered a dead fox much of a present, not even Jake. "Do you want the good news, or the bad news?" he went on.

I sat up in bed, petting my herd of rescue animals as they began wandering in to greet me. "Um, the good news, I guess."

"It's definitely not rabies."

I relaxed a little. "Oh, okay. Good. Wait, then what's the bad news?"

"The symptoms got me curious, so early this morning I called a couple of other vets in town," he reported. "There are three more cases just like this one: a wild animal that has suddenly lost its mind and attacked someone."

Simon would have sounded a little excited by the prospect of a medical mystery; hell, he'd probably be rubbing his hands together. But my quiet, even-tempered cousin couldn't enjoy a situation that involved dying animals. "Attacks? Was anyone hurt?"

"Mostly the other animals were too small to do much damage, but a college kid did get his arm scratched up pretty good by a squirrel." Jake replied. "The hospital gave him the rabies treatment right away, although an autopsy revealed that the squirrel didn't have it."

"So what did it have?"

"No idea. I've never seen anything like this. It's probably some sort of new virus that can go from animal to animal—but not to humans. It happens sometimes." Humor crept into his voice. "And before you ask, the college kid did *not* turn into a zombie. That was Dani's first question."

I had to smile at that. Jake's daughter Dani was probably my favorite of all my cousins' kids. "All right, well, thanks for getting back to me. I'll keep an eye on the herd when they're outside, just in case."

"Good idea. Meanwhile, the Department of Natural Resources is looking into it."

We spent a few more minutes catching up on family news. Dani was thinking about trying out for the volleyball team in the fall, which would be her first team sport. She had also been exchanging e-mails with Grace Brighton, who was the daughter of my friend Sashi, the healing witch in Las Vegas. Grace was a couple of years older than Dani, but apparently they spent hours playing some online game together on the weekends. Jake and his wife Cara were even talking about going down to Vegas for Dani's thirteenth birthday in a couple of months.

When I eventually hung up the phone, it was with some trepidation. I was a little nervous about the two sides of my life—boundary witch and family member—intersecting in any way. Then again, Grace didn't know anything about the Old World, and Sashi was doing her damnedest to keep it that way.

At the same time, I couldn't believe Dani was nearly a teenager. I could swear I'd been changing her diapers a week ago. I felt a stab of nostalgia. Soon she'd be too busy to come over here and play with the herd, and too grown-up for our Pixar movie nights with the other kids.

Feeling old and tired, I considered just staying in bed. But I could never fall back asleep after one of those dreams, not without Quinn, anyway. So I let the animals out and took a quick shower, put salve on my burn, and dressed in jeans and an old purple shirt that used to be my sister's. Sam had given it to me while she was pregnant with Charlie, complaining that it was too tight around the middle and it would never look good on her flabby mom belly again. Smiling a little at the memory, I padded into the kitchen to check my calendar. I was pretty sure I had to work at the Depot at one, but since becoming semi-nocturnal, I'd gotten the days mixed up before.

The doorbell rang before I made it to the living room. I jumped a little, and all around me dogs began barking hysterically, working extra hard to make up for the fact that they hadn't heard anyone approach. Generally the only person who could surprise the dogs was Quinn, because he was vampire-sneaky. "Dropped the ball, guys," I muttered.

The animals swarmed the front door, and I had to wedge myself between them to get to the little glass window. When I peeked through, I saw an unassuming Caucasian man with his hands stuffed in his pockets. When he saw me, he held up his hands slightly in an unconscious nonthreatening gesture. Somewhere in the back of my mind, I automatically thought *salesman*.

He said something, but I couldn't make it out over the barking. I cracked the door, jamming my body in it to keep the dogs inside, and opened my mouth to get rid of him. He overrode me.

"I'm sorry to just drop in on you like this," he called over the noise, "but I didn't have a number for you. My name is Emil Jasper, and I . . . well. I'm your biological father."

Chapter 7

"You're . . . what do . . ." I sputtered. I was having a hard time rear-ranging my entire worldview in a few seconds.

Sam and I had never celebrated an adoption day the way some families did, and most of the time I barely remembered that we weren't biologically Luthers. But I knew the story. My birth mother had walked into a Denver hospital in the middle of a terrible rain-storm, dripping wet and well into labor. She wouldn't give her name or any background information, but she spoke with an accent, and the hospital's assumption was that she was likely an undocumented immigrant.

The doctors would have questioned her further after we were born, but then I went into distress—something about fluid in my lungs choking me. While they were busy saving me, our mother was suddenly bleeding out. And then it was over. I'd wondered who my birth father was, of course, but I'd never actually expected to find out.

Unable to form any actual sentences, I snapped my mouth shut and looked him over more carefully, tuning out the barking. Jasper was just over six feet tall, with dark blond hair silvering to gray and a neat goatee. He carried a little extra weight around his middle, but it was mostly disguised by his simple, forgettable clothing: khaki pants and a plain charcoal button-down, with new-looking casual oxfords. The only remarkable thing about his clothes was the awkward way they fit. His shirt bunched a little just below the collar, and his pants hung low, as though the pockets were filled with change. I'd had a lot of practice looking for weapons under clothing, but this didn't seem like guns or knives, just . . . weighed down.

At first glance he had appeared to be about forty, but now I saw the signs of age: sag under his chin, lines around his mouth, and the small potbelly despite his wiry forearms. I put him just north of fifty. His eyes were cornflower blue, exactly like mine. And Sam's, and Charlie's.

That itself wasn't proof of paternity or anything, but the more I looked, the more similarities I spotted. Our noses. Our thick eyelashes. I glanced at his hands. Even his fingernails were shaped like mine.

"Why are you here?" I blurted, and immediately felt like a jerk.

But he didn't seem offended, just nervous. His fingers kneaded together at his waist, as though he were holding an imaginary hat. "I was hoping to meet you. Speak to you. Explain why . . ."

He trailed off, looking so mortified that I took pity on him. "Are you okay with animals, Mr. Jasper?" I asked. "Dogs and cats?"

"Yes, of course. And please call me Emil." For the first time, I noticed his unusual accent. His vowels were long—like someone from Canada or the Midwest—but there was also an odd lilt I couldn't place.

"Okay, well. Come in."

I ushered him ahead, catching a familiar scent. Cigar smoke. I'd known a few guys who smoked them on deployment. As soon as Jasper—Emil—was through the door, Chip and Cody were falling all over each other to lick his face. Emil dodged gamely, hunching down a little so he could scratch their backs while they were on the floor. We went into the living room, where I motioned him toward an easy chair, heading for the opposite couch. I couldn't keep myself from perching on the very edge, as though my body still expected him to go for a weapon. Emil turned to greet my gray cat Gus-Gus, who literally stepped onto his back by way of greeting. "Hello," he murmured, scratching Gus-Gus under the chin. You can tell a lot about a person by how they are with animals, I had learned, and Emil certainly seemed to be passing that particular test.

Then I remembered how everyone said Hitler was a dog person. "Um, would you like something to drink?" I said, because the internal voice of my mother would have been scandalized if I didn't. "Coffee, water? Or I think I have soda . . ."

I trailed off, but Emil shook his head. "I'm fine," he assured me. "I had coffee on the flight." Once Emil's eyes were off the animals and on me, they roved over my face like he couldn't stop himself. Like he'd finally found the pot of gold at the end of his rainbow.

I had a sudden, juvenile urge to throw off that blissful expression. "Tell me about my . . . my mother," I said, wincing at the word. It felt too much like a betrayal of my real mom, who had raised me and loved me and worried about me every day. But at the same time, what else could I call the woman whose uterus Sam and I had once shared?

Emil's face shut down a little. "Her name was Valerya," he said, as though he had practiced the words in front of a mirror. "We met in Russia, when I was there on a student visa."

His hands moved up suddenly—I had to make an effort not to flinch—but he was just fumbling at his pockets. He pulled out a photograph and reached across the coffee table to hand it to me. "That was us."

I took it with an automatic reverence. I'd seen all the paperwork on our adoption, and a newspaper article from shortly after we were born, but there were never any photos. The picture that Emil handed over showed a trim, youthful Emil with his arm around a young woman. She looked maybe twenty or twenty-one, and for a second I honestly thought Emil had Photoshopped in my sister. Valerya looked that much like Sam, or rather, Sam looked that much like Valerya. Only two things were different from my sister: the eyes—Valerya had brown eyes, unlike the blue that Sam had shared with me and, apparently, Emil. Valerya's hair was different, too. Despite the faded picture, I could see that instead of Sam's dark chestnut, our mother's hair had been reddish-brown. Just like mine.

I felt my eyes prick with sudden, unwelcome tears, and I had to blink hard to keep them back. In the shot, the two of them were wearing simple, relatively timeless clothes that looked homemade. They stood in front of a barn—the faded photo had turned it more rust than red—that could have been anywhere. Anywhere with bright sunshine. "Where was this taken?" I asked.

"Australia. We were visiting my brother at his farm."

Valerya was smiling for the camera, but her expression was pained and uncomfortable, like she wanted the photographer to put the camera down and let her escape. Maybe she just didn't like having her picture taken. I felt a sudden rush of protectiveness for this woman, ten years younger than I was now.

"Why weren't you with her?" I demanded, finally looking at Emil. My voice had come out harder than intended. "When we were born," I added, trying to soften my tone.

His face clouded over. "We had a fight when she was eight months pregnant. It was my fault," he added immediately. "I wanted her to give up boundary magic until the baby was born. I had no real reason, other than it unnerved me for her to be playing with life and death when she was growing new life inside her." He motioned to his own stomach.

So Valerya had been a boundary witch, like me. And this man knew at least a little about the Old World. I didn't think he was a boundary witch himself—we age slowly, our cells reluctant to die. Unless he was *really* old . . .

"The argument got heated," he continued. "We were both yelling, but then I . . . I grabbed her by the shoulders, shook her. She ran from me." Regret had drawn new lines around his mouth, and he dropped his eyes, looking ashamed. "I thought she would stay with friends for a night, maybe two, and we would make up. But I never saw her again."

I handed the photo back, but he waved me away. "You keep it," he said. "You should have a photo of her."

I set it on the coffee table carefully, placing a hardcover book over the photo to protect it from turning into a dog toy. Chip and Cody had wandered off as soon as Emil stopped petting them, but Gus-Gus made himself comfortable in the man's lap. I watched him pet the cat for a moment, trying to formulate my next question.

"You're talking about her in the past tense," I said finally. "So you know she's dead?"

He nodded, his face grave. "When more than a week went by, I took some hairs from Valerya's pillow and brought them to a trades witch I know. He did a locating spell, but she wasn't anywhere. That only happens when the person has . . . passed on.

"I went to two more witches, but each had the same result. I had nothing with which to locate you—no hair, no fingernails—but I did try finding you my own way."

"What does that mean?"

He leaned sideways so he could reach into his hip pocket, pulling out a small piece of glossy stone, perfectly round and perfectly black.

"This is a scrying mirror," he explained. "I have boundary witch-blood, like your mother, but like most males I can't activate it. But I can use natural magics. That's how I eventually found you, by scrying."

Natural magic. Simon had mentioned this once or twice, but he usually called it gravitational magic, because it pools in certain places. It's the same magic that keeps vampires from entering someone's home without permission, although that was about all I knew about it.

I suddenly felt like an idiot. I'd been so caught up in meeting Emil that I hadn't stopped to wonder how he'd found me. Careless. "What do you mean? Why would it work now and not then?"

He put the black stone back in his pocket. "I'm not sure. For years, whenever I tried to scry for the baby, the results were . . . confused. It was like the baby's location was bouncing back and forth, which made it impossible for me to pinpoint." He lifted his empty hands in a helpless gesture. "Eventually, I restricted myself to checking once a year, then every two years. I moved to Nova Scotia, opened a shop there, but I kept my ear to the ground. Last month I was at a small business conference in Chicago. An old friend had heard about a powerful boundary witch who had appeared in Colorado, seemingly out of nowhere. Honestly, my heart just lit up." He beamed. "I tried scrying again, and this time it led me straight to you."

I barely heard this last part. My thoughts were stuck on the words *bouncing back and forth*. "Twins," I blurted. "There were two of us. That's why you couldn't find us when we were little."

He started. "Two of you? The ultrasound never . . . there must have been a mistake."

He stood up, displacing Gus-Gus, who stalked away indignantly. Emil walked a few feet away, staring out the window. "Of course, of course," he muttered. "I'm such an idiot; I should have realized . . . two babies." He paused to look at me. "Was it a second girl? Is she an active witch, too? Do you—"

"She's dead," I said. It came out harsher than I expected. "She died last year."

His excitement faded, and he sank back down into the chair. "I'm so sorry, Allison."

People call me that by mistake all the time, but this time it sort of stung. "Nobody calls me that," I told him. "It's Lex."

He nodded absently, taking that in stride. "May I ask how she died?"

"She was murdered by a werewolf in Los Angeles." It was on the tip of my tongue to add "she left behind a daughter," but some instinct kept my mouth shut. The guy didn't need to know about Charlie, not until I was sure I could trust him.

Then a stray thought caught up with me. "Wait. If Valerya—if my mother was a boundary witch, why did she die in childbirth? Why didn't the magic bring her back?" I had personally died three times, and Valerya sounded stronger than me. More practiced, at least.

He nodded as though he'd expected the question. "I gave that a lot of thought," he said, "after the location spells revealed that she was dead. I realized there was only one thing that could have happened. You—or perhaps your sister—must have been at risk. Dying. Val was powerful; she would have been able to access the magic to trade one life for another." He spread his hands again.

Tears began to run down my cheeks as I put it together. Me. I had been in distress, and Valerya had given her life to save mine. Because that's what mothers do.

I stood up abruptly. "I'm sorry, I—I—"

"It's all right," Emil rose, too. "I've given you a lot to absorb in a very short time, Al—sorry, Lex. I'd like to speak to you more, if that's all right?" I did something with my head that was sort of like a nod. "Yes, well, I'm staying at the St. Julien for a few days. You can give me a call there when you're ready."

My birth father was alive. I had a biological family. I think I walked him out, but I don't remember anything else either of us might have said. This was just . . . too much.

I longed for someone to talk to about it, but who? John would have been good, but he was at Disney World, and he was still upset with me anyway. I hesitated to call anyone from the Luther family, because any interest I expressed in my birth parents might hurt them. Quinn was dead until night fell, and Simon and Lily . . . well, I was indirectly the cause of much of the turmoil that was currently affecting their whole clan. It didn't seem right to call and complain about my own family.

I dropped back onto the couch, ignoring the cat and two dogs that vied for my attention. I was kidding myself. There was only one person I wanted to talk to just then, but she happened to be dead. Last year I'd learned that I could talk to her spirit in my dreams, but I hadn't been able to contact her in months, not since my Iraq nightmares began.

I desperately wanted to talk to her, but I didn't think I could handle any more nightmares quite yet. But in the past, hadn't I been able to call her whenever I really needed her? Maybe if I went to sleep, I would see her?

In the end, my body sort of made the decision for me. I'd only had a few hours of sleep, and when exhaustion began to sink in, I laid down on the couch, prayed for my sister, and let sleep come.

Chapter 8

When I opened my eyes again, I was *not* in the desert.

I sighed with relief, looking around the walls of the bedroom that Sam and I had shared as teenagers. I didn't know if I chose this place or if Sam did, or if it was some combined effort of our subconsciouses, but this was where we always spoke, and it looked just like it always had. The old familiar posters, the bedspread, the stacks of books on the small desk we shared—everything was as it should be.

And there was my sister. She was sitting cross-legged on her bed, leaning against the wall to face me. This was how I'd last seen her in life—brunette pixie cut, black leggings, draped top that hid her little postpartum paunch. She was grinning so hard she was practically bouncing in place.

A rush of relief, love, and grief poured into me at once. "Hey, Sammy," I said.

"Hey, babe! Long time no see."

My smile fell. "Yeah. Sorry about that. Wait—am I sorry? Is it my fault?"

She grinned. "That you're having those dreams, and they've completely preempted my channel? No, of course not. I know you let those memories back in to help Charlie." Her smile faded. "But you should really see someone about it. What about that shrink at the VA?"

I scowled. "Don't Mom me, Samantha. I already have Mom for that."

She held up her hands. "Sorry, you're right. That's not what we do. I'm just worried about you."

I was never sure how much Sam knew about my day-to-day life. She wasn't omniscient, but she seemed aware of things beyond my own experiences. She wouldn't—or more likely, couldn't—tell me how it worked. So I asked, "Do you know why I wanted to talk to you?"

Her face turned serious. "Yeah. Emil, right?"

I nodded. "Do you know anything about him? Should I trust him?"

She gave me a wry look, opened her mouth, closed it for a moment, and then said carefully, "Valerya talks about him sometimes."

My mouth dropped open. Apparently my dead sister was communicating with my dead birth mother. That was huge. That was more than she'd *ever* told me about where she was and how she was doing.

"He hasn't always done the right thing, historically," Sam went on, "but she thinks he's basically okay."

Before I could ask any of my thousand follow-up questions, she shot me a warning look that I could understand as easily as if she'd spoken aloud. *I can't give you details. Watch what you ask or I'll disappear again.* Out loud, she said softly, "I can still listen, you know."

Whatever I was about to say next got stuck in my throat, and I had to swallow several times to choke it down. Instead, I said the one thing that I could *only* say to my sister. "I'm scared, Sammy. I don't even really know why. He seems nice, I guess, but it just feels really . . . big. And I've already got an awful lot of big on my plate right now."

"I know, babe." Something flickered across her face. "I am limited in what I can say here, you know that," she said slowly. "But maybe being cautious isn't such a bad thing. There are many things I can't see from where I am, for one reason or another."

I studied her, not understanding. Was she telling me not to trust Emil? Or was this about something else? "There's some weird new animal disease going around," I offered, but she just nodded. "And John is pissed at me."

Sam rolled her eyes. "You know he's not. He's angry, period, because his kid's been threatened. But he can't be mad at Charlie because she's a toddler, and he can't be mad at me because I'm dead." She gave me a rueful smile. "That's one benefit to dying, I guess. He mostly only remembers the good stuff."

That made me sad, somehow. I remembered childhood fights with Sam, her pulling my hair and me making her cry. I remembered the times we did what she wanted to do, because Mom and Dad treated her like the baby and she milked it. But that was all part of her: not a saint, not a martyr. A full person, with faults and mistakes and baggage.

"Should I tell him that I can talk to you?" I asked her. "I could pass along messages, I guess . . ."

She shook her head. "Thank you, but it would be too hard on him. He wouldn't be able to move on, assuming he even can after Morgan." She brightened. "But I liked what you told him before, about being able to sense that I was proud of him. That was perfect."

I swallowed hard. She knew it, of course, but I had to say it anyway. "I miss you so much, Sammy."

"I miss you, too." She cocked her head for a moment, like she was listening to something, and then screwed up her face.

"You're out of time," I guessed.

"Almost."

"Any advice? In the movies, spirit guides give advice."

"How would you know? You haven't been in a movie theater since the millennium," she countered. More seriously, she added, "Remember the griffin, Lex. Remember why it's yours. And don't be afraid when you finally figure out your mission. I've got your back, and so will John."

"Sammy, that's so cryptic—"

"I know, but that's how it has to be," she interrupted, talking fast now. "You think I *like* speaking in riddles?"

"Hell, yes, I do."

She didn't even acknowledge that. "One more thing," she rushed to say. "Emil, you *have* to ask him what he—"

Abruptly, she blinked away.

Chapter 9

"Son of a bitch!"

My eyes flew open and I grabbed the throw pillow beneath my head and flung it as hard as I could at the armchair, causing several dog heads to lift in confusion as they assessed the room for threats.

I threw a second pillow. Ask Emil what he *what*? What he wants from me? What he plans to do now that we've met? What he looks for in an ice cream topping? "*Dammit*, Sam!" I said aloud.

I'd done enough research on boundary magic by now to know that back in the day, it was mostly used for predicting the future or seeing things you couldn't see from your own vantage point, like an event on the other side of the world. But how did talking to ghosts help if they only spoke in riddles that I put together after it was too late?

What bothered me most about Sam's "advice" was the part about figuring out my mission. I'd done that, hadn't I? Charlie was my mission. Keeping her safe, keeping her alive, that was all that mattered. So what was Sam talking about? Something else I was supposed to be doing at the same time? But then why would John be involved?

I eyed the couch, but I was out of throw pillows to chuck. There was nothing to do but get up and get dressed for work.

• • •

The rest of the day was blissfully uneventful. I called Quinn's body shop, and his contact promised they'd have the Jeep as good as new by late afternoon. They would bill Maven directly, and even drop off the Jeep in its usual parking spot behind the coffee shop. I was a little amazed at the speed and service, but for all I knew Maven had pressed everyone at the garage to give her special treatment.

I had an afternoon shift at the Depot, but business was slow with all the students obsessing over finals, and I got to spend a quiet afternoon restocking shelves and solving simple problems for the cashier. Customer's coupon won't scan? No problem. Give me bad coupons over snake monsters and paternity issues any day.

In between customers and restocking, I couldn't stop thinking about Emil's visit. Even setting aside whatever Sam had been trying to tell me, I had no idea what our biological father wanted from me. If his goal had been to let me know he wasn't a deadbeat who'd abandoned Sam and me, the message had been received. But what if he wanted a relationship? How would that even work? I'd heard of adopted kids who found their biological parents (or vice versa) but those stories were always about children or petulant teenagers, not witches in their thirties. If Emil wanted to spend time with me on holidays or . . . I don't know, go to baseball games or something, I had no idea how to handle that.

Besides, I *had* a family. A really great family. And two jobs, and a vampire boyfriend. Even if I wanted to spend time with Emil, where would he fit into all of that? I could just picture my mother's crestfallen face if I told her I wanted to start prioritizing time with the biological father I'd just met.

Sam's voice spoke up in the back of my mind. I never knew if this was her actual spirit talking or my subconscious's interpretation of what she would say, but I'd gotten used to it. *Setting aside what he wants from you, what do you want from him?*

That was the problem, wasn't it? I had no idea.

The sun wouldn't set until nearly eight, so I had time to kill after my shift ended at five. I had originally planned to go home and work out before getting ready for date night, but while I was still brooding at the Depot I got a whole series of silly texts from my cousins Anna and Elise. They were at the Pearl Street pedestrian mall, getting manicures at Ten20 and shopping for a birthday present for Elise's girlfriend Natalie. Now they were demanding that I join them for dinner. They sent increasingly silly threats—one involved breaking into my house and putting my underwear in the freezer—until I had to text my surrender. Vampires can't eat anything other than blood and a few sips of water, so I couldn't imagine Quinn taking me out to dinner for date night. I might as well eat. Smiling, I turned the car toward downtown.

Only a year earlier, I would have blown off my cousins, certain that they were just throwing me a pity invite. I'd felt that way a lot in the months after Sam's death—not just grief-stricken, but rudderless and resentful. The army had spit me out, Sam was gone, and I was an empty shell. I just assumed any request for my presence was made out of guilt or obligation. Who would actually want to spend time with someone who so obviously couldn't get her shit together?

Really, it was Charlie who had saved me. Keeping her safe from the Old World had given me something to focus on, and then I'd been pulled into this whole other life. Quinn and the Pellars and Maven and the other vampires, a big new world of complications.

Was I better off? That, I couldn't answer. But I did know that I could go enjoy my cousins tonight, when a year ago I couldn't.

I found a metered parking spot downtown and walked through the pedestrian mall to meet Anna and Elise. It was a beautiful spring evening, and there were plenty of people out strolling the shopping district. I paused for a moment to smile at the kids climbing on the big stone-and-metal animal sculptures near the toy store. I'd brought Charlie here back in March. She'd clambered up and down the statues for over an hour, and I'd had to bribe her with ice cream when it was time to go. God, I missed her.

Something in my peripheral vision sent up a red flag in my mind. I twisted my head, expecting to see someone staring at me. Nothing. I scanned the crowd of shoppers, but no one froze or quickly turned away. So why did I suddenly have that familiar panicky feeling that there was a target on my back? I stayed there for a long time, scanning the crowd with heightened awareness, but I didn't see anything that could explain my sudden paranoia. It was maddening, but eventually I had to just move on.

The moment of panic made me late, and Elise and Anna were waiting for me outside Illegal Pete's, a burrito joint right on Pearl Street. Anna was twenty-seven and just finishing up a graduate degree. She had a big heart and had spontaneously developed a New Age streak as a teenager. Elise, on the other hand, was a uniformed officer with Boulder PD and my closest cousin in age and temperament. Both of them had the Luther biological trademarks of dark brown eyes and honey-blonde hair, although Elise's was cut short and Anna's flowed down her back. They looked like they could be sisters, and I felt a stab of displacement.

Shake it off, Lex, I told myself. Emil's arrival was getting in my head.

As we stood in line to order, they showed me the scarf they'd found for Natalie, the criminologist who Elise had been dating for the last six months. I gave my approval, and Elise told us about the birthday dinner she'd planned for the following night. "If I don't get called in for overtime," she added. "Nutjobs are coming out of the woodwork this week."

We had to stop talking to place our orders, going down the line to customize our burritos and quesadillas, but while we were waiting to pay, I asked Elise what she meant.

She made a face. "Nothing, I've just had two shifts in a row where I had to take a guy to the psych ward at BCH."

"Homeless people?" I didn't want to pigeonhole, but the homeless led really difficult lives. Elise had told us before that some of them acted crazy now and then to get a warm bed for a few nights. Then again, it was May.

"One was, but the other was just some dude, like twenty-six, decent job, girlfriend."

We collected our food and made our way to a table in the front, but not too close to the windows. My cousins automatically gave me the seat against the wall, a tiny courtesy that never failed to move me. "So what made him a nutjob?" Anna asked, looking curious.

"He just sort of lost it. Raving, waving his arms around, frothing at the mouth, trying to attack anyone who came near him." She reached up and pulled back her bangs, displaying a small purplish bruise. "I got this when he backhanded me."

Anna made a sympathetic noise without putting down her quesadilla. I hurried to swallow my own bite of veggie burrito so I could ask Elise, "Did you say frothing at the mouth?"

"Yeah, you know, white spittle. I've been spit on before, but this was very . . . dramatic."

My brow furrowed. Could this be related to the animal attacks? For the first time since Lily had used the word "rabies," I wondered if the crazy animals might have a connection to the Old World after all. I made a mental note to ask Simon as soon as possible. Meanwhile, there could still be a garden-variety scientific explanation.

"You should talk to Jake," I said to Elise. "He's seen a few animals with some weird virus that made them do the same thing. One of them was a fox that trashed my basement. Maybe it's related."

Elise looked skeptical. "Isn't it like, next to impossible for humans and mammals to get the same diseases?"

I shrugged. "What's the harm? It's not like Jake's gonna yell at you for asking."

Elise snorted at the idea of Jake yelling at anyone for anything, but she agreed to give him a call. We spent another twenty minutes gossiping about the family. Our cousin Brie was having another baby, which no one had really seen coming. Elise's younger brother Paul had recently decided to move to New York to pursue his music, and my aunt and uncle were not thrilled. In their defense, pretty much all of the Luthers had settled within an hour of where we were sitting. We'd all gotten spoiled by family dinners, well-attended celebrations, and a complicated, good-humored tangle of exchanged favors for childcare, pet sitting, and the lifting of heavy objects. It was weird to think of one of us moving away for good.

After spending the whole afternoon thinking about Emil Jasper, this casual time with my cousins was a nice reminder that I already had a place where I belonged.

Well, as long as I didn't tell them any details about my job, my new friends, or my boyfriend.

Anna announced that she had to pee and took off for the restaurant's iffy bathroom. While we waited, Elise surprised me by asking if Quinn and I wanted to go out to dinner with her and Natalie sometime. "Nat really likes you, and I'd like to get to know Quinn," she said.

My thoughts briefly tripped up on the idea that someone else at the police department liked me. Then I absorbed what she was asking. "Uh . . ."

"I—uh, that's really nice, but I'm not sure," I stammered.

Elise gave me a concerned look. "You never bring him to family stuff. You guys are still together, right?"

Before we were really dating, I *had* brought Quinn to my dad's sixtieth birthday party, months ago. But my family hadn't had any contact with him since, and for good reason. I gave Elise the same statement I'd given everyone in the family for six months now. "Yeah, we're together, but it's pretty casual."

Unlike my parents or my other cousins, however, Elise wouldn't take my word for it. She raised an eyebrow, putting on what the rest of us called her cop face. "Is he married?"

"*What?*" I cried, genuinely insulted. "Of course not! How could you even think that I—"

"You've been together for like six months," she said matter-of-factly. "Yet you barely seem to spend time with him. You act like it's this temporary relationship, but your face gets all girly whenever you mention him." She shrugged. "Ergo, married."

"No," I said through my teeth. "He is not married. And you take back what you said about my face."

Elise's probing look didn't waver. "Is he homophobic?"

"Of course not!" *Geez.* She'd managed to offend me three different ways in the space of two minutes.

"Great, then we'll do dinner," Elise said with a sweet smile. "I'm camping this weekend, but maybe next weekend?"

"Uh . . . I'll have to check my schedule," I said, fidgeting with my shirt and pushing my hair behind my ears. I'd been wearing it down more, now that I wasn't seeing much of Charlie. She considered my hair her personal toy property.

"Hey, you're wearing the earrings I got you!" Anna exclaimed, returning from the bathroom. She pointed at my earlobes, and I automatically reached up to touch one of the little studs she'd given me ages ago, when I was home between tours. They were in the shape of tiny curled-up griffins. My cousins didn't know about my tattoos—I wasn't sure how my family would take the fact that I suddenly had full-on ink sleeves covering my forearms, so I'd kept them hidden.

For a second I was *this close* to blurting out, "That's funny, Sam was just talking about griffins today." My brain caught up to my mouth just in time. "Yeah. I love them," I said instead.

"How come I never got a spirit animal?" Elise complained. "You only assigned one to Lex."

"Um, because you guys gave me shit for years for even bringing up the words 'spirit animal'?" Anna retorted. "Besides, Lex is special. She needs a griffin more than you do."

Elise rolled her eyes in a dismissive, Anna's-being-Anna way and started gathering up her jacket and bag. But I looked at my younger cousin with new interest. I'd always assumed she'd decided griffins were connected to me because of the whole army thing—in mythology, griffins symbolized courage and boldness, which was soldier stuff. Meanwhile, Sam had told me that griffins were the guardians of priceless treasures. I'd associated that with protecting Charlie. "What do you mean, I need one more?" I asked Anna.

"We talked about griffins when we were studying heraldry—you know, coats of arms and symbols and stuff," she said. "Griffins were drawn to powerful monsters, and they stood for military strength and leadership. I just thought you could use one." She grinned, gesturing at my earrings. "Or two."

"Huh." All along I'd associated myself with the griffin, but Anna had been barely thirteen when I'd gone to Iraq. She had hoped for a griffin to watch over *me*. "Thank you," I said sincerely. "That means a lot."

It was only when I was walking back to the car that I considered the rest of her words: griffins were drawn to powerful monsters. Like Maven? Or Quinn?

Then I remembered how good—how *right*—it had felt when I used boundary magic, and I shivered. Or was *I* the monster?

It's just a symbol, Lex, I reminded myself. Symbols only have the significance that we bring to them.

Right?

Chapter 10

I fought the commuter traffic so I could get home and take care of the herd, who were as glad to see me as ever. When they all stopped trying to scale my clothes and settled down to their dinners, I slipped into the bedroom to change for date night.

It was only then that I realized I had no idea where we were going. I wasn't really a movie person, unless there was a theater playing *Singin' in the Rain* or *Mr. Smith Goes to Washington*. Maybe a night hike? Then I probably shouldn't dress up, right? But it was a date . . . ?

I sighed. I hated girl problems.

In the end, I settled on my newest jeans and a short-sleeved silk blouse, sapphire blue to set off my eyes, and a cream-colored linen jacket to hide my tattoos and the shredder I strapped to my right forearm. I half-assed some makeup and spent a couple of minutes straightening my flyaway hair, and that was as primped as I got.

When I was ready, I checked the clock and realized I still had an hour to kill before sunset, when I would meet Quinn at Magic Beans. For once, I didn't feel like being alone, knowing I would just start to obsess over Emil's visit again. My first impulse was to stop at John's house to visit him and Charlie, but they were in Orlando, and besides, John didn't want to see me.

On a whim, I decided to swing by the Basement of Dr. Moreau to check on Simon. It had been ages since we'd just hung out.

Simon's lab was a converted two-bedroom apartment off Longbow in the same building where several of the Boulder vampires lived. Because it was one of Maven's properties, the building had been renovated so that the basement dwellers had a separate entrance from the humans who lived aboveground. By mutual agreement, everyone in the building left their neighbors the hell alone.

I had a key to the outer door that led to the basement, in case there was ever a security concern. When I knocked on Simon's door, he opened it just wide enough to stick his face out. Tall and lean with a nerdy-surfer thing going on, Simon was probably the crush of every undergraduate girl at CU . . . most of the time. Tonight, he looked exhausted and distracted, and he was wearing a blood-spattered lab coat and I-just-murdered-someone leather gloves. "Hey, Lex," he said wearily. "What's going on?"

"Um . . . hi. Can I come in?"

"Oh. Right." He opened the door, ushering me in quickly. It was a little pointless, given Maven's total control over the building, but it never hurt to be cautious. Inside, the apartment had been refitted with lab gear, including several enormous machines that I couldn't have identified if my life depended on it. If it had been anyone else, I might have suspected the gear was just for show, but I was pretty sure Simon used every bit of equipment in there. There was even an enormous aquarium against the back wall, which contained skin beetles that spent their lives eating the flesh off Unktehila bones. I purposely didn't look at it. I'd made that mistake before.

As usual, the air smelled like formaldehyde, Simon's cologne and a bunch of other scents I had no interest in identifying. "How's teaching?" I asked him. "Don't you have finals soon?"

He blanched for a moment, then shook his head. "Class is over, and my exams are already written, so there's not much going on this week."

I nodded. So much for the theory that school was making him look like that. "Have you learned anything new about the sandworm?" I asked tentatively. Six months was a long time to spend examining one dead body—even one as massive as the Unktehila—but Simon was working around a full-time job and his responsibilities for the witch clan. I knew his progress had been a lot slower than he wanted.

He opened his mouth to answer, stopped, and shook his head, looking frustrated. "I've managed to confirm a lot of what we suspected about the Unktehila's evolutionary ties to other species. It has no direct genetic connection to any of the human-evolved magic species, which is interesting. But I still have no idea why magic bonded with only certain creatures, or why the Unktehila was apparently immortal." His shoulders slumped. "And I've mostly run out of things to test."

"What were you hoping to find?"

"It's not that I had a specific goal like that, just . . ." he blew out a breath and removed one of his gloves to scrub a palm through his hair.

"What?"

"Generally, when I—or any other scientist—have an experiment, I can consult hundreds of years' worth of older tests. But this is the Old World, where everyone just writes everything off as 'magic' and goes on with their day," he grouched. If there were rocks nearby, he probably would have kicked at them.

I looked around for a second, and then dragged a metal lab stool over to where he was leaning on a counter. There *was* an actual kitchen table meant for the consumption of food, but I'd never seen Simon use it for anything but paper storage. "Aren't there some things that can only be explained with magic?"

I could tell from his face that this was the wrong question. "Maybe, but maybe not. How will we ever know for sure unless we look for answers? But I can't get any help, and if anyone else in the history of mankind has ever looked into these questions, there's no way to know."

"What about the internet?"

He gave me a look like I'd just walked into his class twenty minutes late. "Lex, there are hundreds of thousands of people online claiming to be witches. Even more claiming to use or study magic. How could I begin to weed out the real from the crazies without violating the law about never telling humans about the Old World? And any other actual witches would be bound by the same law, so they wouldn't be forthcoming either." He sighed. "It's impossible. There could be a dozen other Simons out there asking the same questions I am, but there's no way of finding them or talking to them."

I studied my friend. All these months of round-the-clock work, and he hadn't found the answers he wanted so badly. He looked so forlorn that my Luther family reflexes kicked in, and I impulsively stepped forward to give him a hug. "Trust me," I said over his shoulder. "There are no other Simons out there."

I didn't really expect him to reciprocate, but Simon's arms went tight around me, and he craned his head to bury his face in my neck. "Oh, hey," I said, surprised. Awkwardly, I rested my hand on his upper back. He was so warm, compared to Quinn, who only maintained as much body heat as he needed to pass for human. "It's okay, Simon."

I'm not a psychologist—if you can fail at therapy, I definitely flunked my VA sessions when I returned from Iraq—but even I could see whatever was bothering Simon wasn't just about the Unktehila experiments. So I held onto him, feeling the exhaustion in his body. He'd been pushing too hard. If he'd really run out of things to test with the Unktehila remains, what was he still doing in this depressing basement? Simon may not have had a wife and kids, but he had two jobs and a family, same as me. Something else was going on.

"Have you heard from Tracy?" I ventured. He and his longtime girlfriend had broken up months ago, but she was a witch, too. They still had to see each other.

Simon stepped back, looking away. "We don't really talk, no. The whole clan's been . . . disrupted. We didn't even celebrate Beltane this year, for the first time since I can remember. I barely feel like a witch these days."

I winced. I'd worried about how the Pellars were handling Morgan's betrayal, but I hadn't stopped to think about how it must be affecting the other witches in Boulder. Morgan was supposed to have been their next leader. And now she was gone, and the remaining Pellars were distressed and off-balance. Of course that would have ripple effects in the clan.

Simon stepped back a little and looked at me, realizing for the first time that I didn't look like all my clothes came out of a Goodwill store. "Hey, you look beautiful. Quinn's a lucky guy."

I blushed and looked away, mumbling a thank-you. I never did learn to take a compliment, but in this case I was especially embarrassed. Simon and Tracy's breakup was still fairly recent, for one thing, and I didn't want to rub my relationship in his face. But if I was being really honest with myself, it wasn't just that. I'd felt a little spark of *something* between us ever since I'd used my boundary magic to save Simon's life—or, rather, bring him *back* to life. I wasn't sure if it was a real attraction, or if all boundary witches felt that way about people they'd brought back. I had long since decided not to find out.

Simon, perhaps picking up on my thoughts, took another, more awkward step away from me. "How is Quinn?"

"He's good," I said. "He says you owe him a call about playing . . . um . . . Border . . . Redemption? Something like that." Simon and Quinn had been friends for years, though for appearances' sake they often pretended they couldn't stand each other. Until I started sleeping over at Quinn's, I hadn't known that they played video games in secret, like a weird online bromance affair. A vampire and a witch being friends wasn't forbidden or anything, but it was a little weird. Then again, I was a witch *sleeping with* a vampire, so I was even weirder.

"Right. Yeah, I'll do that soon," Simon promised. "And you guys are good?"

Were we? Well, probably as good as a witch-vampire relationship could be. "Yeah. But, Simon—"

"Listen, I should probably get back to it," he broke in. "Some of these tests are time-sensitive."

I studied his face for a long moment. He wasn't ready to talk. I wished I could cheer him up somehow, and then with a mental head-slap I remembered that I could.

"Hey, do you want to meet my father?"

He raised his eyebrows in confusion. "Like, to get a discount on shoes?"

"No. Well, yeah, I can set that up, but I don't mean my actual dad. My biological father came by this morning and introduced himself. He says he has boundary blood, and I bet I could talk him into a blood test."

Simon's face lit up.

Of course, introducing Simon to Emil meant that I'd actually need to call Emil. I hadn't really thought that part through, but I decided it could wait until the next morning. By then it was time for me to meet Quinn at Magic Beans. He would need to check in with Maven for the night before we could go out.

I expected the coffee shop to be crowded with students cramming for finals, but to my surprise, the "Closed for Private Party" sign was hanging on the door when I pulled up, and there were no cars parked in front. I frowned. Maven doesn't actually rent out the space for private parties; that sign only goes up when there's an Old World crisis—but no one had called me. I turned off the ignition and pulled out my cell phone. Nope. No calls. I tried the coffee shop line. When no one answered, I dialed Quinn's cell, but he didn't pick up either.

Not good. I drew the shredder out of the bands on my arm, climbed out of the car as quietly as possible, and stalked around the side of the building, keeping my steps soft. I was going to feel really silly if Maven and Quinn were just running late to work, but no, that couldn't be right. Magic Beans was open twenty-four hours a day. If it was dark like this, someone had cleared out the customers and sent home the daytime staff. Only Maven, and maybe Quinn, had the authority to do that.

When I reached the end of the brick building, I paused and peeked around the corner to look at the tiny lot behind the building. The lighting was bad back there—just a single dim bulb that buzzed and occasionally flickered. But as far as I could tell, it looked the same as ever. One of those exit doors with no exterior handle, a Dumpster, and a few bits of trash that had blown in from the alley. You could fit a couple of cars back there, and sure enough I saw Maven's Jeep, washed and looking as good as new. As far as I could tell, no one was inside it.

I was about to go knock on the back door of the building when I heard a muted metallic "thump" from behind the Dumpster, like someone was hiding back there and had bumped into the side. Shit. I held the shredder at shoulder height and crept forward as quietly as possible. When I reached the Dumpster, I carefully circled the first corner and then stopped again, intending to peek around it to see the trespasser.

Before I could do more than shift my weight, though, something unnaturally fast came up behind me and clutched at my upper right arm, grabbing me hard enough to knock me into the Dumpster. For a moment my face pressed against the metal, and I felt warm liquid spatter my hand. I looked down, trying to regain my balance, and realized that the hand clutching me was covered in blood.

Chapter 11

This was probably the moment when most people would scream. Instead, I pushed off the Dumpster, got my balance, and swung my left hand with the shredder in a fantastic roundhouse that would definitely have done catastrophic damage if Quinn hadn't ducked just in time.

"Shit!" I yelled as the stake hit the Dumpster and splintered, the impact shooting up my arm. I dropped the ruined stake and shook out my hand. "Quinn, what the hell—"

"Sorry." He was bending over, clutching one bloody wrist. More blood had run down his clothes and all over both hands. I didn't see any wound other than the wrist, but he was alabaster-pale, and his eyes burned like he had a fever. "Help her," he said weakly. "Maven."

"Where?"

"Keep going," he said, and I stepped around the Dumpster and looked down, my heart thudding in my chest.

Maven, the cardinal vampire of all of Colorado, was lying still on her back with her hair fanned out around her, like a princess in a fairy tale. Except usually the princess's hair isn't orange, and she's not wearing bag-lady clothes, with blood splashed all over her mouth, neck and face. Her eyes were closed, and she wasn't breathing, although vampires didn't technically need to.

I looked back at Quinn. "What—"

"Belladonna."

I cursed and darted forward, ignoring the blood that was pooled on either side of her head as I crouched down. Behind me, Quinn stumbled forward and dropped gracelessly to his knees on the other side of her. "How could this happen?" I asked.

In answer, Quinn stuck out the arm that wasn't bleeding and opened his hand, revealing two small, clear-glass cylinders, each with a needle on one end and fins on the other, like a pool dart. A dart gun. Someone had shot her with a dart gun. Dammit, I should have thought of that.

"I tried to give her my blood," Quinn continued, looking woozy. "Had to keep opening the vein . . ." He trailed off.

"Can vampires even drink vampire blood?"

"For a quick fix, not long-term," he mumbled. "Worked for a bit, but she started choking. Spit it out . . ." His eyes lost focus, and I knew he'd given too much blood. I didn't think it would kill him anytime soon, but he'd be weak until he fed again.

"Sit down," I ordered. Quinn sort of half-nodded and leaned back against the Dumpster. "You have a knife?" Vampire teeth are sharp enough to cut through skin, but most of them prefer to use a blade. Easier to explain the wounds later.

He pointed to Maven's body, and I leaned forward to see a large Swiss Army knife tucked against her arm where he'd dropped it. I picked it up and, trying to not give myself enough time to get grossed out, made a cut on the back of my right hand, like I'd seen Simon do once.

"Drink," I told Quinn, starting to move my hand toward him.

"No!" He lurched to his feet, slower than usual but still faster than most humans. "I can't." He pointed at Maven. "Help her. She's dying."

"Quinn—" I was planning to argue with him, but then I glanced down at Maven, just for a second, and realized something was seriously wrong. Her face seemed to be . . . not aging, exactly, but her skin was going gray and papery, like . . .

Like it was beginning to decay. Which happens when vampires die. Panic jolting through me, I slapped the back of my hand over her open mouth, praying she could drink it. Vampires *can* feed off witchblood, but if she couldn't swallow Quinn's . . .

Blood dribbled into her mouth, and for a long moment she remained completely motionless. The decay didn't progress, but it didn't reverse, either.

I cursed under my breath. It wasn't working. I looked to Quinn for help, but his eyes had drifted shut again. "If you're wrong about this, Nellie, so help me . . ." Wincing, I turned one of Maven's wrists over and used the knife to make a deep slash down the main vein. It was clumsy and I had no idea if I'd gone to the right depth, but blood erupted out of the cut like it was evacuating her body, spraying straight up. That didn't seem normal, but then again, what did I know about vampire baselines?

I reared my head back and managed to avoid most of the spray, but some of it got into my hair and jeans. A voice in the back of my mind started chanting *ew-ew-ew*, but I didn't have time to listen. I clamped down on Maven's cut with my left hand and positioned my bleeding wound back over her mouth. "Come on," I urged. "Please, *please* drink."

Maven didn't stir during the cut or the gushing of blood, and she didn't stir now. But after only a few seconds I saw her throat work, once, twice. I blew out a relieved breath.

Slowly—agonizingly slowly—her skin lost the papery cast and looked . . . well, it was still whiter than was humanly possible, but at least it looked like skin. "It's working." I dared to lift my left hand a little, and saw that the cut on Maven's wrist wasn't bleeding anymore. Thank goodness. I pushed back a strand of hair from my eyes, not caring that I was probably smearing more blood on my forehead.

I looked up at Quinn, but he had slumped sideways against the Dumpster, his eyes closed. "Quinn!" I yelled, and to my immense relief, he straightened up a little and looked at me. "Did your wound close?" I said, trying to keep my voice low and calm.

He looked down. "Yeah." He sighed, and his eyelids began to flutter.

"Hey! Quinn!"

When he was looking at me again, I said, "We need help. And blood. Who do you trust?"

He gave me a slow blink. "Don't know. If anyone finds out . . ."

He didn't finish, but he didn't have to. Maven controlled supernatural activity in the whole state. If anything happened to her, it would break the peace between vampires and witches and leave the state wide open for werewolf activity—or for Morgan to come back and stir up trouble all over again. And then there were all the other powerful supernatural creatures who would be interested in coming in to take the state for their own. Nature abhors a power vacuum.

And without Maven's protection, Charlie would be fair game.

This was not good.

Besides Quinn, there were only two people in the Old World whom I fully trusted—but pulling Simon and Lily into this would put them in the very awkward position of keeping a powerful secret from their own mother. Again. Hazel Pellar was the most powerful witch in the state, but she had strong feelings about helping the vampires. Her loyalty to Maven was iffy at best: although they had a bargain in place, it didn't exactly favor the witches. It limited them. Besides, if something were to happen to Maven, Hazel's eldest daughter would be able to return to Colorado to be with her children. Not to mention Hazel herself could have a go at ruling the state.

At the same time, though, what choice did I have? If I didn't get some help, Maven was gonna die, and possibly Quinn, too.

Still feeding Maven with one hand, I pulled out my phone with the other.

Chapter 12

My knees started to hurt after a few minutes of crouching, and I had to give up and sit down cross-legged, feeling lukewarm blood saturate the back of my pants. I told myself to think of it as a puddle of water, which actually helped a little.

I fed Maven for as long as I dared, but when I got light-headed and started to see spots at the edges of my vision, I had to stop and clutch my hand, trying to slow the bleeding. Luckily, it was only about five more minutes before I heard Simon's Chevy pull into the little alley between Magic Beans and the next building.

Simon happened to be having dinner at the Pellar farmhouse when I'd called, so he and Lily had made some excuse and driven over together. They climbed out of the car and rushed toward us, each holding a backpack. With a grunt of greeting, Simon unzipped his pack and pulled out the same lantern he'd used when we were hunting the Unktehila, setting it up next to Maven's body. The blaze of light was almost shocking, and I squinted away from it. I wanted to tell him to turn the lantern off—what if someone saw us?—but we were tucked in a tiny lot behind a Dumpster. I doubted it could be seen from the street.

I'd warned them to wear old clothes, but I didn't realize how much blood my own outfit had collected until Lily rushed over to me and I followed her shocked gaze downward. My jeans were saturated, my silk blouse and blazer were decorated in damp dark blotches, and my skin was stained red in patches that ran from my arms to, probably, my face. It looked like I'd fallen into a bathtub of red dye. Luckily, I was just too dizzy to be properly grossed out. "This is why I can't have nice things," I mumbled to myself.

Lily crouched down near Maven's head, right next to me. On the other side of her, Simon was pulling out what appeared to be his own personal vampire feeding kit, which included bandages, sterilized needles, IV tubing, and surgical knives. "You're really going full-time with the Dr. Frankenstein bit, aren't you?" I asked weakly.

"Frankenstein was just misunderstood," Simon said, his tone so serious that I couldn't decide if he was kidding or not. He handed the IV kit to Lily, who'd done a couple of years of medical school. She had already put on surgical gloves, and she expertly inserted an IV into the back of Simon's hand. It was attached to a long tube with some sort of one-way stopper on the end. Quinn had passed out again, so Simon unceremoniously poked the end of the tube through his lips, provoking a hilariously confused expression from the vampire.

"Hey, dipshit," Simon said brightly. "Let me get the first round." Quinn rolled his eyes and held the tube to his lips.

Lily was stripping off her surgical gloves. "Can you feed Maven?" I asked her.

"In a minute. You're too pale." She took my wrist, checking her watch with her free hand. "Tachycardic," she muttered to herself. She reached toward me until she could put both hands on my face, like a mother feeling for a fever. "Shit. You're clammy. You lost way too much blood."

"Yeah, I was just starting to think that myself," I said unsteadily.

"This a severe hemorrhage, Lex. You could go into shock."

"Later."

"You need a blood transfusion—"

"Later," I said stubbornly. I tilted my head toward Maven, lifting my eyebrows.

Lily sighed. "Let me see your hand." She made a clucking noise when she saw the cut I'd made. "Sloppy. But it shouldn't scar, since you got some vampire saliva in there. Stitches or butterfly bandages?"

"Butterflies."

"I figured." As she taped up my hand, I watched Maven's still form. She still looked bad, but maybe a tiny bit better than when I'd first arrived? It was so hard to tell with the change in lighting. I wanted to ask Quinn what he thought of her condition, but he'd have to stop drinking blood to answer, and he needed it more than I needed an answer just then.

"How much belladonna did she get?" Simon asked, seeing my gaze. When I looked back at him, I noticed the old spark of scientific curiosity in his eyes. I cocked an eyebrow, and he blushed. "Sorry. I didn't mean for that to come out . . . *excited*. I've just never actually seen any of the Solanaceae in action before. Do you know how strong the dose was?"

"No, but she took two vials in the back." While waiting for the Pellars, I'd checked Maven for puncture wounds. There were two marks right next to each other in the middle of her back, between her shoulder blades.

"They shot her in the back?" Lily said, wrinkling her nose in disgust. "That's so . . . tacky."

"Yes, it is." I heard the anger in my own voice. It really bothered me that I hadn't thought of the possibility of a dart gun.

Lily had finished bandaging the back of my hand and was digging into her own pack. She pulled out a half-gallon container of orange juice, with about a third of the juice still inside, and a package of Newman's Own cookies, handing them to me. "This is what my mom had available. You need the glucose and hydration."

As I took the food, she picked up the IV kit again and began swabbing the inside of her arm. "I get better veins there," she said when she saw me looking. "Simon?"

Her brother leaned forward and helped Lily insert the IV needle, moving very slowly so he wouldn't disturb the needle and tube taped to his own hand. For a moment, watching the two of them literally tying themselves to vampires, I was overwhelmed with gratitude. Simon may have been Quinn's friend, but neither Pellar really owed the vampires anything. They'd come because I'd asked, and they had done so without a second thought. My vision blurred a little. I told myself it was just blood loss.

"Lex?" *Whoops.* Simon had been talking to me.

"Sorry, what?"

"I asked if you thought there were multiple shooters. Shouldn't she have been able to dodge after the first dart? The poison can't work that fast."

I shook my head. "Dart guns are single-shot weapons. There's no way someone would have time to reload, which means two weapons firing simultaneously." Being careful of the bandage, I held out my hands in front of me to demonstrate. "Two shooters is possible, but I'd put my money on one shooter with a sidearm-style tranquilizer gun in each hand. It would be the easiest way to make sure the shots were simultaneous."

Simon frowned. "If I'm remembering right, those darts don't hold all that much liquid, though. Would that amount of belladonna really put Maven down?"

"Those weren't the only shots," Lily said suddenly, staring at Maven's linen top. All three of us looked at her. "Look." With her free hand, she pulled down the neckline, stopping just above the vampire's breasts. I leaned forward and saw an angry red puncture wound, the size of a really big needle, right over Maven's heart. I'd completely missed it, having stopped searching after I found the shots in her back.

"Jesus," Simon breathed. "They shot her twice in the back to incapacitate her, then put a syringe straight into her heart."

"That's really cold," Lily said, awed.

I just stared. It *was* cold. It was also brilliant.

"What are you guys going to do?" Simon asked, looking between Quinn and me.

I met Quinn's gaze. His color wasn't all the way back, but his eyes were alert. He tapped Simon on the shoulder and nodded to indicate that Simon could stop the IV. Taking the tube out of his mouth, Quinn said flatly, "Right now, we have to get her the hell out of here. And we need to get rid of all this blood."

"Are we sure it's safe to move her?" Lily said.

Quinn leaned forward, getting his face right down next to Maven's skin, and inhaled deeply. The Pellars and I exchanged a glance, but none of us had any idea what he was doing. After a couple more sniffs, he sat up with a little nod. "When I first found her, she reeked of decay," he explained. "She was right on the edge. I don't smell any now. I think it's okay to move her, but she won't be out of the woods until we can get her heart to start beating again."

"Oh! I took Nellie's advice," I said, remembering suddenly.

"You went back to see Nellie?" Lily said, at the same time that Simon asked, "What was it?"

"She said we had to drain some of the poisoned blood out first, letting the vampire's blood pressure drop. Then give them untainted blood. We thought she was messing with us, but—" I pointed to the mark on Maven's arm. It should have been completely healed by then, but it looked like a fresh scar. "When Quinn's blood wasn't working, I tried it."

"So now what?" Lily asked.

"We're supposed to give it twenty-four hours," I said. "That will, um, redistribute the poison in her current blood supply. Then we do the same thing again."

"None of us are going to be able to donate much in twenty-four hours," Simon pointed out.

"Especially you, Lex," Lily added. "You still need to go to the hospital. At least for fluids."

"Relax," I told her. "I can't die, remember?"

She didn't look comforted. "Maybe not, but if your blood pressure drops off the scale, you can't function, either."

Quinn frowned at me, but all he said was, "I'll talk to my blood bag contacts to see if it's possible to get a large supply without drawing attention."

"Which brings us to the immediate problem of where to keep her," I said, looking at Quinn. "Where are you keeping the other two infected vampires?"

He shook his head. "One of our warehouses in Denver, but we can't take her there. People know about it, and we don't know who we can trust."

"What about one of the, um, portable vampire storage units?" I asked, referring to the empty, clean septic tanks that Maven had stashed all over the state for emergencies.

"Too many of us know where they are."

Duh, Lex. "Right."

Quinn looked at Simon. "Say, dumbass . . . how many people know about your new lab?"

Chapter 13

Quinn had parked down the street, so Lily, who was the cleanest of all of us, went to his car and backed it into the parking lot, blocking the alley. Quinn popped the trunk and pulled out plastic tarps. He had a lot of them for . . . well, I won't say situations like this, because none of us had heard of anyone attacking Maven and surviving, but it was his job to deal with the bodies. Mine, too.

Lily put a tarp down in the Jeep's vampire storage compartment and draped the extras on the seats. Quinn put Maven in the storage compartment, and then he matter-of-factly stripped down to his boxers and wrapped his bloody clothes and shoes in another tarp. Lily didn't wolf whistle when he undressed, which told me a lot about how freaked out we all were. Maven was down. We were dealing with it, but mostly on autopilot, because . . . God, *Maven was down.*

Quinn rummaged around in the very bottom of the trunk, which was basically his own version of Mary Poppins's bag, and eventually came out with a garden hose, the kind you could get at any home improvement store. He hooked it up to a spigot on the back of the building, which I'd never even noticed, and began rinsing away the blood, trying to move it in the direction of the nearest sewer grate. I wanted to offer to help, but I was having a little trouble sitting upright at the moment.

I rested my eyes for a second, and then suddenly Quinn was pulling me up, helping me stumble toward the Jeep. He gently dug my keys out of my pocket and tossed them to Lily. Then he wrapped a tarp around me like it was a blanket and planted me on the passenger seat.

I dozed against the window for a bit, barely registering when the vehicle stopped and then started again. We stopped a second time, and I almost toppled out when Quinn opened my door. I would have landed on my face if he hadn't caught me.

"Come on," he said gently. He started to pick me up, but I shook my head. I did not want to be carried like a princess. "I am not a princess," I said out loud. I doubted he followed my train of thought, but he just nodded, put one of my arms over his shoulder, and gripped me around the waist. At some point he had put on a T-shirt and athletic pants. He had a plastic bag in his other hand, and I could hear it swishing as we stumbled into the building.

He dropped me on a stool at the kitchen counter, where I lay my head down in my arms between Simon's instruments, burrowing from the light. The blood on my clothes was getting tacky, but as filthy as I was, I just wanted to sleep.

Then Lily was there, taking one of my arms and prodding at it. "Hey," I mumbled, too out of it to be indignant. "Where's Maven?"

"Hidden in the back room," Quinn said over my shoulder.

Lily turned my arm over, examining the underside. "She's got too much blood splashed on her. We need to clean her up so there's no infection."

So Quinn and I took a shower together—but only because I needed him to help me stay upright. I kept both hands on the shower stall while he scrubbed at the bloodstains on my skin and washed my hair. It probably would have been tender and romantic if I didn't kind of feel like throwing up. Every few minutes I started to list to one side and he had to right me.

At least the hot water was waking me up a little. "This isn't how I pictured our first shower together," Quinn remarked.

"I never planned to have a shower together at all."

"No?"

"No. Sex in the shower is like buying a convertible or getting a perm. It seems all fun and sexy in theory, but what actually happens is discomfort and weird hair."

He threw back his head and laughed, a sound that I felt in my stomach. I'm not a funny person, but man, I *loved* Quinn's laugh.

He dressed in the same outfit he'd been wearing and helped me dry off. I hadn't thought to keep a spare outfit in the Jeep, so I had to put on some of Simon's clothes: a clean pair of boxers and a CU T-shirt, which just generally made me look like it was the morning after at a frat house. But at least I wasn't covered in vampire blood.

When we were decent, Quinn sat me down at the metal table in the kitchen and Lily, who had cleaned up in the other bathroom and dressed in more of Simon's clothes, pounced on me with a new IV kit.

"What are you doing?" I asked, my words coming out thick.

Lily shot me a surprised look. "You don't remember? Damn, you *are* out of it." She held up a clear plastic tube filled with liquids, as though she were displaying a prize fish. "Your boyfriend got you IV fluids!"

I smiled. "And it's not even my birthday."

A few minutes later, Lily and Quinn had rigged up a makeshift IV stand out of a coat tree, and I was shivering in my chair. I always forget how cold IV fluids feel going into you. The damp hair hanging on my shoulders didn't help much. Lily pulled her chair right up next to me and lined up the side of her body with mine, adding a little warmth. Quinn stood by the table with his hands in his pockets, restless because he couldn't do anything. His body temp was barely warm enough to pass for human.

Simon came out of the bedroom rubbing his wet hair with a towel, dragging a flannel comforter. "This should help," he said, tucking it around me. The comforter smelled like Simon—a whiff of farm, a bit of lab chemicals, and Old Spice. I smiled my thank-you.

Quinn and Simon sat down, and Quinn began to explain the situation to both Pellars. He went through the whole story, from the moment Maven had called us in until the moment I'd called them for help.

The mood sobered quickly as the enormity of what was happening began to sink in. Even assuming that Maven recovered, we had no idea how long it would take. According to Simon, it could be weeks or months. And although Quinn was Maven's right hand, we all knew he didn't have the raw power to hold the state if anyone came after it. We needed another plan.

"Basically," Quinn concluded, "We have two choices. We can try to cover up Maven's current condition, or we can ask someone else to step in and take control in her absence. Like an interim cardinal."

"Is that a thing?" Lily asked.

He shrugged. "It's happened before, often during belladonna attacks." Lily and Simon didn't notice the note of negativity in his voice, but I picked up on it.

"What?" I asked.

Quinn grimaced. "I'm worried about perception. Things were just beginning to settle down after the Unktehila mess, which itself was right after Maven killed Itachi to get Colorado, at least from a lot of peoples' perspective. Maven's enclave is running low on faith and high on uncertainty. To come forward and say that Maven let herself get attacked—"

"But there's no way she could have seen this coming," I protested, but he held up a hand.

"I know that, and you know that. But most vampires won't see things that way. If you succumb to an attack, it's *always* your fault. You left an opening."

There were a few seconds of quiet as we all digested this. "Okay, I get that," I said finally, "but at the same time, hiding the belladonna attack doesn't seem feasible long-term. We could make up a story for a night or two, but there's all the practical stuff with the coffee shop—schedules, deliveries, paydays—plus, if one of the vampires from somewhere else in the state walks in with a problem and doesn't find her here, there will be hell to pay."

"And whoever did this may be motivated to stir up more shit," Lily added. "They could either go public with Maven's absence or come after her again."

My phone buzzed on the counter. I automatically started to get up, but Quinn waved me down at the same time Simon darted for the phone. Rolling my eyes, I held out my free hand for him to pass it to me. I glanced at the caller ID—St. Julien Hotel—and hit "Ignore." "Emil?" Simon asked. He'd taken a peek at the screen, too.

I nodded. "I'll call him back."

Quinn looked at me with a question on his face, but I just shook my head. I hadn't even had a chance to tell him about my birth father yet, but obviously the attack on Maven was a hell of a lot more important than my personal identity crisis. I'd tell him later.

The boxers I was wearing didn't have pockets, so I set the phone on the table in front of me. When I looked up, though, Simon was staring at me. "What?" I asked.

He shook himself, and then said haltingly, "No offense, Lex, but it does seem like a pretty big coincidence that your biological father arrived in town right before Maven was poisoned."

"Wait, *what*?" Lily exclaimed. Quinn raised his eyebrows at me, which for him was pretty much the same as Lily's outburst.

I gave them a brief explanation of Emil's visit that morning. Lily was obviously bursting to discuss it further, but I turned back to Simon. "I agree that the timing seems fishy. But the poisoning started weeks ago," I pointed out. "Emil just flew in yesterday. Besides, I can't see any reason for him to go after Maven or the vampires."

"Neither can I," he conceded.

"Where were we?" I asked, glancing at Quinn. He looked thoughtful.

"The way I see it, two things need to happen." He looked at Simon. "I need you to work on the belladonna. Figure out if there's some shortcut to waking Maven. Failing that, see if you can predict how long it'll take her to snap out of it if we continue with the transfusions. And test the darts we found to see if they tell you anything about the makeup of the poison. Anything that might help us figure out who did it."

Simon nodded, brightening. "I can do that."

"I can help," Lily chimed in. "I might not know much about evolution, but I know biology as well as Si does."

"Well, maybe not *as* well," Simon said under his breath. Lily just rolled her eyes at him.

"What about us?" I asked Quinn.

"We're going to figure out who did this and kill them. And we're going to do it really, really fast."

The best way to trace the belladonna, Quinn explained, would be to figure out who was dealing in the area. He gave Lily and Simon a sidelong look. "I'm not accusing you guys of anything, but you know most of the witches in the state, and the herbs are witch magic."

"Fetters," Simon corrected.

"Hmm?"

"The big three—wolfberry, belladonna, and mandragora," he explained. "We call them the fetters of magic. And they're *not* witch magic. The witches were just the first to discover their uses."

"Okay," Quinn said, "But historically, the majority of people who work with the, uh, fetters, are witches, right?"

"Only because we had to," Lily said, a little snappish. "No one would goddamn help us, and then you-all started treating us like we were drug lords."

I blinked, surprised. We had suddenly jumped into a *very* old argument about how vampires hadn't stepped in to save witches during the Inquisition. If we got into this debate, we might never leave it.

"No one has ever treated you like a drug lord, Lily—" Quinn began, but I poked my free hand out of Simon's comforter and waved at them to stop.

"Guys, enough. Quinn knows you have nothing to do with the herbs, right, Quinn?" His jaw was a little set, but he nodded. I turned to Simon and Lily. "But if you absolutely had to acquire some belladonna, what would you do? Who would you go to?"

The Pellars exchanged a look, and then Simon shrugged. "Billy Atwood, probably," he said. "But he's . . . um, dead."

That was a nice way to put it. Atwood was the witch I had sort of killed in order to save Simon's life. "Atwood dealt belladonna?" I asked.

Lily finally tore her glare away from Quinn. "Atwood dealt everything. But there was never much of a market for the fetters in Colorado, since my mother made peace with Maven."

"Okay, so who would take over Atwood's business?" I asked. The Pellars shrugged, clueless. "What about the Atwood farm? You said he was the last descendent, but there must have been a cousin or distant uncle or something who would inherit."

I couldn't quite interpret the look that passed between the two Pellars—God, I missed sibling insta-communication—but it was Simon who spoke. "Ardie Atwood," he said softly.

"Who's she?"

Simon looked at his sister, giving her room to speak. Finally Lily sighed. "She's Billy's second cousin, the family black sheep. Because she actually went to college and made something of herself."

I knew Lily well enough to know when she was holding something back. "And?"

She stared at the table, looking a little sullen. "And she's my ex."

Chapter 14

Lily decided that I needed food to go with my IV fluid, and everyone but Quinn needed coffee. She went to the apartment's little kitchenette and began banging around, muttering under her breath, as Simon told Quinn and me the story.

Lily and Ardie had attended CU at the same time—Lily as an undergrad, Ardie as a masters student in ecology. They knew each other a little from witch business, but CU was the first time they'd met on neutral territory. Both were from old witch families, both were idealistic and optimistic about magic, and both wanted to break out of the family mold. The way Simon told the story, it was almost inevitable that they would start dating.

Unfortunately, both families objected. The Atwoods were homophobic, not to mention worried about dying out. They wanted Ardie to have babies as soon as possible. "They had actually tried to push Ardie at *me* a few times, hoping to increase their political capital, but I was with Tracy," Simon told us. "Anyway, they got pissed about Ardie dating a non-reproductive option, even if she was a Pellar."

Meanwhile, Hazel Pellar couldn't care less about bisexuality, but she considered her children, and the Pellar line, better than the "backwoods Atwoods," who would surely drag Lily down into the mud with them.

Tensions increased, and then the Atwoods made Ardie an offer: full tuition for as much education as she wanted, plus a down payment on a house anywhere but Boulder. And although women didn't usually inherit in their clan, her family offered to make her the Atwood heir should anything happen to Billy—which was a safe bet, since he was already something of a cretin. All Ardie had to do was agree to leave Lily and have kids with a man.

When she heard about the offer, Lily got ready for a knock-down, drag-out battle for love, assuming Ardie would feel the same. But Ardie took the money.

"I'm not sure she ever cared as much about Lily as Lily did for her," Simon said in a low voice. "But at any rate, she was Lily's first big love, and getting dumped kind of crushed her. Especially because Ardie would sneak back into town now and then to, um . . . reconnect. And then she'd leave again."

My eyes narrowed. "So she used Lily."

Simon nodded. "For years." He looked angry and sad, but also just . . . tired. This was an old story, one that all the Pellars had wanted to forget. Now we were dredging it up again.

"You said she studied ecology," I said, trying to sound tactful, even though I wanted to slap this woman I'd never met. "Isn't it possible that Ardie grows belladonna?"

Simon shrugged. "She'd know how, sure, but so would my mom, or pretty much anyone with a rudimentary understanding of gardening. Or an internet connection. *Growing* it is easy. The hard part is finding the belladonna seeds from the ancient strain."

"But if Atwood had it on the property, and Ardie inherited . . ." Quinn spoke up.

"No." Lily banged down a sloshing coffeepot. Simon hastily took a mug from the counter and began filling it while Lily set a couple of granola bars in front of me. "Keep eating," Lily told me. To all of us, she added, "Ardie *always* said the fetters were too dangerous to dick around with. She's many things, but she's careful."

"Calculating, more like," Simon muttered into his mug before taking a long sip. Lily glared at him, but he just shrugged and swallowed. "She might have changed her mind about the belladonna, Lil. Or she might have moved to Finland, and she's got nothing to do with any of this. We haven't seen her in years."

A guilty look flitted across Lily's face, but Simon didn't notice. I didn't want to call Lily out in front of the others, so I got to my feet, not needing to feign the shakiness. "Lily, can you help me in the bathroom for a second?" I asked.

She looked a little surprised by the request, as did Quinn, but she unhooked my IV bag from the coatrack and led me down the hall, helping me weave around Simon's piles of equipment. When we got into the small bathroom, I closed the door and sagged against a counter. "You've seen Ardie recently?" I said gently.

Her dark skin flushed, but she nodded. "She stopped by last year, after Billy's funeral. But I still don't think she'd mess with the fetters."

"Do you have her address or phone number?"

Lily bit her lip. "Simon made me delete her numbers from my phone . . . but I know she works at the Denver Botanic Gardens. She's a horticulturist."

"Okay. Quinn and I are going to need to pay her a visit."

"I know." Lily switched the IV bag from one hand to the other, uneasy. "I should go with you."

"I don't think that'd be a great idea."

"She might not talk to you."

"Oh, she'll talk to me." Something in my face must have hardened, because Lily took an unconscious step backward, the IV tubing wobbling between us. "You can stay here and give Simon a hand, okay?"

She nodded again, and I turned to grab the doorknob. Before I could turn it, Lily reached out and touched my arm. "You're not going to ask me about sleeping with girls?"

I shrugged. "None of my business."

Something sad and bitter touched her eyes for a moment. "Some women would be worried that I was secretly lusting after them."

It hadn't occurred to me, but I cocked an eyebrow as dramatically as I could. "Lily, are you secretly lusting after my body?"

An actual giggle spilled from her lips. "Not so much."

"Well, obviously you have no standards and I pity you."

She threw her head back and laughed.

Lily made me sit still through two more bags of IV fluid. While I did that, Quinn called his contacts to dig up Ardie's home address. I didn't know much about how he got that kind of information, but I didn't really want to know, either. Simon and Lily, meanwhile, worked out a schedule for the next couple of days so one of them would always be in the apartment with Maven. As long as word didn't get out that Simon was hiding her, they would be okay. Even if someone did come for Maven, Simon was living there, which meant a vampire would have to be invited in. Lily or Simon could probably handle any other unwelcome guests with apex magic.

By the time I finished the last bag of fluid, I felt like I'd been brought back from the brink of death . . . although since I actually *had* returned from death a couple of times, I suppose that was hyperbole. At any rate, I also really had to pee. When I got back from the bathroom, Quinn was waiting with a Post-it Note in hand: Ardie Atwood's address in Denver.

The two of us made a quick stop at my cabin to change clothes—he had a drawer in my room—and feed the herd, since I wasn't sure when we'd be back. I also put on an unseasonably heavy jacket, still chilled from the IV fluids.

Then we were on the road.

Chapter 15

I kept my eyes in my lap while Quinn drove us in the Jeep. Part of me was hoping I'd eventually get used to the sight of a translucent, half-decapitated man wandering the intersection at 30th and Arapahoe, or the two little girls who ran skipping into the street every night on Baseline Road. At the same time, though, I didn't *want* to get used to it. I didn't want the horror of their deaths to fade into normality. I had a sudden flash of memory: the ghost of Hugh Mark, former manager of the Boulderado, begging me to help the hotel's remnants cross the line between living and dead. He'd wanted me to make them whole again on the other side, but I had no idea how to do that. I reminded myself that when this was over I needed to go back and push Nellie for more information on boundary magic. For now, though, I just stared at my hands and hoped no one had died in Ardie Atwood's house.

I didn't need to worry. Ardie Atwood lived in a fairly new "planned community" neighborhood in Aurora, the kind of place where the homeowner's association forbids large dogs and everyone has to have their lawn cut to regulation length. It was after one a.m. by the time we pulled into the driveway, but there was a small light on in one of the upstairs bedrooms. A reading lamp, maybe.

When we rang the doorbell, I instinctively braced myself for barking out of habit, but this house remained silent. After a long moment, I reached for the doorbell again, but Quinn stayed my hand. A light had popped on inside, and a moment later the small window in the door revealed a woman in her late thirties padding down carpeted steps.

I'm not sure what I was expecting from Ardie Atwood, but it was definitely on the supermodel side of attractive, like one of those celebrities who's so good-looking they could seduce men, women, and most forms of plant life. But the woman who opened the door seemed like nothing special: shorter than me, blonde hair chopped short, fashionable square plastic glasses. She was in her late thirties or early forties, and wore old-fashioned button-down pajamas with slippers, along with a few extra pounds on her hips. There was a faint odor clinging to her, and after a moment I realized she'd been smoking pot recently. "Yes?" she said, frowning up at us.

I let Quinn take the lead. "Ardie Atwood?"

"*Doctor* Atwood-Kazinsky," she corrected, straightening up. "Who are you?"

"I'm Quinn, this is Lex. We represent Maven's interests."

When he mentioned Maven's name, I watched Ardie carefully. She reacted, certainly, but I couldn't tell if it was an "oh shit what does she want" reaction or an "oh shit the vampire I conspired to murder" reaction.

After a glance behind us for witnesses, she opened the door wider. "You'd better come in, I suppose. You're lucky my husband and children are out of town this week." She turned on her heel, assuming we would follow.

Quinn and I exchanged a look, but trailed her through a beige hallway into a small, tidy living room. Ardie had said she had children, but you would never know that from seeing the house, or at least the downstairs. There was no sign of any toys or clothes, let alone the cheerful clutter that always infested John's house. The paint, carpeting, and furniture were all different shades of beige and gray. It was like a conservative dentist's office without the old magazines.

"You can sit there," she said, pointing at a sofa. She dropped into the opposite armchair. "What is this about?"

By unspoken agreement, Quinn and I remained standing, even though I still felt a little light-headed. "Several of the Denver vampires have recently succumbed to belladonna," Quinn said, his voice even.

If Ardie was uncomfortable with us standing, she didn't show it. She leaned back and crossed her legs. "I don't know anything about that." She paused and waved a hand. "Well, of course I know about the plant—I'm a horticulturalist. But I have nothing to do with the fetters."

"Your cousin Billy dealt them," I pointed out. "And you inherited his property."

"Which I sold three months ago," she said, barely glancing at me. "Cleaning out that junk heap cost me a fortune, but it's close enough to Boulder to still turn a profit. If I remember correctly, the buyers are currently building a new house on the property." She stood up. "If that's all?"

"'If that's all?'" I repeated, not bothering to keep the incredulousness out of my voice. "You're trying to tell us you just . . . *delegated* the removal of hazardous and illegal materials, and we're supposed to smile and skip out the door?"

Atwood crossed her arms, reddening. "I don't care what you believe. That's what happened, and you have no right to come into my home—"

"*You* have no rights here," I snapped, taking a single step toward her. "You don't get it, Ardie. We're not the police, and we don't answer to anyone but Maven. For *anything*."

Something in my face scared her, and she swallowed whatever she had planned on saying. Quinn glanced at me, and I saw a flash of curiosity and amusement cross his face before he turned to Ardie. He wasn't usually the one playing good cop. "Dr. Kazinsky, you must understand why we need to cover our bases here. Vampires were poisoned fifteen minutes away from your house. You work with plants, and at some point you had access to the herb in question." He spread his hands helplessly, as if to say *what choice do we have?* "We would look awfully stupid if we didn't at least come speak to you."

Taking a deep breath, she rubbed her eyes with the heels of her hands for a moment. When she lowered them, her gaze seemed clearer. "I suppose I can understand that," she said with a rueful smile. "And I *do* want to help however I can. Let's try this again, all right?" She gestured to the couch. "Please."

She sat back down in the chair, and I followed Quinn to the couch, perching on the edge. I was immensely relieved to be sitting, but I tried not to let it show on my face. "Would you like something to drink, Lex?" she asked. "Hot chocolate, or perhaps something stronger?" Her eyes were eager, hoping to please me. But I wasn't falling for the new ass-kissing strategy.

"No," I said flatly. "But I would like to know where Billy Atwood got the belladonna."

"Ah." She leaned back in her overstuffed chair, getting comfortable. "Now there's a good question. Unfortunately, most of Billy's contacts were out of state."

"How would you know that, if you weren't involved with his business?" Quinn asked reasonably.

She didn't take offense, just pushed up her glasses with one finger and explained, "You have to know a little about our family. The Atwoods, as I'm sure you've heard, have something of an unsavory reputation, but we weren't always this way. Once we were as respected in this state as the Pellars, maybe even more so. We are trades witches, but we have a bit of a talent for growing things. Obviously I've inherited it, given my career choices." She smiled again, her eyes sparking. For the first time I saw it: energy and joy, an enthusiasm that went beyond enjoyment and into the realm of passion. It made her beautiful. *Okay, Lily, I get it.* "Anyway, most Atwoods were farmers, but a hundred years ago, my great-grandfather Amos decided to set a new course. He set up shop as a spiritualist in Sterling, along a branch of the Oregon Trail." Her smile fell away. "He made a fortune. At first, anyway."

"Spiritualist?" I asked.

She winced. "'Medium' would be a better term, I suppose. He led séances."

"Was he a boundary witch?" Quinn said.

"No, of course not." She sounded disgusted, like Quinn had asked if Amos had married his favorite sheep. "He could do a little trades magic, but he was really quite weak."

"So he duped people," I put in. "Tricked them out of their money."

Her eyes hardened, but only a little. "He *wanted* it to be real, though. He developed contacts in the Spiritualist community, but in those days it was easier to travel north and east than to venture into Denver and Boulder. Eventually he got hold of some mandragora."

"Which brings people back from the dead," I said quietly.

She sighed. "In theory. You need a hell of a lot of power to make it happen, though, and Amos didn't have it, even with a coven of twelve behind him."

"He died?" Quinn asked.

She nodded soberly. "And took all twelve witches with him."

A chill ran across my shoulders. Thirteen people dead, just so Amos Atwood could prove there was life after death. No wonder people thought the Atwoods were idiots. "None of that explains Billy selling the fetters," I reminded her.

She leaned forward, resting her elbows on her knees. "It does, in a way. What happened to Amos had . . . *reverberations* for us, for generations. No one in the Colorado Old World wanted anything to do with the Atwoods after Amos died. So my immediate ancestors became thieves and swindlers, taking Amos's relatively benign calling and turning it criminal."

"Why not just leave the state?" Quinn asked. "Start over somewhere else?"

"Some of us did," she answered. "But there were a few who insisted that we had no reason to leave our territory. They were the same Atwoods who thought Amos was unfairly maligned. Billy's father was among them."

I'd never heard anyone mention Billy's father. It probably showed on my face, because Ardie nodded as if I'd asked a question. "Oh, Jay was a piece of work. When Billy was quite young, Jay found Amos's journals in an old wardrobe. He became convinced Amos was innocent, that his spell had been sabotaged. He left Billy's mother to retrace Amos's path all the way up to South Dakota and east to Omaha. He reestablished contact with the kinds of witches who . . . well, let's just say they wouldn't help the Atwoods' reputation any."

"And that's how Billy got the plants," Quinn concluded.

She nodded again. "Jay's gift to his son," she said wryly. "Personally, I think Jay intended for Billy to use the fetters against the Pellars somehow, tear everything apart. But Billy was never smart enough to make a move."

But *Ardie* sure seemed smart enough. "And where do you fit into all this?" I asked. "This story about the Atwoods being trashed, it really only gives you more motive to use belladonna against the vampires."

She arched an eyebrow. "You've got it backward. This story is exactly why I would never mess around with belladonna. Playing with the fetters is like giving a child a loaded gun."

I glanced at Quinn. Vampires can't exactly smell lies, but I knew he'd be able to pick up the sound of an elevated heartbeat and scent any fear coming off her, which were both pretty good indicators of whether someone was lying. His face remained blank.

"Besides," she added. "You're right. I work with plants, I'm related to Billy, and I live close to the vampires who were poisoned.

But I'm not an idiot. If I wanted to kill a vampire with belladonna, I certainly wouldn't do it in my own backyard, where I would be the world's most obvious suspect."

As soon as our car doors closed, the windows at Ardie Atwood's house began to darken. I looked over at Quinn. "What do you think?" I asked, leaning back in the Jeep's plush seat. All those tarps seemed to have worked—I didn't see any bloodstains.

"If she's lying, she's good." He started the car and began the drive back to Boulder, looking thoughtful. "Although the marijuana could easily be numbing her enough to fool me."

"When Lily and I were talking in the bathroom at Simon's," I began, "did you overhear us?"

He squirmed in his seat. "I wasn't trying to eavesdrop—"

"I know. Vampire superpowers. My point is that we can't trust Ardie. From the way Simon and Lily tell it, she's a sociopath who uses Lily."

"You're so protective of her." He smiled, then glanced over at me. "It could also be that Ardie's lonely, that she's not happy with the deal she made, that she can't stay away from Lily any more than Lily can say no."

I thought it over for a few minutes before I grumbled, "Touché, I guess. But what do we do now?"

His eyes flicked down to the clock on the dash. It was almost two. "Would you recognize the belladonna if you saw it?"

"Not yet, but I could study."

"Let's take a drive up to the Atwood farm and take a look around."

I was happy to have an excuse not to look at the road. While I scanned through images of belladonna on my phone, Quinn spent most of the ride on the phone with the human crew at Magic Beans, explaining that Maven had a family emergency and would be gone for a couple of days. He gave them an elaborate story about a sibling in a hospital with no cell service, and was so convincing that *I* almost bought it.

I told him that after he hung up the phone, but Quinn just gave me a wan smile in return. "The humans are easy," he said. "Maven is a good manager, but she still looks nineteen, and at that age people expect you to disappear every now and then. The problem is going to be if anyone in the Old World comes looking for her."

"Is that likely?" I was only called in for daytime errands or Old World emergencies; I had no idea what Maven's day-to-day—well, make that night-to-night—schedule looked like. It was starting to hit me how much work she probably had to do to keep the trains running on time.

Quinn glanced over, looking troubled. "There's really no way of knowing when she'll get a call about Old World business. Most cities have their own leadership that's fairly self-sufficient, but there's squabbling. She might go a week without any disputes, or there might be three in one night. But this will help." He reached into his pocket and held up a cell phone.

"Maven's?"

"Yeah, this is the Batphone. If someone calls with a minor problem, I can text back as Maven. Hopefully it'll buy us at least a couple of days."

"Smart."

He shrugged. "All it would take is one phone call from someone with a huge problem."

"No pressure or anything."

Chapter 16

The Atwood place was on the outskirts of Gainesville, a tiny town that existed mostly as a gas stop on the way to better things. At one time the Atwoods ran a working farm, but the land had been sold off in patches for decades now. The last time we'd been there, to save Charlie, all that had remained was a shitty house and an old barn. When we arrived, I saw that both structures had been razed to the ground. The rest of the property still looked neglected, so it all resembled the "before" photo in some HGTV show. My heart sank. What were the odds we would find anything useful here?

But we tried. Armed with my cell phone and a flashlight, Quinn and I spent the next hour tramping around the property, looking for anything resembling belladonna. I had to go slow, and a lot of my energy was devoted to hiding how weak I felt.

It was, unfortunately, a complete waste of time.

"It's too overgrown here," I said finally, panting a little. "There could be belladonna under or between any of these plants and we'd never know, especially in the dark."

"You're right." He checked his watch, looking defeated. "It's almost four. We might as well go back to your place. You look like you're about to fall over."

"I'll have you know," I said severely, "I've got another six or seven minutes of standing before I fall over."

"Color me chastised, then." He offered his arm so gallantly that I had to accept.

We called the Pellars on the Jeep's bluetooth, but Simon was a little snappish at the request for an update. He suggested that I get some sleep and try him in the late morning. Well, he didn't so much suggest it as bark it and hang up. We headed back to the cabin.

Walking through the front door felt wonderful. I'd locked the dogs in the back bedroom when we stopped to change clothes—animals don't much care for vampires—so my bedroom was blissfully empty. I was ready to collapse onto the bed, but Quinn closed the door behind him and pounced on me. Lifting me by the hips so his face was level with my belly, he blew a raspberry into my skin. "Hey," I said, laughing. "What's gotten into you?"

He let me slide down his body until we were face to face. "Nothing, I just . . . feel weird all of a sudden."

"Weird how?"

"Sort of . . . calm."

I stroked his cheek. It was true, the shadows of Maven's attack had fallen away from his eyes. "Is that a bad thing?"

"Of course not, but . . ." The little thinking wrinkle between his eyes grew deeper, which I privately found adorable. "You have to understand, humans feel this huge variety of moods and emotions, but we don't usually operate on that kind of scale. To have my mood change all of a sudden, especially in the middle of a crisis—" he broke off abruptly, ducking his head to kiss me. It started out relatively chaste, but then Quinn's tongue darted into my mouth and it got interesting really quick. "Sorry," he murmured when I finally came up for air. Quinn didn't technically need it. "Was I saying something?"

"I think you were suggesting we move to the bed."

• • •

Afterward, I pushed aside a tangle of sheets so I could rest my body against his. He kissed the top of my head, and I tilted my face up to look at him.

"So, Elise wanted to know if we'd go out with her and Natalie."

"A double date? Like, with me?" he teased.

"None of the other guys I'm seeing are available," I informed him.

He laughed, then went quiet, the smile fading off his face. "You know why we can't, right?"

"Yeah, I know." He wasn't human. If Elise saw the two of us together, she'd start to wonder why our relationship didn't seem to be progressing, why I still wasn't bringing him to family events. Once that domino fell, it was only a matter of time before she started asking dozens of other impossible-to-answer questions. Why didn't we hang out in the daylight? Why didn't he ever eat? Why did my animals hate him? Right now, my entire family thought of Quinn as that guy from my old softball team who was my occasional plus-one. None of them could ever think Quinn and I were serious.

Which meant that in addition to my witch abilities, there was another big part of my life my family could never know about. I felt the chasm between my two lives get a little wider.

Quinn saw it on my face. "You wish we were a normal couple," he said quietly.

"It's not that. I mean, yeah, it would be nice if we were both just human, and if Charlie was just human, too, but . . . I guess I'm realizing for the first time that I *like* some of that cheesy couple stuff," I confessed. "Double dates. Game nights. Saturday afternoon trips to Whole Foods."

"We could have a game night. Let's see, we'll get Maven, Hazel, the werewolves, of course—"

I tried to smack him with a pillow, but he yanked it out of my hand with vampire speed. "No fair," I complained.

A grin spread across his face, and he propped his head up on his elbow. "Okay, here's something normal we can do. Tell me something about you that no one knows."

I wrinkled my nose at him. "Seriously?"

"Yep. We're doing this." He turned sideways, propping his head on his hand. "I'm waiting."

I thought it over for a moment, but nothing came to mind. I don't actually keep a little mental database of things I don't tell people about myself. "There's nothing. I'm an open book."

He threw back his head and laughed that full-throated, unrestrained laugh that I loved. "Lex, you are one of the most self-contained people I've ever met, and I mostly hang out with vampires."

"Fine. I . . . um . . . I've been going to school."

His eyebrows lifted. "To CU?"

"Yeah. I've been auditing classes."

"Since when?"

"A couple of months after I got back from Iraq."

He sat partway up in the bed. "That's why you have so many books on your living room shelves." I nodded. "Why don't you enroll for real? Get your degree?"

I snorted. "In what? And for what purpose? I don't exactly need a BA to be a register monkey. And there are no other day jobs that would let me dick around with my schedule so I can work for Maven when she needs me. Plus, I don't have time to deal with homework and exams and all that." I shrugged. "I just like to learn."

He leaned forward to kiss me, but I poked him in the ribs. "Your turn. Tell me something that no one knows about you. And make it good."

The mirth dropped away, replaced by a grimace. "I have a daughter," he said quietly.

That brought me up short. Quinn *never* talked about his life as a human in Chicago. All I knew was that he hadn't started working for Maven by choice, and that at some point he'd hurt or maybe killed his human wife when he lost control of his hunger for blood. In the back of my mind, I'd presumed the two things were sort of connected, like maybe he'd accidentally attacked his wife and the Chicago cardinal vampire had shipped him off to Colorado. But he'd never mentioned having a child, and I hadn't asked.

Now I wasn't sure what to say. Finally, I settled on, "What's her name?"

"Holly." He smiled, eyes full of memory. "Holly Noelle. She was born Christmas Day, and my wife insisted."

It was so strange to hear him talk about this. I checked myself for any signs of jealousy or anger, but I was just sad for him. His family thought he was dead, and the man he'd once been really *was* dead. At the same time, if Quinn wasn't that man, who was he? I stroked his cheek.

"How old is she?" I asked.

"Twenty, now." Quinn had been in his mid- or late thirties when he was turned, and now he'd always look that way. "She can't know I'm . . . still around, for obvious reasons, but I keep tabs on her, within the rules."

Vampires weren't allowed to have any contact with their old lives, but Quinn had found a work-around. He probably kept an eye on her online—that was easy these days—but I decided not to ask. Then I could never be made to tell.

"Does Maven know about her?"

"Of course. Holly is the leash I come with," he said sourly. "'Here, take Quinn, and if he ever disobeys you, use his daughter against him.'"

"You really think Maven would do that?"

"I don't know," he said. "She's been decent to me—as domini go, I have no complaints. But all my experience with other vampires has suggested I can't trust them."

There it was again. *Them.* "You know," I said carefully, "You've never told me about how you were turned."

He was quiet for a long time. I let the silence play out, not sure if he was avoiding the question or trying to decide how to answer. "I was a cop, you know that part," he said finally. I nodded. "I *lived* for my job. I had a wife and a little girl, but I was never focused on them. I always wanted to get back to work. I think . . ." He paused for a moment. "I loved my wife, but I rarely thought about her when she wasn't right in front of me. I treated her like an accessory." The bitterness was back in his voice, but this time it was all directed at himself.

"Anyway, a few years after I made detective, I got this weird case: young women in their twenties, very beautiful, were vanishing into thin air. Five of them went missing within about three months. I thought maybe I had a serial killer on my hands. And I was *thrilled.*"

His voice was full of pain and regret, but there was plenty of anger there too. "I dug into the disappearances, and realized they didn't play out like the average murder, or even the average sexually motivated attack. Each woman packed a bag before she disappeared, which implied they knew they were leaving. But none of them said anything to their friends, their families, or their jobs. At first I thought maybe the murderer had convinced each of them that he was taking them away for the weekend or something, but that didn't explain why they didn't tell a soul they were leaving town. One woman's mother was dying in the hospital; you'd think she'd at least say goodbye. It didn't add up."

"So you kept digging."

"Yes. I was sure this was the case that was going to make my career. At the same time, I would often sort of lose interest in it, practically forgetting the whole thing. Then I would go back to the office and find notes all over my desk, and I'd get interested again. I kept another set of notes at home, and sometimes it'd work the other way around. Later, of course, I realized I was being pressed to forget, but at the time I thought someone was drugging me. I started leaving myself little notes, little clues to remind me to keep pushing. And then I . . . I pushed too hard."

His voice quieted, so I prompted him. "The women," I said. "They were being turned into vampires?"

"The ones who survived the process, yeah. As it turns out, there's this vampire pimp in St. Louis, Oskar. He wanted to add to his stable of hot vampire girls, but we're not allowed to stay in the same city after we turn."

"So he came up to Chicago to recruit."

"More or less. I never did find out if the girls really wanted to be vampires, or if they were being pressed to think something else was happening. All I know is that I eventually got too close to this guy, and he . . . *noticed* me."

His voice caught at the end, so I tried to help him skip ahead in the story. "And turned you."

But Quinn shook his head. "No. The vampire that Oskar sent after me was supposed to kill me."

"How did you survive?"

He winced as his eyes filled with the memory of pain. "I was dying, but I managed to get to my gun. I shot her once in the heart, once in the neck. It didn't kill her, but it was enough to get her to back off while she healed. I crawled out into the street where there were too many witnesses for her to finish me off."

"You got her blood on you?" I had only a rudimentary understanding of vampire biology, but I thought you needed to ingest vampire blood in order to turn.

He nodded. "I was in too much shock to realize it in the moment, but I'd nicked her carotid artery at close range, so blood went all over my face and into my mouth." He gave me a wan smile. "Still, I shouldn't have turned—the odds are terrible. But here I am. I refused to swear troth to Oskar after that, so he sold me to Maven."

"I'm sorry," I said softly.

Quinn shrugged. "It was a long time ago."

It really wasn't, not to a vampire, but I didn't say that. I considered asking him about attacking his wife, but decided it wasn't the right time. "Thank you for telling me," I said instead.

He rolled over on top of me, holding himself up on his elbows so our bodies pressed together. "If you *really* wanted to thank me," he began very seriously, and my laughter rang through the house.

I woke up alone the next morning, as usual, but this time I felt exceptionally relaxed and peaceful—and I hadn't had a single dream about Iraq.

I stayed in bed for a long time, staring at the ceiling, thinking over the case, feeling lazy. Eventually, I reached out to check my cell phone. I'd missed a text from a number I didn't recognize. *Lex, this is Emil. I don't mean to pressure you, but I need to leave town tomorrow night. Can we talk today?*

I started to text back a "sure," but before I could hit "Send" my phone rang and a picture of Simon replaced the text screen. I answered.

"Hey, Simon," I said through a yawn. "Good morning. Or noonish or whatever. What's up?"

There was a momentary pause. "Um, are you okay?"

"Yeah, I'm great. *You* sound stressed, though."

"Have you seen the news today?" Simon asked. "The thing about Gunbarrel Ave?"

"Nope, I just got up." I flipped off the covers and got up, stretching. The dogs on my bed looked up, tails wagging hopefully. Quinn must have opened the back bedroom door before he'd left. I patted my leg, and they stampeded off the bed en masse. They were so loud that I missed the next thing Simon said to me.

"Sorry, what?"

"*Lex*," he yelled. "Listen to me. The police found a body last night."

Chapter 17

I blinked, frozen with my hand on the doorknob. "Anyone we know?"

He sounded exasperated. "No, but Boulder averages like, one murder a year. Doesn't it seem like an awfully big coincidence that someone is killed right after the attack on Maven?"

"Huh."

"Yeah, 'huh.' You should call your cousin to see if it was a vampire."

My brow furrowed. "But Elise doesn't know about vampires."

I heard a noise that sounded suspiciously like Simon thunking his head against a wall. "No, I mean a vampire might have killed the guy. You know, drank all his blood?"

"Oh. Right."

"Are you high right now?" he asked.

I considered the question. "Not unless Lily put something special in my IV."

Simon didn't laugh. "Then can you stop by the lab? I need to talk to you about my findings."

"Sure, I can do that," I said.

There was a pause. "Maybe get some coffee or something, too, Lex."

Simon hung up without another word, and I shook my head a little, trying to clear it. I did feel awfully foggy, although physically

I felt pretty good. I must just need coffee, I decided, and padded out to the kitchen, humming the theme song from one of Charlie's favorite kid's shows.

After I let the dogs out and finished my first mug, I remembered what I was supposed to be doing. I turned on my computer and checked the newspaper's online home page. Sure enough, the top story was about the body of a forty-year-old man that had been found in a Dumpster behind a tech park. There was no information about the man's identity or the cause of death, so I called Elise. She was working day shifts that week.

"Hey," came Elise's low voice. "Hang on a second." Louder, she yelled something that sounded like "a hamburger and fries," and I realized she was at a drive-thru. It was almost noon—of course she was getting lunch.

After a tinny voice told her to pull ahead, Elise was back. "Listen, today's crazy, I've got like five minutes to eat—"

"That's okay. Are you working the body thing?"

"*Everyone's* working the body thing," she grumbled. "I've been pointlessly knocking on doors all morning."

"Can you tell me how he died?"

There was a long pause, and then a muffled exchange while Elise got her food. When she spoke again, she'd put on her professional cop voice. "You know I can't talk about it, Lex."

"To the newspapers and the public, yeah. But I'm not looking for trade secrets here, just what's going to be on the Daily Camera website by close of business."

She sighed. "We don't know how or why he died, okay? There wasn't a mark on him. Right now the ME's suggesting an aneurism, but that's kind of what she says when she has no idea."

"So it might not have been murder."

"We don't *know*," she said impatiently, her mouth now full of food. "Why are you asking, anyway?"

I paused. Why hadn't I figured out what to say before I called? "Just curious, I guess," I said lamely. "It wasn't anyone we know, right?"

"Nah, just some electrical engineer from Fort Collins, worked in the tech park. Listen, I've *really* got to go. Love you."

She hung up before I could say anything else.

I looked down at Chip and Cody, my two Lab mixes, who were looking at me with identical eager expressions. "Why is everyone hanging up on me today?" I asked them. Chip licked the air in front of his face, and Cody bumped his nose into my leg. "Okay, well, as long as it's not me." I shrugged and went to get dressed, humming.

As I got closer to Simon's lab, I started to feel the pressure again. Maven was paralyzed for God knew how long, whoever did it was still running around free, and we had no leads, unless Simon had pulled a CSI miracle and traced the source of the dart guns. Somehow I doubted that.

When Simon opened the door to the Basement of Dr. Moreau, I nearly took a step back. His eyes were red and his hair was wild, like he'd been trying to pull it out by the roots. There were coffee stains down his shirt, and he looked haggard. "Whoa," I said, handing him a fresh coffee. "You, um, look like you've been working hard. Where's Lily?"

He took the coffee and ushered me inside, his movements slow, like it was hard to move his limbs around. I reminded myself that he'd lost a lot of blood the night before, too. "Taking a nap in my room."

We went to the small kitchen table, which was now covered in binders and scribbled notes. I sat down in my chair from the night before.

"Did you talk to your cousin?" Simon asked.

"Yes. They actually can't figure out how the guy died—no external marks—but the current theory is aneurysm. Doesn't sound like a vampire attack."

He sighed with relief. "Well, thank God for that. Mom called me this morning, worried it might have been an Old World attack."

"Has Maven improved at all?" I asked.

"That's kind of the problem," he began. "Still no heartbeat, and her color isn't any better than it was last night—I've been taking photos and comparing them. It's like she's frozen exactly where she was after you fed her last night."

"You mean after Lily fed her."

He shook his head. "No, I don't. That's why I called you here. Lily and I have been running tests with samples of Maven's blood." He gave me a rueful smile. "It's possible that Lily's a tiny bit better than I am at human and vampire physiology, but don't tell her I said so. Anyway, we examined both the intravascular changes to Maven's blood, compared to a sample of Quinn's, and the belladonna has created a reaction that pretty much mimics the effects of disseminated intravascular coagulation—"

"Simon," I interrupted. "I need the idiot's guide to this explanation."

He sighed and rubbed his face with his hands. "Right, sorry. Basically, we looked at how different donor blood reacts to her tainted blood. Vampire blood does almost nothing for her. Human blood sustains her, so she doesn't starve, but it doesn't actually counteract the belladonna. It will just keep her in stasis until the poison eventually wears off. Nellie's method of bloodletting may help a little, but judging from the reaction I'm getting from her cells, I'd estimate six to eight weeks before it's out of her system."

I cursed and got up from the table, pacing a little. That was way too long. We were going to have to go with the interim solution, but who could hold the state for two months? Clara was powerful, but I'd pressed her *hard* to keep watch over Charlie, and I'd never tried to undo a press. Besides which, I had no idea how to organize Maven's contacts to get Clara back from Florida.

Simon's voice behind me was soft. "Um, there's one other thing, though."

I spun around to look at him. "*Your* blood is different," he said. "It's like . . . well, 'antidote' is too strong a word, but it actively counteracts the belladonna. I can't really explain it, except—"

"Death in my blood," I finished for him. "The connection between boundary magic and vampires."

He nodded. I started pacing again, planning now. "So I donate again tonight. And tomorrow night. Lily can keep giving me IVs—"

"No, Lily can't," came a tired voice from the doorway. I looked up and saw Lily leaning against the doorframe, yawning. Her hair was mussed and she looked nearly as exhausted as Simon.

"Sorry, baby sister," Simon murmured. "We didn't mean to wake you up."

She shrugged it off. "Too much coffee to sleep well, anyway." She began eyeballing my coffee cup where I'd abandoned it on the table. I motioned for her to help herself, and she seized it like Charlie attacking graham crackers. After her first sip, she turned to me. "Lex, you can't donate again for at least a couple of weeks. Your body can't handle it."

"I can't—"

"Die, I know," Lily interrupted. "But you don't heal any faster than anyone else. Your body can't replace blood any faster."

"So I'll feel shitty for a few days," I reasoned. "How bad could it be?"

Simon arched an eyebrow and gave me a little *you shouldn't have said that* smile. Lily marched over to his whiteboard and picked up a marker. "The human body is roughly seven percent blood. You weigh . . . what? A hundred and twenty pounds?"

"One twenty-five."

She wrote the number on the board and did some complicated math that involved long division. "That means your body has approximately three point seven liters of blood, which is, what? Almost eight pints?"

She glanced at Simon, who'd pulled out his phone and was using a calculator app. He nodded. "Seven point eight."

"Right." She wrote the number on the board. "Last night you lost almost a third of your blood. You were damned lucky you didn't go into shock. If we did that to your body every night, without allowing it time to replenish—" She shook her head. "You could go into a coma."

"So? I'd wake up, right?"

Simon and Lily exchanged a look of annoyance. "It could cause neurological damage, Lex," Simon told me.

"We are not taking that chance." Lily's voice was firm.

I threw up my hands. "What choice do we have? We're talking about risking the *possibility* of neural damage to one person versus the possibility of a supernatural war breaking out in Colorado."

"You're thinking like a soldier." Simon's voice was mild, but he brought me up short. When I looked at him, his eyes were fixed on the whiteboard. "There might be another way."

"What are you thinking?" Lily asked him.

"Lex isn't the only person in Boulder with boundary witchblood."

I blanched. "You're not serious."

"Who? Charlie?" Lily said, looking back and forth between us. "She's a null, she won't have the boundary magic in her system—"

"No," I said heavily. "Simon wants us to call my biological father."

Chapter 18

As usual, Lily got straight to the point. "Do you trust him?" she asked me.

"I . . . don't know if I trust him. I can't figure out what he wants. Why would he contact me?"

"What do you mean?" Lily looked confused. "You're his daughter. He wants to get to know you."

I shrugged, uncomfortable. "Honestly, I haven't really had time to process the whole thing. I just found out yesterday morning. And then Maven was shot, and everything went to hell."

"And we all got distracted." Lily concluded. She looked at me abruptly, like something had just occurred to her. "But why didn't you call me right after he showed up?"

Her tone was so indignant that I had to smile. "I didn't feel like dumping my family problems on you right now, give everything that's been happening with . . . um . . ."

"Morgan," Simon supplied. "You can say her name."

"And yes, it's complicated, but this is huge news, Lex," Lily said. "You shouldn't have worried about my feelings."

I held up my hands. "Okay. I promise, the next time my biological parent shows up out of the blue, I will call."

"That's all I ask."

Simon raised a hand. "Can we get back to the issue? You told me that Emil has boundary blood."

"But it's not active," I pointed out. Like most males with witch-blood, Emil had never had the chance to activate his magic. "Will it even work, with dormant witchblood?"

Both Pellars fell silent. "I honestly have no idea," Simon said finally. "But I don't see how it could hurt to try. Even if he's human, the blood would at least help sustain her."

"But assuming he agrees to this," I said, "he would know where we're keeping Maven. Unless we get him to donate somewhere else, bring it to Maven in bags?"

A smile spread across Simon's face. "I don't think that will be necessary," he said. "One thing we know for sure about dormant witches—they can be pressed."

We did a little more planning, and by midafternoon, I was ready to call Emil. I asked him to coffee, and I picked a location off the beaten path: Naked Lunch, a little café that was buried in a big apartment and retail complex off Arapahoe. It was cute, utilitarian, and the kind of place where people mostly tracked in and out with to-go cups rather than sat and chatted. We would have relative privacy while still being in a public space.

I had to make a quick trip to the cabin to change my clothes and take care of the herd, so Emil got to the café before me. When I walked in, he stood to greet me with a broad, nervous smile. He was wearing nearly the same outfit as the day before: chinos that hung awkwardly near the pockets and a slightly lumpy polo shirt with a tiny reptile over one breast. Maybe he had a heart condition and needed to wear an external pacemaker or something.

I really didn't want to hug him yet, so I was relieved when he held out his hand for me to shake, taking it in both of his warm ones. "Good to see you again, Lex," he said, beaming. He gestured toward the counter. "What can I get you? Coffee? Pastry?"

"Coffee and a cookie-dough ball, please," I said. Ordinarily I would have fought one of my own family members—er, one of the Luthers—for the check, but it was obvious how badly he wanted to please me. I felt a little guilty that I was going to try to use that against him, but I could always make it up to him later.

When we were settled at a table, Emil and I chatted for a while about inconsequential things. I told him about my job at the Depot and my second job doing some "security consulting for a local business," which was how I'd explained my nighttime hours to my family. He smiled when I asked how he liked Boulder. "It's a fascinating city," he said, the corners of his mouth lifting with amusement. "A smoke shop on each block, dreadlocks on all the white college students, and everywhere I go, it takes me five minutes to throw away my trash in the appropriate containers."

I laughed. We talked a little bit about Emil's life, which I hadn't really bothered to ask about the day before. He lived just outside Halifax in Nova Scotia, where he owned a small New Age bookstore. He gave a little dismissive shrug when he talked about it. "Most of what I sell is garbage, but I know enough about witchcraft and magic to help the customers a little bit here and there: a candle, a symbol, sage to cleanse a new house. That sort of thing." He had come to Boulder to meet with a potential new supplier, an appointment he'd made mostly to have an excuse to meet me.

"Do you . . . um, did you ever remarry? Have other kids?" I felt awkward asking such a personal question, but there was a part of me that longed to hear that I had a sibling out there. As soon as I had the thought, though, I felt disloyal to Sam.

It's okay. I want you to have someone, too.

At any rate, Emil shook his head. "I've dated here and there, and right now I have a nice friendship with a lady who lives about an hour away." He smiled ruefully. "I don't think we'll get married, though. We're both too independent. Solitary."

That sounded familiar. "And what about you?" he asked, brightening. He leaned forward. "Do you have someone special? Any kids? I would love to be a grandfather."

I shook my head. "No kids. I spend a lot of time with my cousins' children, though. And I'm seeing someone, but we're both sort of"—I borrowed his word—"independent."

He studied me. "A vampire?"

I blinked, not bothering to hide my surprise. "How did you know?"

Emil shrugged. "Just a guess. My father died when I was young, but my mother, Sophia, is a black witch—sorry, I always forget the preferred term. A boundary witch. She has been with a vampire for decades now. I've seen the"—he waved a hand, looking for a word—"the *allure* between boundary witches and vampires." There was a note of disapproval in his tone, and I suspected some serious family drama there. "That attraction is, unfortunately, part of why boundary witches are so scarce now. There just isn't enough breeding with other witches."

I wrinkled my nose at the word "breeding," but Emil didn't see it. Despite Sam—and by extension, Valerya—saying this guy was okay, I didn't like the way he talked about boundary magic. There was a reverence in his voice that was nearly worshipful.

At the same time, though, it was nice to meet someone who didn't either cower or snarl at the very mention of death magic. Besides, didn't every family have these prejudicial disagreements? I had an uncle who still thought homosexuals shouldn't marry, despite living in liberal Boulder. And as much as I loved my parents, I was pretty sure my mother privately thought all my rescue animals should be put down before they ruined my house any further. Were Emil's opinions about boundary witches needing to have babies really any different?

I was also really interested in Emil's mother, Sophia. I didn't know a single other boundary witch—with the exception of Nellie, who was dead. The idea of having someone I could actually call up on the phone for advice really appealed to me. And I could use some help with training, since Simon and Lily had pretty much maxed out their knowledge.

"Is your mother, um . . ."

"Still alive? Yes, although these days she's often mistaken for my little sister." He smiled and added, "You remind me of her, actually. She's also very . . . contained."

"What does she do?"

"She's mostly retired, although she works part-time at the shop for me. She's actually running it this week while I'm gone." He put down his coffee cup very gingerly, as if trying not to spook me. "You should come and visit us sometime. I'm sure Mother would love to meet you."

I spun my own cup in quarter turns, not sure how to answer. "Listen, Emil," I began. "I need to ask you for a favor."

His eyebrows lifted, genuinely surprised. "Of course, anything."

"Well, wait until you hear the favor." I took a deep breath and gave him the story Simon and I had worked out. One of the Denver vampires had been poisoned by belladonna. I had fed her some of my blood the night before, but she needed more death-magic-infused blood to help her wake up. I watched Emil's face carefully as I spoke, alert for any sign that he knew about the belladonna attacks, but his expression remained puzzled and interested, never guilty.

"So you'd like me to donate some of my blood to this vampire," he said slowly.

"Mmm, it's a little more than that. We'd also like to press you to make sure you forget what she looks like and where she's located."

I held my breath, certain he'd be offended, but he just looked sort of perplexed. "I'm not sure I understand. Why is this person so important to you?"

I had been expecting that question. "She's my friend," I said, and was surprised when it didn't even sound like a lie. "I'm not even sure your blood will work, but if you're up for it, I'd truly appreciate if you could try."

"I don't know either," he admitted. He paused for a moment, then plunged on, "Lex, I know you don't know me well, but is it really necessary to press me? I have no interest in telling anyone about the Old World here in Colorado."

"I understand," I assured him. "But remember when I said I'm a security consultant? It would look really bad for me if I let just anyone—no offense—know where we're hiding an injured vampire."

He tilted his head for a long moment, thinking that over. I took a few bites of my dessert, giving him a little space to consider.

"I realize that you didn't have to tell me you were planning to press me," he said at last. "You could have just done it, and I never would have known the difference. I appreciate the honesty."

I nodded. Quinn had argued against warning Emil we were going to press him, but I'd insisted. I had no idea what my relationship with this man would end up looking like, but starting it with a betrayal, even a small one, wouldn't help.

"I will do this for you," he pronounced. "But in exchange, I'd like for you to seriously consider coming to visit Sophia and me in Halifax."

It seemed like a small price to pay, and I wasn't actually promising anything, so I nodded. "It's a deal."

We made plans to meet at nine o'clock—he could feed Maven anytime, but we would need Quinn there to press him afterward.

Then I went home, resolved to do some research online about belladonna, even the regular variety. When I walked through the door, though, I suddenly felt exhausted . . . and oddly satisfied. We had a plan, we had the help we needed, and maybe things would be okay. I could probably afford to take a little nap. I collapsed on top of my covers and immediately drifted off to sleep.

There were no dreams at all.

I woke up to a slight, scraping pain on my hip: the familiar sensation of a dog gently clawing for my attention. I cracked open an eye and saw Cody and Chip panting happily at the side of the bed, their humid breath on my face. There was a much-abused tennis ball rolling slowly toward me. Dopey, the mentally deficient Yorkshire terrier, was on the bed next to me, her tongue hanging out as she scratched at me again. "You're working for them now?" I complained, looking around. The clock on my bedside table said six p.m., which meant I still had a few hours before I had to be anywhere. Next to my knee, Pongo lifted his head and gave me a particularly mournful look, as if saying, "I *told* them not to wake you."

I laughed and sat up, the willing victim of yet another dog conspiracy. "All right, mongrels," I said. "We'll go play."

I put on my oldest hiking boots and we all tromped out to the yard, where Chip and Cody terrorized the tennis ball while Dopey scampered back and forth twenty feet behind them, pleased as hell to be involved. Pongo ignored all of us and flopped over in the shade next to the house. We played for a long time, until Chip began to flag, letting Cody get ahead of him to the ball. "One more throw and we're going in, you guys!" I called out to them.

I reared back and threw the ball as hard as I could, sending it all the way to the back fence at the edge of my property. Chip and Cody gamely trotted after it, but both of them stopped twenty feet short of the fence. I squinted, trying to figure out what they were doing. They were just standing there, apparently staring at the ball. Maybe a squirrel was distracting them?

I rolled my eyes and started toward Chip and Cody, with Dopey prancing next to me. When I reached the other dogs, I saw that they weren't just standing there—both of them had their limbs locked in tense body language. They were whining, and the hair on Cody's neck was standing up a little. "Guys?" I said, and whistled. Both dogs glanced back at me, and then trotted toward me with sudden gratitude, pressing against me. "Was it a bear?" I asked, puzzled by their reaction. In the years I'd been living there, we'd seen a bear near the yard exactly once, but when it happened I couldn't get them to stop barking. I took a few cautious steps toward the fence. The dogs whined a little, but none of them followed me. I rested my hands on the back fence and looked left and right, scanning for any movement low to the ground. What would unnerve Chip and Cody? I shrugged to myself and turned to walk back to the house.

On the first step, my foot landed on something hard and round. I jumped back, a little spooked, but relaxed when I realized it was just a rock. I bent and picked it up. A purple stone, the size of my palm, in a perfect cylindrical shape. The sides were smooth and shiny, like they'd been polished. Okay, that was weird, but for all I knew it could have been there for ages—I didn't mow this far back, in the scrubby plants.

The dogs abruptly rushed me, crowding around me with waving tails like I'd just escaped a grizzly attack. "Hey, goofballs," I said, laughing to myself. We were a long way from the house, and I suddenly remembered Jake's warning to keep an eye on the dogs. "What am I doing?" I said out loud, feeling like an idiot. There were sick animals in the area; we shouldn't be playing outside. I took off for the back door at a jog, absently shoving the rock in my pocket on the way.

Chapter 19

I got cleaned up and made dinner for everyone, including live bugs for my three-legged iguana Mushu. While everyone was munching, I picked up the phone and called Jake to check up on the mysterious animal illness.

"Oh, yeah," he said after I explained why I was calling. "I haven't heard back from the DNR." "Have there been any more attacks?"

"Not that I've seen, and I've been keeping my ear to the ground in the veterinary community. Of course, it's always possible that someone would go straight to the DNR or not report it at all."

He didn't sound too worried. I hesitated, but I had nothing to lose. Jake wouldn't be annoyed by stupid questions. "Listen, Elise told me about a few recent cases where people went nuts and started foaming at the mouth . . ."

He chuckled, but not unkindly. "Yeah, she called me. I gave her the number for my contact at the DNR, though I honestly doubt the two things are related. There *are* illnesses that can jump from mammals to humans, but they're almost all parasitic," he explained. "Tapeworm, ringworms, that kind of thing. Foaming at the mouth, on the other hand, happens when all the muscles near the mouth contract at once. It can happen to any species that's prone to seizures. I'm sure it's just a weird coincidence."

"Oh, okay." Jake didn't sound worried, which made me feel better. And I couldn't see how seizures could be related to anything Old World. Just to be safe, I texted Lily, who confirmed that she'd never heard of any spells that directly led to foaming at the mouth. I shrugged to myself and went to get ready.

The St. Julien Hotel is probably Boulder's swankiest lodging. Although it doesn't have the charm or history of our other grand hotel, the Boulderado, the St. Julien makes up for it in attractiveness and modern amenities. The entire exterior is made up of sand-colored ledgestone, so the building looks like a palace made from stacked rocks. Although I was twenty minutes early, Emil was waiting out front when I pulled up, sitting patiently on the bench encircling the courtyard fountain. I pulled up and put on the hazard lights, studying him for a moment before I got out. He was wearing the same ill-fitting clothes from earlier that day, but his face seemed guarded—and a little flushed. He kept touching one pocket, as if to reassure himself something was in there.

On a whim, I picked up my phone and Googled his name, along with "new age store" and "Halifax." The top result was a website for Crystal Spirit Books. I clicked on it, and a picture of Emil came up right away, posed behind the counter with a cautious smile. On a whim, I touched the number for the store and raised the phone to my ear.

I was expecting some sort of answering machine, but to my surprise, a female voice answered in a whisper. "Hello, Crystal Spirit Books."

"Uh . . . hi. You're open."

"Yes, we are," the voice said pleasantly. "Madam Sophia is doing her monthly midnight reading tonight. It's too late to sign up for a slot this month, but if you're interested, I could put you on the schedule for June?"

"Sophia is a . . . um . . . a psychic?"

"She prefers the term 'medium,'" said the voice, a tiny bit severe now. "She communicates with the dead."

"Thanks, I'll . . . think about it."

I hung up. Sophia supplemented her income by doing spiritualist readings. Not a bad gig for a boundary witch, I supposed. Emil hadn't mentioned that specifically, but everything about what he'd told me did seem to check out. I took another look at him, sitting alone on that bench. He wasn't twirling a moustache or anything, so why did I suddenly feel unsettled?

You're being stupid, Lex, I told myself. I got out of the car and waved to him.

The drive to Simon's lab was quiet—not tense, exactly, but there was a certain anticipation in the car that seemed to have struck both of us dumb. We mumbled polite "excuse me's" and "thank you's" as I led him down the steps to the basement apartment, but that was the extent of our conversation.

When Simon opened the door, I saw right away that Quinn had already arrived, doing his quiet looming thing in the background. Lily wasn't there when we arrived—her yoga studio had contracted her out to teach a free class at the Twenty-Ninth Street mall. She'd offered to skip it, but I knew she could get fired for that. Besides, it didn't seem like Simon and I would need her for a simple blood transfusion.

I introduced Emil to Simon and Quinn. Simon immediately stepped forward and extended his arm. "It's very nice to meet you, sir," he enthused, pumping Emil's hand. Quinn was at his shoulder, with a polite not-quite-smile for my biological father. He gave a nod of acknowledgment.

"Could I trouble you for a glass of water?" Emil asked, and Simon left to get it. Emil still looked a little flushed, and I wondered if he was nervous. It would be kind of funny if he turned out to be afraid of needles.

"Are you all right?" I asked, and he nodded, managing a smile.

"Just a bit tired. I'm afraid as I get older, it gets harder and harder to fall asleep away from my own bed."

"This way, please," Quinn said, ushering him into the back bedroom. He had gotten Maven out of her earlier spot, curled up at the bottom of the closet, and laid her out on the bed. I saw with a bit of relief that either he or Simon had scrubbed the blood off her skin, making her look less like . . . well, a terrifyingly powerful vampire. Instead, she seemed small and vulnerable, barely more than a child. It made *me* want to open a vein to help, and I was still feeling the effects of the previous night.

"We already removed some of the tainted blood," Simon said in a low voice. "All you need to do, Mr. Jasper, is donate about two pints, and you're on your way."

"After you press me, of course," Emil added, glancing at Quinn with just a little bit of hostility in his tone.

Quinn met his gaze impassively, leaning in the doorframe like he had all the time in the world. "That's right. Just as Lex explained."

Emil began to say something, but then shook his head and turned toward Simon. "Ready when you are."

Simon sat him down in the chair next to the bed and pulled in a folding chair for himself. The room was getting crowded, so I went around and stood on the other side of the bed to watch. Simon, who wasn't nearly as skilled at IVs as Lily, couldn't find a suitable vein on the back of Emil's hand, so he asked him to roll up his sleeve so Simon could check the inside of Emil's elbow. Emil leaned forward, his shirt gaping at the collar, and I saw something under the neckline swing forward on a cord. Something big and shiny.

"Is that a pocket watch?" I asked, gesturing toward his shirt. Emil flinched and put his hand flat against the shirt.

Simon inserted the needle, and Emil shot me an embarrassed look. "Just a good-luck charm, I'm afraid," he said. "Something my mother gave me."

"May I see it?" I said lightly.

Emil glanced at Simon, who was attaching tape to the needle. "I'm a bit embarrassed," he murmured.

"Please? I'm really interested."

Reluctantly, Emil reached into the neck of his shirt and tugged out the leather cord. The necklace spilled across his chest, but it was a lot more than one charm. There were at least eight different stone bars on the cord, and each one of them gleamed with perfection. The smallest was green and the size of my thumb. The largest was nearly as big as a three-pound hand weight. No wonder the guy's clothes were hanging weird.

Simon sat back, staring with frank admiration. "Holy shit," he said. "I don't know much about crystals, but those look like museum-quality pieces."

With his free hand, Emil hurried to tuck the necklace back into his shirt. "Yes, well. Mother wanted me to be protected, even if I don't have magic of my own."

"Do you know much about—" Simon began, but cut himself off, leaning closer to Emil. "Wait. I think your pupils are dilated. Turn toward the light, please?"

"I'm sure it's just the lighting. The IV looks fine. Are we all set?" He looked at Simon expectantly. Simon shrugged slightly and reached for the rubber tubing so he could connect it to Emil's IV.

"Stop," I heard myself saying, though I wasn't sure why. "Something's not right."

Simon and Emil both began talking at the same time, but it was Quinn who strode forward, grabbed the end of Emil's just-taped IV, and yanked. The tape came loose with a small ripping sound, and a tiny trickle of blood spurted out.

Before any of us could process what he was doing, Quinn smeared a finger in the blood and stuck it in his mouth. Then he spat. "Belladonna," he growled.

Before anyone could react to that, he had grabbed Emil by the throat and was beginning to lift. Emil's legs kicked out, blood trickling down his arm.

"Who the hell are you?" Quinn demanded.

"I can explain," Emil began in a reasonable tone—just as he pulled a stake out of one pocket and plunged it into Quinn's chest.

Chapter 20

"*No!*"

I didn't even hear myself scream it; I was too busy scrambling over the bed to lunge at Emil.

He was expecting it. He sidestepped me easily, and Quinn and I went down in a tangle. Out of the corner of my eye, I saw Simon running at Emil, but the older man clocked him in the jaw, using Simon's own momentum against him. Simon fell down, momentarily stunned, and Emil used the opening to bolt out the door.

I ignored him, totally focused on the wooden stake sticking out of Quinn's chest. It was thicker and more crude than the spelled stakes we used, and—oh my God it was in his *body*—

He's not dead, I told myself, though my breath was coming out in a ragged panic. Vampires start to decay immediately when their hearts are destroyed, and Quinn's eyes were open, his hands twitching. Emil had either missed the heart or only nicked it.

"Quinn!" I yelled, but his eyes had gone distant, his body focused on repairing itself. My hands fluttered over the stake. It just looked so wrong sticking out of his chest that my fingers itched to pull it out, even though my old first aid training screamed at me to resist.

I looked frantically at Simon. "Should I pull it out?" My voice came out high and shrill.

Simon didn't answer. He was on his hands and knees, looking dizzy. I hesitantly wrapped both hands around the stake—and gasped in shock as Quinn's hands went around mine.

"I'll be okay," he wheezed. The stake must have punctured a lung. "Go after him."

"I don't want—"

"Simon's got this. Go!"

Groaning with frustration, I staggered to my feet and stepped over Simon, who was giving me a reassuring nod as he struggled to his feet. I stumbled a little as I went through the living room, still a little shaky from blood loss and shock, but by the time I made it through the door, I was at a full run.

The sun was down, which would hide the new bloodstains on my sleeves, but it also made it harder to spot Emil. Then I caught movement in a streetlight down the block—a large figure barreling around the nearest corner. I sprinted after him, feeling slow and discombobulated.

What the hell was going on? Why would my father attack Maven? Wait, was he even my father? Sure, he'd shown me that picture of Valerya, who looked just like Sam, and he and I did look related. I was sure I hadn't imagined that. But why would my biological father want to hurt Maven? Was he the one who'd been after her all along?

Wake up, Lex. Emil had belladonna in his system. What were the odds of two unrelated people having one of the fetters at the same time in the same place? Emil must have been the one who'd originally poisoned her and the Denver vampires. The next time I talked to Sam, I was gonna flip out at her.

I ran harder. Belladonna or not, Emil was surprisingly fast as he hurtled through the streets. I run three or four times a week, but not usually right after losing a third of my blood volume. At best I could only maintain the gap between us, never close it.

After nearly ten minutes I realized that he was running with certainty, like he knew exactly where he was going, and that scared me. What was he planning? Before I could work out what was ahead of us, Emil veered left, racing straight into the traffic on Third Street. I halted, but he managed to weave neatly through the cars, hitting the other side and regaining his stride. *Shit.* I was gonna have to follow.

I bolted forward, watching the incoming traffic and zigzagging as much as I could. I was so busy making sure I didn't get hit that I nearly missed Emil's sudden left turn. He circled the outside of a deserted parking lot, and now I was convinced he *did* have a plan. I imagined a map of Boulder in my head. The busy street to my left had to be Longbow Drive. But where was Emil going? There was nothing over here.

Then I remembered.

Boulder has so many tourist-friendly attractions that it's easy to forget about the less-flashy ones, such as the Leanin' Tree Museum and Sculpture Garden. It's kind of a funky combination of a greeting card factory and a historical art museum. I'd never actually taken the indoor tour, but I liked to come to the sculpture garden sometimes for the quiet. It was a small, simple space, just grass interspersed with bronze figures in classic Western scenarios: an elk with his head lifted to bugle, a buffalo, that kind of thing.

Sure enough, Emil ran across the paved entrance that led to the museum grounds, barreling toward the sculpture garden. For a moment I thought he'd be trapped against the eastern wall of the garden—it was closed at night, and the entrance was around the side—but Emil ran straight into the chest-high hedges that formed the border, barely slowing down as he crashed through them and disappeared.

When I finally caught up, I paused just outside the broken hedges. There was no sense of movement inside, but he couldn't have raced all the way through the garden and out the other side by now. Was he trying to ambush me? I squinted, but it was too dark to see anything but shadows. In the dim light, the statuary seemed strangely ominous.

I crept forward, cautious. "Emil?" I called. No reply. "Is that even your real name? Are you actually my father?"

No answer again. I didn't like this. The garden was shaped roughly like a rectangle, with a corresponding oval-shaped path inside. Visitors could stroll around the oval walkway and see the statues on the grass. I stepped toward the path, strangely reluctant to cross onto it. This whole situation had "trap" written all over it.

Then again, what could happen? Emil didn't have magic, and I would have noticed if he carried a firearm. "Okay, fine," I yelled. "How about you tell me what you have against Maven?"

Somewhere in front of me there was a low, dry chuckle that lifted the hairs on my neck. "This isn't how I wanted to do this," said his voice, wafting out of the darkness. He was panting, out of breath. Well, good. "But you forced my hand. You really are quite like your mother that way."

I fought the impulse to shiver. "So you did know my mother," I called back, trying to keep him talking. The sound bounced off the walls and the bronze sculptures more than seemed natural. Where *was* he?

"He'll be cross with me," the voice went on, as though I hadn't spoken. "It wasn't supposed to go like this. But I think he'll forgive me. If you survive, he'll know you're worth all the trouble."

Fuck it. I was not going to stand here and play mind games with shadows. I stepped forward, crossing the oval path into the inner courtyard.

At last, I saw him. He was crouching next to my favorite statue, a life-sized female settler with her baby strapped to her chest. I felt a bizarre spark of indignation, like he was defacing the sculpture just by being next to it. His hand was on the ground, resting on something cylindrical that was nearly as long as my forearm. A piece of glass?

"Who? Who will be cross?" I asked.

When he spoke, his voice curled with reverence and fear. "Our father," he said, and twisted the glass sideways.

There was an explosion of smoky light—no, several small explosions, dotting across my vision. There was no sound, but the lights began to move closer to me, forming shapes. Human shapes. They were ghosts. I backed up, heading away from the settler statue, but when I turned to run, I saw there were more of them behind me. I whipped my head around, looking for Emil, but he'd vanished.

I couldn't even process that, though, because the ghosts were getting closer, surrounding me in a shrinking circle. I was starting to make out details: the bloodstains, the missing limbs, the gunshot holes. Their faces were twisted with anger and their mouths opened and closed soundlessly as they glared at me.

A jolt of recognition hit me. Oh, God. I'd seen these things on Halloween, when they had to return to their graves, but this time they had a terrifying sense of purpose. They reached out for me, and with every step, they seemed to solidify further.

Emil—whoever he was—had found a way to weaponize the wraiths.

Chapter 21

As the wraiths advanced, I spun in a circle, counting. There were eight of them, and they were moving slowly, but they were still closing in. The light coming off them had faded, and they were now terrifyingly solid-looking, even more so than Nellie had been when the ley line was active. My best option was to act quickly, while there was still enough space between them to run. I picked the two that were farthest apart and sprinted for the space between them.

The woman on the right couldn't have been more than twenty when she died, and her hairstyle suggested the sixties or seventies. The ghost on the left was a cowboy in his forties, his eyes bulging out and an angry line of red running across his neck. His clothes were probably from the mid-nineteenth century, although it was too dark and I was moving too fast to look closely. I put my head down and ran, hoping that if they closed rank I would slide through them.

But that's not how it happened.

The woman didn't react in time, but the man leaned sideways into my path and held out a rigid arm, clotheslining me at the chest. My legs flew forward and my torso flew back, my back slamming into the ground. The man planted a heavy boot on my chest, squatted, and wrapped his hands around my throat, his face twisted in a snarl.

I panicked.

My legs kicked out wildly, ineffectively, while my fingers scrabbled at his hands. They were locked tightly around my throat—real, so real—and now the young woman was coming around to help him, trying to trap my legs. I was focused on evading her, unwilling to be completely pinned down, but that meant my attention was divided and I couldn't get the man off and I couldn't breathe—

Stop reacting like a victim, Allie! Sam's voice screamed in my head. *Show this fucker who you are.*

With enormous effort, I shut down the panic and assessed. These two had me pinned, and there were more behind them, eager to help restrain me. I wasn't going to get out of this by physical force. It took every bit of concentration I could muster, but I managed to drop into my boundary mindset, expecting to see these things as glowing blue images, like the fox. Instead, the human-shaped figures crouching over me were completely colorless—swirling, silver-black pieces of light that felt *wrong* in my mind. No, not just wrong—*wronged*. Something had been done to these things without their consent.

But that didn't make them any less deadly. My concentration was beginning to waver, and I knew I was on the verge of losing consciousness. *Think, Lex.* I let go of the cowboy's iron fingers and focused on his essence, trying to manipulate it the way I usually did—pulling it toward me with imaginary fingers. I couldn't get a grip, though—the oil-slick surface was too slippery.

But the wraith felt my clumsy attempts and paused in confusion, his grip loosening long enough for me to get a few desperate gulps of air. I was so grateful for the oxygen, though, that I lost control of my mindset, and the wraith's grip on my throat tightened again. The female was sitting on my legs now, trapping me, and I couldn't even see past her—the other six wraiths had surrounded me, packing tightly around me like I was at the bottom of a football dogpile.

Panic rose in my chest again, but I pushed it down. I was *not* going to die like this, goddammit. I had been through too much to be killed by a bunch of costume-party rejects. I forced myself into the mindset again, examining the cowboy wraith's swirling, polluted aura. Okay, I couldn't pull it. But I extended my imaginary fingers again, and this time I *stirred*, sending the swirls of sickness dancing frantically through his form like bubbles in boiling water.

The ghost let go of me, and I could sense its confusion and bewilderment. I didn't stop to see what happened, though. I rolled over as hard as I could, disrupting the female wraith on my legs and sending her off-balance. I crawled through the jumble of ghostly bodies, pushing aside legs and arms. Now their numbers worked to my advantage. There were too many of them to grab me properly; they kept tripping over each other. They were clumsy, like they'd forgotten how to move in the physical world. I crawled forward and stumbled to my feet, but the cowboy, who seemed like the strongest of them, grabbed hold of the back of my shirt and yanked, sending me stumbling. I whipped around and swung a roundhouse at him, but it was like hitting a pillow—the ghost absorbed the force without even moving.

Then he hit me. And it was not at all pillow-like.

His open-handed blow struck the left side of my head and clubbed me to the ground as effectively as a baseball bat. I sprawled on my face in the dirt path, and immediately felt the cowboy crouch on my back like a demon, his forearm sliding beneath my chin so he could strangle me again. My vision blurred, and there were wraiths on my arms and legs again. I felt myself fade and wondered if a boundary witch could die like this, at the hands of the dead. It looked like I was going to find out.

Then all of them abruptly vanished. Every single one, like someone had flicked off a switch.

I couldn't hold up my head, and it plopped down into the dirt. Someone hunched down in my field of vision, a warm hand that pushed hair out of my face.

"Lex? Lex!" My eyes focused just long enough to see Simon, who was holding the long, translucent piece of glass. Then I was out.

Chapter 22

The first thing I felt was a cool hand squeezing mine. I knew that temperature. Quinn.

When I opened my eyes, he was leaning over me with worry etched in his face, which seemed odd to me. I wasn't used to seeing Quinn with actual emotional expressions. I opened my mouth to say I was fine, but nothing came out but a dry rustle.

"Shh," he murmured. "Lily said you shouldn't try to talk yet. Whatever got you, it damn near crushed your trachea." He gave me a thin smile. "Of course, she used a lot more words to explain it. Those Pellars and their big science words."

I chuckled, which made me dizzy with pain for a second. It must have showed on my face, because Quinn winced, his hand stroking the uninjured side of my face. "Sorry, I'm so sorry. No more jokes. I'm glad you're okay."

My eyes dropped to his chest. He was wearing a clean button-down shirt, although I could see a tiny smear of dried blood near his collarbone. He followed my eyes down, touched the spot on his chest where Emil's stake had pierced him. "Oh, yeah, I'm fine. I drank some of the bagged blood I got for Maven, and it's almost healed. I'm a lot more worried about you."

I couldn't say anything yet, so I just smiled at him. The left side of my face ached with the movement. Quinn's eyes softened, but didn't leave my face.

I glanced around without moving my neck, recognizing the concrete walls and the sparse furniture. It was the Basement of Dr. Moreau, but this was Simon's bedroom. Probably Maven was still in the spare room. I flexed my arms and legs, trying to feel for broken bones. My body was weak and exhausted, not to mention sore, but generally okay. Quinn saw the movement. "You're going to be fine," he assured me. "Scrapes and bruises on your back and chest. You've also got a pretty impressive bruise on your cheekbone, and your throat will hurt for a few days, but Lily said you just need rest and some ice packs."

Emil? I mouthed.

His face clouded over. "He got away. Simon and Lily are working on a locator spell using the crystals we found, but it's already failed twice. I went back to the St. Julien and pressed a bellboy to get into his room, but it was empty." He kissed my forehead again. "I'm going to go get that ice pack."

When he was gone, I began to drift off again. My last thought before I sank into the dark was: *crystals?*

The next time I woke, the clock next to Simon's bed said 7:42, presumably in the morning. Someone had left the little lamp on the dresser switched on, so I had no trouble making out the figure huddled in the bed next to me, snoring lightly. Lily.

"Hey," I tried to say, but it came out as an unintelligible rasp. Lily's eyes popped open anyway. "Hi!" she said, relief heavy in her voice. She sat up, folding her legs in a lotus position. "Thank the goddess. I was a little worried when the ice packs didn't wake you up. Here." She twisted at the waist and picked up a sweating glass of water from the nightstand. There was a bendy straw inside. "You need to keep drinking, or we'll have to do the IV again."

I took an experimental sip of water. My cheek hurt when I closed my lips around the straw, but swallowing wasn't as bad as I'd expected. The cold water felt wonderful and painful at the same time. It was like trying to drink when you have strep throat. Or after the tracheotomy I'd gotten the previous year.

Lily was watching carefully, giving me a little nod of approval when I was able to get the water down. "Good. Your trachea is swollen, but the hyoid bone is intact. You might be a little nauseous or light-headed today from the hypoxia, but you'll be fine in a couple of days."

She called for Simon, who leaned in the doorway and gave me a tired smile. "Welcome back to the living," he joked. Lily smacked his arm, but without much energy. They both looked exhausted.

The cold water soothed the back of my throat, so I tried a whisper. "Did you find Emil?"

Simon's face darkened. "No. Our locator spells aren't working."

Lily gestured helplessly. "We need either something that belongs to him or something that's a part of him, like hair or fingernails. But the only thing we have is the crystal he left behind, and that's gravitational magic, so it's all wonky."

"His blood?" I whispered. There must have been a little bit left in the IV tubing.

But Lily shook her head. "We tried, but the belladonna in his system messed it up. It was like when Emil tried a locator spell for you and your sister at the same time—the results were all confused."

"No matter how many times we tried," Simon added, dejected.

That's why they looked so tired. They'd been up all night trying spells. For me. "Where does your mother think you are right now?" I whispered.

Simon and Lily exchanged a complicated look. It hit me in that moment that by dragging them into this mess, I had more or less asked Simon and Lily to choose loyalty to me over loyalty to their own mother, to their own kind. Shame burned my cheeks as I absorbed the size of that.

But before I could apologize or beg for forgiveness, Lily answered me, her words rushing out in a burst. "We had to tell her, Lex." Her hands twisted together in knots.

"You . . . Hazel knows about Maven?"

Simon looked away. "This whole thing has sort of snowballed out of control—" Lily began, apologetically.

I waved a hand around for her attention, and she cut herself off. "It's okay," I croaked. "I get it. What did she say?" A terrible thought occurred to me. "Is Maven—"

"She's fine," Simon assured me. "Or in the same condition as she was last night, anyway."

"We told Mom about the attack and your father trying to kill her. She said that as long as there's a chance of Maven recovering, she'll stand by her promise," Lily explained.

"But," Simon added, holding up a finger, "she said she can't really help us, especially if it takes a while for Maven to wake up. Mom's not just the witches' leader—she's their representative. If the other clans learn that Hazel Pellar had the chance to usurp Maven and didn't take it, there will be problems."

Lily batted her eyes with great innocence. "If, on the other hand, Hazel Pellar's reckless younger children decide to go rogue and help the vampires, that's certainly not Hazel's fault." Despite the difference in their skin tones, Simon's smile matched his sister's perfectly.

I bit my lip. "If the other witches find out you guys are trying to save Maven . . ."

"There'll be a witch hunt, so to speak," Lily said cheerfully.

"But if we can resolve this quickly, there's no reason for them to find out," Simon finished.

I felt the prick of tears in my eyes. I blinked hard, not knowing what to say. I had pledged loyalty to Maven, and more importantly, I still believed she was my best chance to keep Charlie safe. As long as she was—well, whatever passed for alive for vampires—I had to do everything I could to keep her in power. But if she died, or someone found out she was paralyzed and took action against her, I wasn't the only one who would suffer. We would all be screwed.

"So," Lily said, "what do we do next?"

Slowly, I pulled myself into a sitting position and swung my legs over the side of the bed. Lily's hands hovered nearby to spot me. The movement was awful, but I'd had worse.

"I need everything you know about crystals," I told her.

Chapter 23

Ten minutes later, Simon, Lily, and I were sitting around the little kitchen table. I kept eyeing the empty chair where Quinn should have been sitting. He'd gone to ground for the day, of course, but I hated planning things without him. It felt like riding a bike without one of my arms.

Simon had been examining the small sample of Emil's blood, but the only thing he'd determined was that we were right about the belladonna. "There wasn't enough in his system to kill him, but given how far gone Maven is, it would likely have killed her," he told me grimly.

"How was he able to run if he was half-poisoned?" I asked, keeping my voice just above a whisper. Lily had crushed up four Advil and given them to me to swallow, but talking still hurt like hell. "I know you didn't see him, but he was fast."

Simon nodded like he'd expected the question. "I didn't get a great look at all the crystals he was wearing, but probably one of them was boosting his stamina."

I wanted to follow up on that, but before I could, Lily placed a hand on mine. "I'm so sorry, Lex," she said. "We both are."

Guilt flashed across Simon's face. "Right, yeah. Sorry about your father being a . . . um . . ."

"Murderer?" I suggested.

"Yeah." He glanced at Lily. "If anyone knows how rough it is to have evil family, it's us."

"Thank you," I said, meaning it. "But he's not my father."

Their eyebrows rose in the same way, at the same time. "Um, he looks just like you," Lily ventured.

"He's my brother."

The two of them exchanged a worried look—not in an *oh, that explains it* kind of way. More like an *uh-oh, being strangled has degraded poor Lex's brain* kind of way. "What makes you say that?" Simon asked carefully.

"When I confronted him, he said someone was going to be pissed that he screwed up. I asked who, and he said, 'our father.' Then he ran."

"Leaving you to face . . . whatever the hell those were," Simon finished for me.

"They were wraiths," I whispered, shuddering as I remembered the cowboy's rage and desperation, his vise grip on my throat.

"But that's impossible," Lily protested. "Wraiths are tied to where they die, except on Samhain." She looked uncertainly at her brother. "Right?"

He pushed up his glasses. "Right. And nothing I've ever read suggests that they can interact with the world physically." He gestured to the bruises on my neck. "That's some serious physical contact, Lex."

"Trust me," I said shortly. "They were wraiths. I could feel it. But they'd been trapped or directed somehow. They were being *made* to attack."

Simon and Lily fell into awed silence. "How is that even possible?" Lily asked in a hushed voice.

"That big crystal," I croaked. "Did you bring it back?"

He nodded. "And it wasn't the only one."

Lily got up and went to the counter, bringing back one of those reusable shopping bags from Trader Joe's. She upended it on the table, and a bunch of gleaming stones tumbled out. Most of them were a sort of translucent gray, but there were a few chunks of dark green in there as well. They were just as shiny and cared-for as the purple stone I'd found in my backyard. "These were scattered all over the sculpture garden in a sort of circular pattern, similar to many witch spells," Simon told me. "I wanted to document their placement a little more, but we were worried about you."

"Do you have the jacket I was wearing?" Someone had pulled it off me while I was unconscious, probably to make me more comfortable. Lily got up and retrieved it from the hall closet.

When she handed it to me, I dug the purple stone out of the side pocket and placed it on the table with the others. "I found this in my yard yesterday. I didn't think anything of it at the time, but the dogs reacted to it like they do to magic. Do you recognize it?"

Lily picked it up and examined it, then shrugged. "If I had to guess, I'd say amethyst, but I really only know about it as a birthstone. I don't know much about crystals."

I looked at Simon. "Me neither," he said.

Now it was my turn to be surprised. I'd sort of assumed that as trades witches, Simon and Lily would know all about using stones in magic. "You don't?" I asked.

They both shook their heads. "Crystals and stones are gravitational magic," Simon told me. "We don't know much more about it than the average citizen of Boulder."

"Why not?"

"Because," he said patiently, "most gravitational magic doesn't work with witch magic."

I looked back and forth between them, confused.

"Crossed signals," Lily explained. "Sort of like . . . having the bluetooth and the wireless turned on in your laptop. Makes everything slower and clumsier. So we don't use it."

It scared me a little that I almost followed that. Simon held up a finger. "There are a *couple* of crystals that are compatible with witch magic," he cautioned. "For example, pretty much every witch I know has a bracelet or a necklace made from labradorite."

"Oh, that's true," Lily said with a nod. "I have a brooch."

"But other than that," Simon continued, "the important thing to know about gravitational magic is that it isn't limited to the Old World. In theory, anyone can use it."

So Emil really didn't have access to boundary magic. He'd just found a work-around. "Like scrying?" I offered.

"What do you know about scrying?"

"That's how Emil said he found me." I described the shiny black stone disk he'd shown me when we first met. "I never really gave much thought to how he could do that without active witchblood. I should have."

"He's a magician, then," Lily said, as if that explained everything.

Simon was nodding, but I was still confused. "Like at kids' parties? Sawing a woman in half and rabbits out of top hats?"

Simon snorted. Lily answered, "No. Magicians are humans who use gravitational magic."

"There are a few things that any human can do, in theory," Simon explained. "It's like an equation: A plus B equals C. It's usually weaker than our magic, but more stable. If your—if Emil knows how to use crystals, he's a magician. There aren't many of them left."

Lily nodded. "But that still doesn't explain how he got the wraiths inside them," she pointed out.

"Sophia," I said abruptly. Looking at them, I added, "He said his mother is a boundary witch, and apparently she looks younger than him. That means she's got strong magic, right? She must have figured out a way to harness and trap the wraiths."

"How do you know he was telling the truth about his mother?" Simon asked. "He lied about being your father."

"But that picture he gave me was real. And I checked, he really does own a New Age shop in Nova Scotia . . . which probably sells crystals. God, I'm an idiot."

"No, he just mixed truths in with his lies," Lily said, rescuing me. "He's smart."

"Yeah, but why? What's the point of all this?" I said, frustrated. My throat hurt, and I felt so far out of my depth it was threatening to choke me all over again.

"He tried to kill Maven," Simon mused. "Twice."

"Does he want Colorado?" Lily said.

Simon looked doubtful. "I only met him briefly, but he didn't seem like the world-domination type. And he's not even a witch. How would he expect to hold a whole state?"

"No, he's working for someone," I concluded.

"Who?"

"Our father. Whoever the hell that is."

Chapter 24

It was obvious that we needed to do more research on gravitational magic, but Simon and Lily didn't have any special resources. Their texts were limited to witch magic.

A few minutes on the internet proved that there was a ton of information out there about crystals, but much of it was contradictory or unsupported.

"We need a library run," Lily concluded. "Or maybe one of those New Age bookstores. There's one downtown where I get my sage."

I started to stand up, but she put a hand on my arm. "Not you," she ordered. Getting up from the table, she went to the fridge and got a bottle of one of those sports drinks with electrolytes. "You need to drink this and go back to bed."

"I have to go home to take care of the herd anyway," I protested. "I might as well go to the library too."

Lily just cocked an eyebrow. "Have you looked in a mirror yet?"

That brought me up short. "Huh?"

"You look like you . . . um . . . saw a ghost," Simon said, with a wince of apology. "If anyone sees those bruises, you're gonna get some attention."

Right. I'd forgotten. I dragged myself into the little bathroom and took a look in the mirror. My jaw dropped open. I looked . . . well, actually, I looked like one of the wraiths. My skin was deadly pale except for a spectacular purplish bruise on my cheekbone, which was just beginning to lighten to blue around the edges. I tilted my head up to get a good look at the matching ring of bruising around my neck. It was fainter and less defined, but just as purple as my face. Meanwhile, there were dark circles under my eyes, and my hair hung in lifeless clumps around my face.

I sighed. I could come up with a story for the facial bruise, but my neck couldn't be mistaken for anything but strangulation. If I bumped into any of my family members looking like this, they'd frog-march me to the police station to file a report on whoever did this.

I went back out to Simon and Lily. "I can't just let you guys do all the work," I argued. "This is my case."

"Lex," Lily said gently, "you are literally leaning against the doorframe because you're too weak to stand."

I straightened up. "No, I'm not."

It took a bit more negotiating, but I finally agreed to rest for another hour while Lily took care of the herd and stopped at the Lighthouse Bookstore, a New Age store on Pearl that probably had a lot in common with Emil's store in Nova Scotia. It was likely to have some texts that weren't exactly science-based. She would also bring back makeup, clothes, and a scarf from my cabin. Meanwhile, Simon would make a trip to Boulder's main library, where he would bring back everything he could find on crystals. Then we'd reconvene for the actual research.

I fell into Simon's bed with a blissful relief that only increased my guilt.

And opened my eyes in my old bedroom.

Out of curiosity, I reached up and touched my face. No bruises when I was in the dream-space. Interesting. I looked up and saw

Sam, sitting cross-legged on her old bed with her hands raised defensively. "I know, I know," she said immediately, "I got some splainin' to do."

I laughed in spite of myself. "You know what happened with Emil?"

She nodded. "And I'm really sorry. Val and I had no idea he was going to betray you like that."

I noticed that our birth mother was "Val" now and felt a ridiculous stab of envy. "She must have known he's not actually our father," I said.

Sam bit her lip and said nothing. We'd entered into one of those topics she couldn't talk about. Okay, fine.

"I'm not sure he meant to betray *me*," I said, thinking it over. "If he wanted to kill Maven, he could have walked into that room and plunged a stake into her heart before anyone could stop him. If I hadn't seen his necklace, if Simon and Quinn hadn't noticed the signs of belladonna, he could have poisoned Maven and waltzed right out of there. We would have assumed she just succumbed to the earlier poisoning."

"I am so proud of you for using the word 'succumb,'" Sam said seriously.

I ignored her. "My point is, he made himself sick so he could get away with killing Maven on my watch. He wasn't trying to hurt me—it was more that I got in the way of his objective."

"He did send those things to kill you," she reminded me.

"Yeah, after I'd backed him into a corner. I'm not saying Emil's a good guy, but he didn't set out to get me. Whoever he's working with, their goal is to kill Maven, not me."

She leaned back with her spine against the wall, and I recognized her expression. Sam is—was—always the charming one, the life of the party. It sometimes seemed like that was all there was to her—charm and good humor. But anyone who underestimated my sister learned pretty quickly that she was also smart and shrewd. "You have to find out who he's working for," she said at last.

"Well, duh. Can't you help me with that?"

She shook her head, looking perplexed. "Even if I was allowed to tell you, I don't know. I can't see—" she broke off, tilting her head in that listening gesture. I waited. "Emil's boss isn't human, I can tell you that much," she said. I wondered if she'd been about to tell me that her perception of the living was limited to the Old World. Or to humans. Or to magic? Damn, this was frustrating.

"But it's a he," I said. "Male. And he's possibly our father, right?"

Sam scrunched up her face helplessly. She couldn't talk about that. I gritted my teeth.

"This is ridiculous, Sammy. People could die if I can't figure out—"

She said it so softly that I almost missed it. "People *have* died."

I froze—and woke up to Lily shaking my shoulder.

"Sam," I gasped as my eyes flew open.

"Um, no. Lily." She held up a paper grocery-style bag. "I have books. And Simon brought food from that place you—" She registered the look on my face and went still. "What is it?"

"People *have* died," I repeated. I climbed off the bed, only wobbling a little, and staggered into the kitchen. "Si, do you have the newspapers?"

Simon, who was sitting at the table, raised his eyebrows. "In the recycling. Why?"

I went to the cupboard underneath the sink and dragged out the recycling bin. I pulled out the stack of newspapers and picked through them until I had the front section from the last three days. The rest of the stack I let fall to the floor. Simon had been right:

there were very few murders in Boulder every year, which meant they would undoubtedly make the front page.

Simon and Lily had spread books about crystals all over the table, but I laid out the newspaper sections right over them. There was nothing interesting on the front pages for Tuesday or Wednesday, but the headline for yesterday's paper screamed POLICE ON ALERT AS BODY FOUND IN DUMPSTER. I scanned the first few lines, enough to confirm that the story was about the engineer from Fort Collins that Elise had mentioned on the phone.

I mumbled to myself, "Plural, she said people, *plural.*" Then I glanced up at Simon. He and Lily were both giving me bewildered expressions. "Humor me a minute. Where's today's paper?"

Simon went to his messenger bag and pulled out a folded newspaper. "The paper boy leaves it outside the building. I haven't even looked at it yet," he said, handing it over.

I practically tore it open. The headline above the fold read SECOND BODY FOUND.

I scanned the opening paragraphs. The second corpse was a college student from Oregon, no obvious connection to the first victim, although the article spent some time speculating on possibilities. Her body had snagged on a fallen tree in Boulder Creek and been spotted early this morning by hikers in Open Space and Mountain Parks. The police had no idea where the body was originally dumped, but the victim was wearing a fitness tracker that had stopped transmitting at 9:05 p.m., which must have been when she'd gone into the water. I automatically glanced at the clock on the microwave. It was after eleven. I rounded on Lily and Simon. "You let me sleep for over three hours?"

Neither of them looked the least bit contrite. "Your body needed it, Lex," Lily said.

"What are you thinking?" Simon asked, reading over my shoulder. "The bodies really are connected to the Old World? Why?"

"Because Sam said they are."

I didn't bother to watch Simon and Lily react to that. I didn't care if they believed me about Sam. There were too many pieces here, and it was driving me crazy that none of them seemed to fit together.

Ordinarily this is where I would have really wanted to pace, but I was too tired to move. I sat down and closed my eyes, trying to reason through it. "Two and a half weeks ago, the Denver vampires were poisoned. It took two weeks for the news to get to Maven, who sent Quinn and me to Denver to investigate. Ford tried to kill us, and when we killed him, we thought we'd put the belladonna attacks to rest. But Maven was poisoned the next night."

"And the next day, Emil tried to finish her off right in front of us," Simon prompted. "Where are you going with this?"

I opened my eyes and looked at him. "Ford wouldn't work for Emil. Vampires don't do that, especially not a dominus dickhead like Ford supposedly was. So let's say Emil was working for Ford, as unlikely and coincidental as that seems. I could see Ford sending Emil on a sneak attack to kill Maven."

"Then Ford could swoop in afterwards and claim the state, without actually needing to face Maven himself," Simon offered.

I pointed at him. "Exactly. I can buy that plan. But then why would Emil still try to kill Maven after Ford was already dead? And where does our father fit into all this?"

"Maybe Emil didn't know Ford had been killed," Lily suggested. "Maybe they'd already set the wheels in motion before the attack."

I turned that over in my mind, and shook my head. "Emil seems too smooth for that kind of mistake. When I met him for coffee he was incredibly convincing. Besides, Emil didn't kill the college student last night."

"How do you know?" Simon asked.

I jabbed a finger on that morning's headline. "Because he was with us at 9:05 last night, and that was long after Ford died. Neither of them could have killed this student."

"Emil could have set traps in crystals, like he did with you," Lily ventured.

"I don't think so. Setting traps would have required stalking the victims and predicting their behavior. These attacks were random; these people were killed because they were in the wrong place at the wrong time."

Simon studied my face. In some ways, he knew me better than Lily did. "You have a theory," he said.

I nodded. "I think my father killed them with boundary magic."

Chapter 25

This time, the look that passed between Simon and Lily was downright uncomfortable.

"That doesn't make sense, though," Lily said, her voice careful. "Why send a proxy—Emil—if you're also going to come yourself?"

"Plus, boundary magic is extraordinarily powerful," Simon added. "If he used two different people as human sacrifices, he'd have the juice to raise the dead. And that kind of magic makes an impact—empty graves, confused loved ones, empty coffins at funeral parlors." He gestured at the newspaper. "We would have heard something by now."

Lily was nodding along as though Simon was voicing her thoughts verbatim. "Besides," he continued, "we don't know for sure that there's *any* connection between these deaths and the belladonna attacks."

"I do," I insisted. "Look, none of us knows all that much about serious boundary magic, but Emil obviously came here to kill Maven, and he said he worked for *our* father. Presumably the man's a boundary witch, since Emil and I both have strong boundary blood. Ergo, our father is behind the attacks on her, and somehow he's behind this too."

"Couldn't it be Emil's mother?" Lily offered. "You said Sophia was a powerful boundary witch."

I shook my head. "Yes, but she was in Nova Scotia last night. I called and confirmed."

"I've never heard of a male witch being strong enough to do human sacrifice alone," Simon insisted. "And if your theory were true, why did they try to kidnap you?"

I had to admit, he had me there. I had no idea why someone powerful enough to use human sacrifice would want to drag me into this. But my instincts said that I was on the right track.

But Simon and Lily didn't seem convinced. I couldn't entirely blame them for not buying my theory, but it was still frustrating. I needed more evidence. "Let's put a pin in this for the moment," I said, looking down at the cluttered table. I brushed aside the newspapers, revealing a bunch of open books and the stones from the sculpture park. "What have you guys figured out about crystals?"

Both Pellars began to speak at once. I held up my hands in protest, and they exchanged another one of those sibling communication looks, which somehow resulted in Simon speaking first. "A lot of this is New Age crap," he said, waving his hand at the table of research. Then he paused, considering me. "Um, unless you believe that tiny beings from another dimension live inside crystals and have the power to influence the exterior world. If so, congratulations on your wacko religion."

Lily smacked his arm, probably a little harder than I would have. "Hey!" he protested, rubbing the arm with great exaggeration.

"Do the science part," she ordered.

"Fine. Okay, so, the word 'crystal' actually refers to the structure of the material," he began, relaxing into his explanation. Science was a lot firmer ground for Simon. "Rocks with an orderly arrangement of atoms are called crystals. They are unique from other rocks because they can produce a piezoelectric effect—"

"Which just means they can generate an electric charge in response to pressure," Lily broke in.

"Right. Anyway, there are *some* people"—he cut his eyes to Lily—"who believe that because crystals vibrate in different frequencies under pressure, they can affect the human bioelectric energy fields."

"Which is basically the aura," Lily added.

I stared at them, not bothering to hide my incredulity. "Wait, you're saying it's real? I mean, we know crystals do *something*, but are you saying it's common knowledge that they affect humans?"

"Yes and no," Simon answered, tilting his flattened hand back and forth. "Yes, crystals have a measurable piezoelectric effect, and yes, human beings do conceivably have a bioelectric field, which in magic we call the aura. But there's no scientific evidence that crystals actually affect people. In fact, I'd say most of the testimonial evidence comes from crystal users who want to believe in it so badly that they convince themselves it's true."

I looked at Lily. "Okay, now give me the woo-woo version. What do hard-core crystal users believe they can do?"

She took a deep breath. "The idea is that you can program crystals to do all sorts of things. Different crystals can supposedly amplify energy, broadcast information, heal wounds, and affect moods."

"Wait, go back to the word 'program.' What does that mean?"

"Just how it sounds. You program the crystal to do something—heal a wound, ground energy, or whatever—and it does it."

I thought about that. "That's how Emil was able to run so fast when he'd taken the belladonna."

"Exactly."

"And if crystals can ground energy, and Sophia used them to ground boundary magic . . ." I went on.

Simon nodded. "She could store spells in the crystals, and Emil could set them off later. Technically, *he'd* only be using gravitational magic."

"Okay, well, that's one mystery solved." I tried not to think about how many animals—I was really hoping it was animals—had died just so Emil could attack me with wraiths. I looked at Simon. "Why did the spell stop when you picked up the big stone? Is it based on touch or something?"

He shook his head. "Emil had laid these out in a grid system," he said, gesturing at the pile of stones on the table. "The idea is that if you place certain stones in a certain ritualistic pattern, it creates an energy net that the magician can control. That's how Emil was able to activate such a complex spell."

"It's just like witches' circles," Lily said.

"Only more vulnerable," Simon pointed out. To me, he added, "When I picked up the big crystal, I disturbed the grid, and the spell failed. He also probably had a grid around your house, so picking up this one rock"—he pointed to the chunk of maybe-amethyst—"would be enough to break the spell."

Which meant he'd set out a grid of crystals at the sculpture garden before I'd ever picked up last night, just on the off chance that his effort to kill Maven failed. He was a planner.

I sat down at the table and took the amethyst from Simon, examining it. It was pretty, but I didn't see anything particularly special about it. I certainly didn't feel any vibrations, menacing or otherwise. "What was it doing?" I wondered.

"Supposedly, amethyst is a protective stone," Lily said. "But I don't understand why Emil would want to protect you, if the only threat against you is coming from him and whoever he works for."

"But it's hard to say for sure, without seeing the rest of the pattern." Simon shook his head.

I considered that for a moment. "I've felt a little weird at home lately," I said slowly. "But in more of a good way." I told them about how peaceful and relaxing the cabin had seemed over the last few days.

The Pellars exchanged a bewildered glance. "You need an expert," Simon declared. "A lot of the public 'knowledge'"—he mimed quote marks with his hands—"about crystals is based on the theories of a

single guy, who made them up based on his meditative practices."
Seeing my baffled look, he added, "The 'feelings' he got from the
crystals. If you want to know how actual magicians use crystals,
you're probably going to have to find one," Simon told me.

"Great."

"There are at least two crystal stores on Pearl Street," Lily offered.
"Probably more in Denver."

Simon, ever the scientist, said, "But we have no way of knowing
if the people who work there are the real thing, or just wannabes."

I considered that for a long moment. "Hang on, people, I'm
having an idea." I retrieved my cell phone from my other jacket
pocket and called Anna.

"Hey, cousin. What's buzzin'?" she said cheerfully.

I couldn't help but smile at that. "Hey. Listen, do you know
anything about crystal healing?"

"Yeah, of course." Her voice was amused. "You realize that I have
a degree in religious studies, right?"

I paused. I'd never really considered crystals as part of an actual
religion. "Right, so if I send you a picture of a stone, would you know
what it's, um, meant for?"

There was a pause. Simon and Lily were both watching me
expectantly. Finally Anna said, "Maybe, but why don't you just ask
Blossom?"

I blanked for a long moment. "Blossom *Wheaton*?" I said incred-
ulously. "John's mother?" The Pellars exchanged a confused look, but
I waved them off.

"How many other Blossoms are there?" Anna asked me.

"Dude, this is Boulder. Last month I met two different kids
named Dandelion."

"Girls or boys?"

"Anna—"

"Right, anyway. Blossom *Wheaton* works at the crystal shop in
downtown Longmont. You didn't know?"

Blossom lived thirty miles outside of Boulder in a little house with two defense-trained Dobermans and an armful of rifles. I'd never considered what she did for money. "I guess I just figured she ate the kids she lures into her gingerbread house." Simon made a choking noise in the back of his throat.

Anna just laughed. "She's not *that* bad, Lex. She actually helped me with a paper on ceremonial applications for various quartzes. She's just a little . . . mmm . . . prickly."

I had a very distinct memory of Blossom chasing Sam and me out of John's house with a giant butcher knife, because we'd used one of her woven throws as a picnic blanket. "Prickly" wasn't the word I'd use.

"I'm sure this stuff is probably on the internet," I hedged.

Anna made a little grunting noise that perfectly communicated a verbal shrug. "Your call, but Blossom would probably save you some time. Assuming you tip her well. I had to buy, like, eight pounds of quartz to get that paper done."

I sighed. "Thanks, Anna."

When I hung up the phone, I let my head fall to the table with a clunk. "So," I said into the Formica. "I think I might know a magician."

Chapter 26

As I drove northeast on 119, I tried not to think about having to confront Blossom and beg her for information. My efforts were futile. "She's not an ogre, Lex," I muttered to myself. "She's not gonna hurt you."

Some fears run a lot deeper than logic.

Blossom was a full-blooded Arapaho. She grew up on the Wind River Reservation in Wyoming, but after her father died, her mother had married a white man, which caused a serious rift between her and Blossom. As soon as she turned eighteen, Blossom moved to Boulder and began waitressing and taking classes at the community college. She intended to go to CU, but she got pregnant by a man who left her. She wound up quitting school and taking in sewing to pay for the little tract house next door to the one where my parents lived when Sam and I were little.

Some of my strongest memories from those years involve the smell of cotton and the sight of yards and yards of color spread across John's living room and kitchen. Blossom would screech at Sam and me to stay away from her material, cursing us in both English and Hinóno'eitíít, the Arapaho word for their native language. I learned the Arapaho words for "filthy white monster" before I could ride a bike.

At the time, I thought Blossom was a merciless witch, but looking back, I can have sympathy for her: a young single mother, trying to keep the rambunctious neighbor kids away from her only way to put food on the table. She worked day and night—I didn't remember seeing her without a mouthful of needles and a measuring tape around her neck until I was at least eight.

My dad—my real dad—started Luther Shoes out of our little tract house, and when it began to take off, he hired the best seamstress he knew to oversee the stitching. Blossom worked for Luther Shoes for years, and during that time, John more or less lived at my house. My mother helped him with his homework just like she did with Sam and me, and he ate dinner with us every night. Sometimes Blossom, who had never experienced much freedom because she'd had John so young, would take advantage of the free childcare and go out, and John would end up camped on the living room floor. By the time we were ten, his sleeping bag had a permanent place in the corner by the couch. The three of us were inseparable—not like a brother and sisters, exactly, but like best friends who had been given the extraordinary gift of never being separated. We accepted him as a permanent part of our world, as only children could.

Those were great years, but when we were fifteen, Blossom and my dad had a falling out. The company was growing so fast that he needed to move all stitching to machines, even the special orders. Blossom was a brilliant seamstress, but not exactly a people person, and he hired someone else to manage the team over her. He kept her in the sewing department and drastically overpaid her—my dad was passionate about rewarding talent—but Blossom's ego was wounded. She quit in a now-legendary public tantrum, and forbade John from ever returning to our house.

John did not take that well. He may have been quieter and gentler than his fierce mother, but in his own way he was just as stubborn. He went to court, became legally emancipated, and moved in with us. By then my parents had bought their dream house in Mapleton, which came with a small apartment over the garage. John had his own space, and we had our best friend only a few feet away.

The last couple of years of high school were complex and rich and mostly wonderful for the three of us, but Blossom never forgave John for choosing us over her. She saw John's decision as a betrayal not just of his mother, but of his entire heritage. She accused him and my parents of some ugly things, including racism and brainwashing. If Sam and I were around, she would scream at us too, trying to shame us by implying that we were teenage seductresses who'd poisoned John's mind by tempting his body.

By then, though, Sam and I understood that Blossom had completely missed the point. John chose us because he knew us better than he knew Blossom, and he understood that we loved him—because we told him so. For John, it was really that simple.

After high school, John went years without speaking to his prickly mother. It was actually Sam who eventually reached out to her mother-in-law, declaring that she wanted her new baby to know both sides of her heritage. Blossom may have been a shit mother, and she may have hated my parents and disliked Sam and me, but she couldn't resist Charlie. Who could?

Over the past two years, Blossom and John had begun to build a sort of wary, grumbling relationship. She had flown to LA to help with the baby while John was preparing to move back to Boulder, and she'd attended Charlie's first birthday party despite the presence of so many Luthers. Once there, she stood in the corner with a drink, glaring at the other guests, giving only curt responses to anyone who tried to speak to her, including John. But she did come, and when Charlie opened her gift—a little doll that Blossom had sewed herself—I swear, she actually smiled for a second.

I tried to remember that smile as I parked near Blossom's store, Crystals of the World, and walked into it, hearing a strand of store bells jangle just above my head. I *hated* those bells.

The inside was one large, well-lit room filled with glass shelves, so you could see straight through to the other wall if you were so inclined. Every shelf held a neatly arranged pile of stones, which seemed to be in order of color. Some of the crystals had been adapted into jewelry, while some were polished and carved in the shape of hearts or skulls. And still more were set out as raw chunks, unaltered. I noticed that these seemed to be the most expensive.

The girl at the counter looked up with a shy smile. She was in her late teens, maybe early twenties, and at least part Indian, with glossy black hair that was cut in a sharp bob near her chin. Her shoulders looked permanently hunched, as though she spent a lot of time getting yelled at. Despite this, her movements were confident, her hands capable as they worked with a small roll of copper and a pair of wire cutters. Behind her, there was a heavy velvet curtain leading to a back room.

"Hello," she said. "Can I help you find something?" Her eyes were focused on me, but her hands never stopped working, measuring the wire by muscle memory.

Stupid, Lex. What if Blossom wasn't even working today? I should have called ahead. "Um, I'm looking for Blossom. Um, Wheaton." *How may Blossoms do you know?* Sam's voice in my head sounded amused.

The curtain ripped aside, and a petite, wiry woman with graying braids was suddenly glaring at me. She seemed smaller than I remembered. "You. What do you want?" Blossom demanded.

"Hello, Blossom. How have you been?" I said pleasantly.

"Don't sweet talk me, white girl." The young woman blinked in surprise, but just ducked her head in deflection. Her expression said *better you than me*. "You come here looking for me, you must want something." A stricken look passed over her face. "Is my granddaughter okay?"

"Yes," I said hurriedly. "Charlie's fine. She's at Disney World with John and my parents."

I immediately regretted my choice of words. To Blossom, it would seem like I was throwing the Luther money in her face.

Sure enough, she glared at me with fresh resentment and irritation. "Then what do you want?"

I marched up the aisle to the counter and upended my shopping bag of stones, right over the girl's rows of cut copper. There were more stones than ever, since Lily had managed to find an additional dozen placed outside my cabin. They poured out of the bag in a glittering rush and scattered over the counter, filling in all the little spaces between the wires.

The girl gasped, her eyes wide. And for the first time in my entire life, I got to see Blossom Wheaton completely speechless.

It was awesome.

"I need to know what these are used for," I said into the silence. "And how to stop the guy who's using them."

Blossom looked from the stones to me and back again. She picked up the long piece of smoky quartz that Emil had used to activate the spell, examining it under the desk lamp. "Kathy," she said, without taking her eyes off the crystal, "Take your lunch break. Lock the door behind you."

"But Momma said—"

"I don't care what your momma said," Blossom snapped. "If she asks, you can blame me. Go now."

The girl—Kathy—hopped off the stool, grabbed a cheap purse from under the counter, and fled out the door. "My brother's daughter," Blossom groused, her eyes still on the crystal. "Stupid."

She'd been smart enough to run away from Blossom, but I didn't say that out loud. "Does your brother own this store?"

"His wife."

"You're not sewing anymore?"

"Arthritis." For the first time, she took her eyes off the quartz and eyed the bruise on my cheek. "Although I feel better than you. You look like shit, white girl. Someone's been hitting you." It was a simple observation. She did not sound particularly concerned about my welfare.

I touched the scarf around my neck, glad she couldn't see most of the damage. "Do you know what they do or not?"

Her eyes slitted. "Of course I do. But information has a price."

"Of course it does," I countered. "God forbid Blossom Wheaton do someone a favor."

Her face reddened, and I could tell she was about to wind up into one of her hard-core rants, so I held up my hands in peace. "I'm sorry. You're right; I'm not feeling well. What do you want in exchange for telling me?"

I was expecting her to name a dollar amount—Simon, Lily, and I had pooled all the cash we could manage—but her eyes dropped to the stones on the counter. "I want *them*. The whole package."

I almost laughed; it was too easy. I didn't want the creepy rocks anyway. But the greedy way she was eyeing them made me pause. There was power in these stones; did I really want to give it to Blossom?

"Will you use them to hurt people?" I asked finally.

She looked up in surprise. "No. I'm going to sell them."

"And the people who buy them, will they use the stones to hurt people?"

She shrugged. "S'pose they could. But only that big one is outright dangerous. The rest of 'em are high quality, to be sure, but not uncommon."

"Then the big one never leaves your possession," I stipulated. "And you don't use it to hurt anyone."

"Deal."

She was still too eager, for Blossom, so I pushed a little farther. "*And* I want something I can use to stop the guy who used these on me."

I could see her thinking that over for a long moment, then she nodded. "But you'll have to pay for the stock. Crystals ain't free."

I held out my hand. "Deal."

Her handshake was firm and leathery. Without another word, she tugged the copper wires out from under the crystals and moved them to a shelf behind the counter. Then she began sorting the stones into piles, a look of intense concentration on her face. I watched quietly, noticing how quickly she recognized subtle differences in the texture and color of the various crystals. Subtleties that I would never have noticed by myself. I had thought there were four or five different kinds of stones, but before I knew it, Blossom had sorted them into more than a dozen piles.

When all the stones were separated, she stared down at them and reached up to tug on her lower lip. "Two different casts here," she said at last.

"How can you tell?"

She looked up long enough to glare at me. "I just can. Do you want my help or not?" Without waiting for me to answer, she pointed to a small pile of amethyst, which was next to some stones of a slightly lighter purple. "Amethyst and sugilite together . . . interesting."

"Why?"

Her fingers went back up to her lip. "Because it's not a conventional cast; your guy is improvising. Ignore the malachite"—she pointed to a pile of green stones—"that's just a booster. Sugilite and amethyst and dream quartz all together in a grid . . ." She looked up sharply. "It's a painkiller. A deadening of one's senses and instincts. Placing these in a grid around someone's home would be like giving them a heavy narcotic, or maybe one of those date rape drugs."

I tried to keep the shock off my face. Emil had placed that spell around my house to make me less resistant to him. I suddenly remembered how relaxed and happy Quinn and I had felt the other night, and how I'd slept with no dreams of Iraq. Then I remembered that Emil had called that night, presumably to talk me into something. Betraying Maven, maybe? My fingers curled into fists. "Son of a bitch."

Ignoring me, Blossom swept the piles of stones for that spell to one side, focusing on the remaining groups. "Now, this. This isn't just unusual; this is a blitz. Celeste for other dimensions, blue tourmaline to see through the veil, mystic Merlinite for magic, obsidians for the dead . . . and the smoky quartz turns the whole thing into an offensive." Blossom shook her head, taking a small, unconscious step backward. "This is some kind of necromantic attack." She looked up, her hard eyes meeting mine. "Who did this?"

"How do I stop him?" I asked, ignoring her question. "I mean, is there a way of shutting him down remotely?"

"You can't. I've never seen anything like this; it's *old* power. If your guy has more like these"—she pointed to the stones—"and you don't know where he is or where he's setting up . . ." Blossom crossed her arms in front of her chest, a defensive posture. "I don't know of any way to stop him from a distance. You'd have to disturb the grid."

I'd never seen Blossom like this—she looked intimidated, awed. What could scare the meanest woman I knew?

I felt a chill. I hadn't known that crystal grids could be so powerful, which made me anxious about what else Emil could do with them.

And then I realized that after last night, he knew where we were keeping Maven. Oh, God.

"Hang on a second," I told Blossom, stepping away from the counter. I ignored her scowl and called Simon to explain the problem. "You need to move her, Simon. Immediately."

"But how?" he asked. "It's broad daylight out there."

"You must have a box or a big suitcase or something. It doesn't have to be dignified, it just needs to happen *right now*."

"Okay, okay. I'm on it."

I hung up the phone and went back to Blossom. "I need to know how to stop this guy. It was part of the deal."

Her face went hard again, returning to the wizened crankiness I knew so well. "You're not listening, white girl. I can't beat this. I don't know anyone who can beat this. Even—" she cut herself off, her mouth snapping shut.

"Even who?" I demanded. "Don't dick around with me, Blossom."

She scowled, but through clenched teeth she said, "Even Viola. She knew crystals. She taught my brothers and me. When I left the rez, I wanted nothing to do with it."

Viola was Blossom's late mother. "And when you couldn't sew anymore, you had to go back," I finished for Blossom. She didn't say anything, just glared at me. "And I bet that's why you get to keep this job, despite your shitty people skills. You know crystals."

"And what about you?" she snapped. "You pretend to be another half-crazy vet with a crap job, hanging onto your sanity by family ties. But you're more than you let on, aren't you, white girl?" Her eyes suddenly widened. "Tell me. What happens when you touch the stones?"

I stared at her blankly. "I . . . I guess I haven't touched them," I said, frowning in puzzlement. Only the amethyst, and I didn't like handling it for some reason.

"Is that so?" Idly, Blossom picked up the enormous piece of smoky quartz, holding it up to the light to examine it. "There's a little juice left in this one," she murmured. With no warning, she tossed the crystal straight at my chest. I automatically fumbled to catch it—

Just over Blossom's shoulder, a gruesome-looking ghost flickered into view.

It was Sam.

Chapter 27

This wasn't Sam as I knew her in life, or the Sam who visited with me in our bedroom while I dreamed. It was Sam as she'd been when she died, ravaged by a werewolf.

Her skin and dress were shredded, fresh and old blood stained her skin, and there were raw, oozing chunks missing from her belly, her arms, and her legs.

With a shout, I threw the stone on the floor as hard as I could, feeling a rush of satisfaction as it snapped in two. The image immediately disappeared, and I stood there staring at where Sam had been, panting as if I'd run ten miles.

"Now look what you did," Blossom said crossly. There was no indication that she'd seen anything unusual. "Do you have any idea how much that was worth?"

I turned on my heel and bolted from the store. If I didn't, I was undoubtedly going to hit Blossom, and while she may have deserved it, I wasn't sure I'd be able to stop.

When the door closed behind me, I took a step sideways and crouched down, pressing my back against the siding. I clenched my hands into fists, squeezed my eyes shut, and curled in on myself, my breath still jagged. I hadn't reacted this badly since those first few panic attacks when I came home from Iraq. It was Sam who'd calmed me down back then. But Sam was dead, and although I'd known intellectually what a werewolf attack might involve, I'd never let myself imagine . . . I shook my head violently, not caring who might see. *You can't fall apart right now, Lex*, I told myself, rocking back and forth a little. *Too many people need you to keep it together.* It was easy to say, but a lot harder to do. I kept seeing the image, over and over. The look on her face . . .

After a few minutes I heard the door creak open. A presence sat down next to me, and a distant part of my brain realized that it was Blossom. She folded her legs in a lotus position and didn't speak, just sat there next to me.

After a few minutes, a couple of tourists came laughing up to the door. The man tugged on the handle. "What's the matter with you?" Blossom challenged them. "Can't you read? Closed for lunch. Come back later."

There was some grumbling and huffing, but the tourists backed off. We sat in silence again for a long time, until finally I began to uncurl.

"You ask me," Blossom said, her voice rough. She was staring straight ahead. "Some stones are too powerful. That smoky quartz, for example." She nodded to herself. "Probably better to have it separated into two pieces. Still valuable, but it's not so dangerous now."

I felt a faint smile touch my lips. That was as close to an apology as I'd ever get from Blossom Wheaton.

"Who did you see?" she said, and the smile died on my face. "Your sister?"

I nodded.

She let out a little snort. "I should have known."

"Was it really her?" I whispered. "Was that Sam's . . . spirit? Trapped in the crystal?"

She gave me a disdainful look. "No, girl, of course not. Her spirit passed over a long time ago. That stone was used for an elaborate cast, like I told you, but there was a trap on the end. They were hoping if you survived the initial attack, you would pick up the stone. So they got an echo of her, a bit of her hair or clothing, something like that, and they used it to build a tiny remnant. But it wasn't any more real than a snapshot of her."

That at least gave my rational brain something to chew on. Emil must have broken in, probably while I was at work, or maybe even while I was helping Quinn save Maven. It wasn't like it would be hard: there were several boxes in my attic labeled Sam's Things, and he'd already made friends with my animals.

I felt like a fool.

"Whoever did this, he knew your weak spot," Blossom said into the silence. "Knew how to hurt you."

"Yeah."

"Which gives me an idea," Blossom continued. "There's nothing that can stop him remotely, but I can give you something to protect yourself from attacks."

I lifted my head. I had my doubts, given what Simon and Lily had told me about most crystals being incompatible with witch magic. But what was the harm in trying? "Worth a shot."

She got to her feet. "Come on."

When we were back inside, Blossom led me straight through the store, past all the rows of crystals on their glass stands, and around the register. "I thought you were going to help me find a protective stone," I said in confusion.

"Those?" She waved a dismissive hand at the store's stock. "Most of that is garbage for the tourists. Irradiated, dyed, artificial, unclean. They don't know the difference." She pulled back the heavy curtain, motioning for me to follow. "Come with me."

The curtain led to a typical storeroom with metal shelving filled with unevenly packed storage boxes and random supplies—packing tape, bubble wrap, a label maker. The back corner of the room had been turned into a sort of employee area with a mini fridge and a card table. Under the card table, a large black dog lifted its head to watch us. One of Blossom's Dobermans. "You never know when some tweaker will show up for the cash register," Blossom muttered.

Ordinarily I'd try to make friends, but I knew Blossom's dogs feared or hated everyone who wasn't Blossom. I kept my eyes lowered as we walked past.

Beyond the employee area was a narrow door painted to match the walls. It had no doorknob, but Blossom just reached out and slid it sideways. A pocket door, hiding in plain sight.

On the other side of this door was another, much smaller storeroom. Unlike the haphazard room before it, this one had simple wooden shelves arranged with carefully laid-out groupings of stones. Everything was precise and neat. I took it in quickly, trying to understand the order of the grouping. They weren't by color, and I didn't think they were alphabetical, either—there was amethyst, right toward the middle. Maybe something to do with the stones' powers?

Just inside the door was a box of white cotton gloves, simple and utilitarian. Blossom picked up a pair and pulled them on. "Gotta take care of crystals," she said gruffly. "When you handle them, they start working, and like with any battery, the usage drains their power. Crystals gotta be cleansed regularly, not to mention stored and activated properly in order for them to keep working. Part of the reason so many idiot amateurs get no results. They don't know how to take care of the things."

I blinked. It was like she was describing the right way to care for an exotic pet.

"Three things to know about crystals," she went on. "First, different stones are good at different things. You've probably figured that out by now." I nodded. "Second, everything depends on the user's intent. If I have an amethyst and my intentions are for my focus to experience good fortune, the cast works in that direction. If my intentions are to numb and sedate my focus, that's how the stone works."

"Okay."

"But," she said, holding up a finger. "People vibrate at different levels just like stones, which means that we respond differently to different stones, and vice versa. There are a dozen stones with protective properties, but your guy chose amethyst. Partly that's because it's powerful, but partly that's the stone that's attracted to him."

"So that's what we're doing here? Figuring out the stone that works best for me?" I said doubtfully.

"No. Weren't you listening, white girl? We gotta figure out which stone likes *you* best."

She made me open and close my hands quickly to get my blood flowing and my energy concentrated in my palms. Then she started to pick up stone after stone, putting each one into my hand and watching me for any reaction. If there was none, she would drop the stone into a bucket, "to be cleansed later." She mumbled the names of the stones as she went, and soon we'd gone through andalusite, malachite, purple chalcedony, black tourmaline, and amethyst. Nothing happened when I touched any of them.

After a few minutes I started to feel extremely stupid. Nothing was happening, and I had a feeling that Simon was right about crystals not working with magic. The furrow between Blossom's eyebrows was deepening with every failed attempt. Frowning, she left the section we'd been standing near and returned with one cotton glove filled with black rocks. She placed one in my hand with a murmured, "obsidian."

Nothing happened for a moment, and I was about to hand this one back like all the others. But then I felt it: the tiniest buzz, like the stone was vibrating.

Blossom, who must have seen the reaction on my face, nodded grimly, as if I'd just confirmed her worst fears. She picked up the obsidian and thrust another dark stone in my hand. "Cassiterite," Blossom muttered as it started to buzz.

"Yes," I said softly.

Blossom practically snatched it away and thrust something else in my hand: not just a stone, but a clear, gleaming crystal that had been carved in the shape of a skull. This one buzzed more than the last two combined.

"I thought so," she snapped. "Death stones. Threshold stone." Snake-fast, her hand darted out and grabbed my outstretched wrist, pushing up the sleeve before I could make the decision whether to bodily shove her away. She saw the bottom of my griffin tattoo and pushed the sleeve up farther. Her eyes widened, and I heard her suck in breath through her teeth.

Fine. Cards on the table, then.

I let her check my other arm, too, until both tattoos were exposed. Blossom said something under her breath in Arapaho. It sounded like a curse. "Witch magic," she hissed through her teeth. I was used to Blossom's surly expressions, but the look she gave me now was equal parts hatred, fear, and mistrust. She backed away from me, moving toward the curtain, and let out a long, low whistle.

And the well-trained Doberman exploded through the doorway, teeth bared and snarling.

Chapter 28

The storeroom was barely wide enough for the dog to sweep past Blossom and corner me, teeth gleaming in the bright light. It snarled, its paws planted between Blossom and me, but it wouldn't actually attack until Blossom gave the order. I took a slow, cautious step backward—but that incensed the dog, who flew forward until he was a foot away from my waist, barking in a low, terrible voice. I automatically shifted my weight, ready for a fight, but I knew I wouldn't be able to stop him by force.

"Call him off, Blossom," I said over the sound.

"*Witch*," she spat. "Necromancer. Don't know what you're mixed up in, Luther, but I want no part of it. Get out of my store."

I didn't have time to absorb the fact that Blossom knew at least something about the Old World, not when the dog was snarling at me like that. "Not without something to stop the guy," I said back. "Or the stones. We had a deal."

"Deal's off. You think I don't know what's happening here? Some poor slob takes a stand against necromancers, and now you want me to help you squash him? Get out of here before I let Raven tear you to bits."

At the sound of his name, the dog snarled again, the fur on his glossy back standing rigid. I sighed. "You're not thinking it through, Blossom," I said. "If I'm as evil as you think, wouldn't I be able to stop the dog? Please don't make me hurt him. Call him off."

"Fat chance, white girl. You've got three seconds to get out of here."

I weighed my options. I really didn't want to hurt the dog, dammit. I could try the same thing I'd done with the fox, but I wasn't sure I'd be able to de-escalate him without outright killing him. On the other hand, if I walked away empty-handed, how was I going to stop Emil?

I made the decision: I would find another way. "You have to back up so I can get out," I called over the dog.

Slowly, Blossom moved backward, giving the dog a short command to do the same. I moved forward out of the storeroom, looking around in desperation. There was something in this room that would help me fight Emil, but I had no idea what it was or what to do with it. I also wasn't going to kill a dog to find out.

In the main storeroom, Blossom and Raven backed up, Blossom's rigid finger pointing me toward the purple curtain. "Please," I tried one more time. "If I can't get this guy out of town, Charlie's going to be vulnerable."

That brought her up short for a second. "Vulnerable to what?" she demanded.

Please, I prayed. *Please let this be the right choice.* "Charlie's a null. I'm trying to protect her."

Blossom stared at me in wonderment. The dog, sensing the change in his mistress, turned his head to look at her. There was a breathless moment of suspended time while we both waited for Blossom to make a decision. "Wait there," Blossom finally said. She edged around me warily, disappearing into the back storeroom. When she returned a moment later, she had a crystal in one gloved hand. "Mahogany obsidian should protect against psychic attacks," she said gruffly, thrusting a chunk of bronze-and-black-streaked stone into my hand. I felt the little zing of vibration again. "Look up how to care for crystals online," Blossom barked. "Now get the hell out of my store."

It was only later, when I was nearly back in Boulder, that I realized that Blossom must have been *really* upset, because she hadn't even charged me for the stone.

I called Simon and Lily on the way back to town to tell them what Blossom had said about the two casts. They had moved Maven, although I warned Simon not to give me the location over the phone, just in case. The investigation was at a standstill until we could either see the bodies or find Emil. "Maybe he'll just leave town," Lily said hopefully. "Cut his losses."

I shook my head at the phone. "Maven's still alive . . . ish," I said. "He's gonna want to finish what he started. And I think he wants something from me, though I'll be damned if I know what."

When I hung up the phone, it was not even one o'clock, but I had no idea what to do between now and sunset, not without Quinn. He let me take the lead in a lot of situations, but investigating was his thing. I was just a soldier with a creepy connection to death. I ran through my mental list of resources, but I wouldn't be able to speak to Nellie until nightfall, and by then Quinn would be awake. What the hell could I do with the next seven hours?

Then I thought of someone else I could call. I wasn't sure if he could help me, but I didn't think asking him would make things any worse. I scrolled through my phone contacts until I found the number for Jesse Cruz, formerly of the Los Angeles police.

Cruz was the detective who'd investigated Sam's murder, and he and I had a complicated relationship. Although he was a human, he had connections in the LA Old World. Through them, he'd actually helped destroy my sister's body, ensuring that my parents and John would never have the closure they needed.

On the other hand, he was also the one who'd caught Sam's killer. And when I flew to LA last fall in search of answers, he was decent to me. He even gave me back Sam's watch, which I wore every day. My instincts said he was a good guy, and could be trusted—as long as I didn't ask him to compromise his contacts.

He answered on the third ring. "Hi, Lex," he said warily. I couldn't really blame him. The last time we'd spoken I'd just punched his friend in the face. "What's going on?"

"Hey, Cruz. I've got kind of a situation over here. Are you on good terms with any witches?"

He spent a few seconds digesting that before he said slowly, "You could say that. You could also say that my friends don't like me to talk about things on the phone."

Right. The LA Old World was bigger and more complicated than it was here, so they kept off cell phones—which are, in all fairness, basically tiny radios—as much as possible. Ordinarily I didn't like to talk on them, either.

"I'll get a disposable phone and text you the number," I promised. "Can you call me back from a pay phone?"

"Uh, yeah. If I can find one in this town. Call you back."

It took about forty-five minutes for me to get to Target, buy a prepaid cell phone, and get Cruz the number. Within minutes, the new phone buzzed with an LA number. "You found a pay phone," I said.

"In an IHOP, of all places. This better be good. I swear I'm already sticky."

I took a deep breath. "Okay, I've got several things going on, and I can't figure out how they're connected. I think it has to do with witch magic and gravitational magic."

"Go ahead."

As concisely as I could, I told him about the belladonna attacks, the mysterious deaths in Boulder, and the magician using crystals to attack and sedate people. I didn't mention Maven or my familial connection to Emil. "Can you find out if your witch knows anything about people dying with no apparent injuries, in connection with gravitational magic, or maybe boundary magic? Or if she knows anyone dealing belladonna on this side of the Mississippi?"

"I'll try," he said. "I'll call her now, but she probably won't be able to talk until after five."

Which wasn't until six my time, but the sun wouldn't set until eight, anyway. "Thanks, Cruz."

"Call you back at this number."

I went back to the cabin to take care of the herd and check my yard for any new crystals. It seemed clear, although I had no idea how far out he could cast—would the spell still work if the circle was fifty feet away from the house? A hundred feet? In my experience, magic did have to obey a certain amount of logic, and I was guessing that the bigger the net, the harder it was to control. But I didn't know for sure.

After I'd fed and watered everyone, I paced back and forth in my living room, racking my brain for something I could do. I felt like shit, and the bruises hadn't even begun to fade, but I was too restless to be still. I ended up cleaning and loading several firearms, which made me feel a little calmer. Then I finally realized exactly who I wanted to talk to.

He didn't answer his phone, but I barely had time to feel disappointed before he called back. I answered it. "Sorry, we're right by this really long line for rides," he shouted. "I couldn't hear my phone!"

"That's okay. How's Mickey and the gang?"

I knew my dad well enough to picture him rolling his eyes. "Your mother's fallen under the spell, I'm afraid. She's buying souvenirs for all the grandkids, and she thinks we should have Mickey ears for our holiday photo. I'm worried she's going to put them on me while I'm sleeping and take photos."

I grinned, dropping into a chair. "And Charlie? Is she getting any of it, or is it too overwhelming?"

"A little of both. You want to talk to her? She's right here. John's back at the room, taking a nap. He hasn't been sleeping well, poor guy."

Longing and sadness burst through my heart. "Yeah, sure."

So I spent a few minutes chatting with my two-year-old niece. I did most of the talking, but I did manage to learn that she had met Pwincess Anna *and* Pwincess Elsa that morning, which was "awesome." "Awesome" was one of her favorite words, thanks to my cousin Paul's influence.

When Charlie discarded the phone in favor of a caramel apple, my dad picked it up again. "And how are you, honey?" he asked. "Work going okay?"

My family had learned through trial and error that using this phrasing was the simplest way to talk to me about my life and my odd job situation. "Yeah, work is fine. I just miss you guys."

"We miss you, too." Some of the din behind him quieted, and I figured he'd ducked somewhere quiet. "I'm actually kind of surprised John didn't invite you on this trip instead of us. I would have paid for it."

I smiled. Classic Dad: half altruism, half wishing I was the one stuck in line for the Jungle Cruise instead of him. "I wouldn't have let you."

He acted like he hadn't heard me, which maybe he hadn't. "Is everything okay with you and John, honey? Your mother says you haven't been babysitting on Fridays."

I squeezed my eyes shut, but it didn't stop the tears from leaking out. "Everything's fine, Daddy," I lied. "John probably just figured I can go to Disney anytime, whereas you're so old and decrepit you might not have another chance."

My father let out a full-throated laugh, but he caught himself and pretended to grumble at me. Still, I could tell from his hesitation that he wasn't ready to drop the subject.

Dammit, I hated to pull this card, but it was the best way to placate him. "No, seriously, I think he just figured all the noise and crowds would be too much for me. You know."

"Oh, of course, baby. I'm so sorry. I should have realized," he rushed to say, his voice filled with concern and guilt. I immediately felt like an asshole. I'd just used my alleged PTSD to weasel out of a difficult conversation with my father. "We love you so much, Lex, honey. We just want you to be happy."

"I love you too, Dad."

I hung up the phone feeling both better and worse. *At least Charlie's having fun*, I told myself. *And at least she's not part of this.*

I checked my phone for messages and saw that I'd missed a text. Simon and Lily had finished moving Maven, and they were both going to rest for a bit. Good. They needed it. The control freak in me was tempted to call and demand details, but Jesse's cell phone paranoia came back to me. I trusted Simon and Lily. I didn't need to micromanage them.

But where did that leave me? I still had four hours before Cruz would call me back, and six hours before Quinn would wake up and we could figure out a game plan.

I tried to come up with another way to find Emil or my biological father—or both. By now, though, they could be just about anywhere. I wasn't going to find them by kicking in doors, which was unfortunate, because I was really good at that.

I spent some time contemplating Emil's next move. If I really was right about our father pulling Emil's strings, and they still wanted me alive and Maven dead, they would eventually have to come looking for me. Quinn and I had been staying away from all the usual Old World hangouts, including Magic Beans, so Emil wouldn't be able to track our movements through other vampires like he'd done in Denver. Emil *did* know that Simon was involved, but I'd only introduced him by his first name. Even if he managed to identify Simon, Hazel Pellar's farmhouse was well warded against intruders.

As long as we kept Maven hidden away, I concluded, Emil only had two possible moves: he could try to draw me out or he could take a shot at me at home.

But a direct attack in broad daylight wouldn't be Emil's style. This was a man who'd set up several contingency plans just to *meet* me. He wouldn't come to the cabin guns blazing, especially because he would have to assume that I'd have my own firearms. He might risk attacking a position of strength if he thought Maven was on the premises, but hopefully he wouldn't think I was stupid enough to keep her here.

So what was Emil planning? And where was he hiding now?

After a long period of staring at the ceiling, I had to admit that I had no idea. I couldn't predict his moves . . . but maybe I could counteract his best weapon against me.

After a few minutes of internet research, I grabbed my keys and headed out to the car.

Chapter 29

Despite the overcast skies and the smell of impending rain in the air, I felt a lot more relaxed than on my last visit to Nellie's building. The brothel was much more palatable in the daylight; it crossed the line from "horror-movie creepy" back over to "old and rundown." When I was sure no one was watching, I ducked around the corner and went in through the back, happy not to have to mess with a flashlight.

There wasn't any furniture in the brothel, so I just sat down on the steps in the main entryway and opened the paper bag I'd gotten from the metaphysical store in Denver. The new stones were individually wrapped in tissue paper, but I managed to unwrap all of them without actually touching them, arranging them gently on the stair next to me, so they still rested on their tissue paper. I'd left the stones from Blossom in the car—I didn't want to be protected from ghosts this time; I wanted to talk to one.

I pulled out the small encyclopedia of stones and crystals I'd bought, looking down at the cover, which featured a painting of a New Age goddess. Lily would probably know exactly what it meant.

"This is so stupid," I muttered under my breath as I opened the book. But Simon had told me that some stones did work for witches, and I'd felt the little buzz of vibration at Blossom's store. And I had time on my hands. What was the harm?

Blossom had said that crystals had to be cleansed before they would really work, so I flipped through the book to the section on crystal cleansing. Sunlight and running water were two of the most common options, so I gathered up the stones, pulled the bottle of water out of my bag, and headed over to the window where a board had rotted through, allowing for a bright stream of sunlight the size of a paperback. I held up the stones and dumped a thin stream of water over them, feeling like a complete and total idiot.

Back on the steps, I sat down and opened and closed my hands rapidly, warming them up again. The book I'd bought had a lot of information about chakras and meditation, not to mention instructions for things like body layouts and dreamwork, but even I had limits to the suspension of disbelief. I picked up a small, irregularly formed stone about the size of a large strawberry: cassiterite. In the sunlight I could tell it was brown, but without direct light it seemed like more of a milky black. The clerk had promised me that this specimen hadn't been dyed or irradiated, even though I still wasn't sure what that meant.

I just held the chunk of cassiterite between my palms, brought it to my lips and breathed on it. And I hoped.

Blossom had called cassiterite a "threshold stone," and to me, that sounded like something a boundary witch might use as she interacts with the boundary between life and death. I was hoping it might give me just enough of a threshold to talk to Nellie.

I don't know how long I sat there with the stone warm in my hands, but after a few minutes my thoughts wandered and I noticed the shape of it, all the little planes and angles jutting together in a complex non-pattern. My mind started to relax, and the word "threshold" started bouncing through my thoughts. What an odd term. A threshold could mean a doorway, but it could also mean a new beginning, like when someone says they're on the threshold of discovery. Or it could mean someone's limit, like the threshold of pain. Thinking about the word *pain* made the image of Sam's desecrated body pop briefly back into my mind, but I pushed it away determinedly.

Nellie, focus on Nellie, I told myself. I was starting to feel more stupid than I had before, which was saying something. I didn't even know if Nellie's spirit was normally aware during the day, much less—

"Just sits there staring at nuthin' like she's got all the time in the world, when she's been making a big show of being so busy," came a cross, familiar voice. It sounded faint, and from no particular direction. "Meanwhile I could be doing naked cartwheels in front of her nose and not get so much as a how-do-you-do—"

"Nellie?" I said, freezing in place like I was an antenna that had just received a flicker from the right channel.

"And now she's talking to me just like she thinks I'm gonna respond, well!" Usually when Nellie spoke, her voice seemed to come from her body, like a live person. But now it came from everywhere and nowhere, like an echo chamber without the actual echo.

"I *can* hear you," I said loudly, feeling jubilant. I scanned the room. "Where are you?"

A pause. "You're bein' truthful? You can hear me talk?"

"Yes!"

"I'm . . . oh . . . three steps to your left and four steps forward. You canna see me?"

"No." Simon had told me that gravitational magic was weaker than witch magic, so maybe that was why I could only hear her faintly. But it was broad daylight outside, and I called that a win. I had made a telephone to the dead.

Excited, I said, "Nellie, I need to talk to you, and I don't have time to mess around with bargaining and stroking your ego, okay? I don't know how long this crystal thing will work."

There was a very tense pause, and then her wary voice said, "I'm listening."

"Remember I told you there was someone poisoning vampires with belladonna? Well, he's in Boulder, and he's interested in me for some reason. He attacked me with wraiths last night. Angry ghosts," I added, in case Nellie's terminology was different.

"That where you got that bruise on yer face?" she demanded. "And the one on yer neck?"

"Yes." My scarf must have slipped, but I didn't want to let go of the stone to fix it.

There was indiscriminate grumbling. "Doesn't he know who you are?"

"That's just it, he knows *exactly* who I am. He has boundary blood, too, but it didn't activate. That's why he uses crystals." I told her about the wraiths trapped inside the crystals, and how I suspected Emil's mother had helped him trap them in there.

"Aye, the wraiths, as you call them, they can touch us. To them, we are the gatekeepers. I've never heard of 'em being quite this stirred up, though. And I've never heard of anyone using them to kill one of us."

"It didn't seem like he wanted them to actually kill me," I allowed, trying to remember Emil's exact words as he'd sicced the wraiths on me. "It was like he was testing me," I said. "Trying to determine my worth."

"Let me think," was Nellie's gruff response. I couldn't see her, but I could imagine her pacing in her thick pumps, her heels drumming soundlessly on the old wooden floors. I held as still as possible, trying not to think about the dampness on my palms. Would it interfere with whatever was allowing me to use the cassiterite? If it did, would I be able to "call" Nellie back?

"When I was alive," she said finally, "the Christians were mostly done hangin' witches, but there were still those that hunted us. There was a group that was always looking for those with witchblood—but they were only interested in necromancers. Evocators, we were called then. This group was always offering money, favors, power. Whatever it took to find us."

"Did they kill the evocators?"

"Can't be certain," she replied. "There were hints that you could make a good living if you went with them willingly, but that might have been a lie they spun to get evocators to cooperate. I never heard of anyone going with them and coming back."

That didn't exactly seem like information I could run with. "Did this group have a name?"

"Aye. Our mothers used it to scare us. It isn't easy to frighten children who see their parents speak to the dead, but when we were naughty they would threaten to sell us to those people. I remember once, my sister 'n me—"

"Do you remember the name?" I interrupted, and it took all my willpower to maintain my patience. I had this terrible idea that the stone would stop working right before she gave me something I could sink my teeth into.

She sighed loudly. "It were some highfalutin' Latin words. Lemme see. Milt . . . milli . . . *milites mortis*," she said triumphantly. "If that's not it, it's something close."

Finally. Real information. My shoulders sagged in relief. "Thank you, Nellie. I owe you one, and I won't forget."

She cackled. Apparently it was my day for old women to cackle at me. "Oh, I won't let you forget," she said smugly.

I got up and flipped the channel on the television, which would save me a trip in the near future. I was about to say goodbye, when another thought occurred to me. "The wraiths. Nellie, can you tell me how to dispel ghosts?"

Another pause, this one so long that I was staring to fear I'd lost the connection. "I don't know how," she said at last.

"Oh, come on."

"It's true! I never learned."

"Nellie," I said impatiently, looking around the brothel, "this is a two-hundred-year-old building. People must have died here, but I've never seen any remnants, even when I was here at night. Because you got rid of them when you were alive, and you're the last to die here. You know how to banish ghosts."

Her voice went cold. "I got nothin' to say about that."

I could have walked away then, but what if Emil attacked with wraiths again? What if they mobbed me before I could disturb the grid? "Nellie," I called into the empty room. "If you tell me how to banish them, I'll come back every week, myself."

Nothing.

"I'll even bring tea," I tried. "And you can tell me stories about the brothel."

I checked my watch. Ninety seconds dragged by before she spoke again.

"Even if I did know how to banish them back across the line," Nellie said, "how do I know you wouldn't try to banish *me?*"

"You're not hurting anyone, as far as I can tell," I said. "I have no interest in banishing you if you don't want to go."

"I gotta think about it," she said at last. "You come yourself next time, and we can talk."

And no amount of begging on my part would change her mind.

It was late afternoon when I got back to Boulder, and although sunset was still a few hours off, the skies were dark with the threat of rain. I had managed to get grime from the brothel all over my clothes, so I decided to stop at home to change and take care of the animals before I met up with Simon and Lily. I called to find out where they were, but Simon didn't answer. Ordinarily I might worry, but he *had* said he and Lily were going to nap, and given how hard they'd been pushing, I couldn't blame him for turning off his ringer. I left a voicemail briefly outlining what I'd learned from Nellie.

When I arrived at the cabin I parked in the driveway instead of the garage, since I'd only be there for a few minutes. As I hurried up the little pathway to the house, I heard an unfamiliar ringing coming from the car. The disposable cell phone. I jogged back to the passenger door, opened it, and snatched up the phone without looking at the number. "Cruz?"

"Yeah, hey. Listen, I talked to the head of the witches here. She had a follow-up question."

I bumped the door shut with my hip and turned back toward the house, fumbling to get my keys out of my jacket pocket. "I'm listening." I put the key in the lock and paused, missing the next thing Cruz said. Something was wrong. I put my ear against the door—not a single dog was barking. Had they not heard me? I took the phone away from my ear and made a little scratching noise on the door with one fingernail, which would usually drive the dogs into a barking frenzy.

Dead silence.

"Hello? Lex?"

"Yeah, sorry, Cruz. What did she ask?"

"I said, she wanted to know if animals in your town have been going insane. Foaming at the mouth kind of insane."

I went completely still.

And that's when the attack came.

Chapter 30

I caught the movement out of the corner of my eye and instinctively ducked. The phone slipped out of my hand as I flinched to my left, away from the threat. I felt the air over my head shift as a huge hand crashed into the side of the house, right where my right ear had been a moment earlier. When it pulled back there was a fist-sized dent in the metal siding.

I came up with my fists held in front of my face like a boxer, dancing back to get a glimpse of my attacker. And for the second time in fifteen seconds, I froze from shock. Because of the *size* of him. His eyes were at least two feet above mine, which had to make him well over seven feet tall. He wore an enormous, buttoned black raincoat that must have been made for him, because it went down to his midcalves. His body still strained against the fabric, but not because of that carved, gym-rat look. No, his bulk was hard and dense, concrete poured into a man-shaped mold.

My eyes finally made it all the way up to his face, and with another shock I realized that his skin was . . . blue. I blinked hard to make sure the overcast daylight wasn't creating an optical illusion. But no, it was definitely a washed-out, frostbite blue. His features were cruel, commanding, and so remote it chilled me. I had thought that Quinn's expressions were impassive. This guy looked like he came from another planet.

No, that wasn't right. He *should* have looked silly, too big and too alien to fit in against the background of the world around him. It should have been absurd. But there was such an intense quality of menace coming off him that I could nearly taste it on the air. It turned my insides to snow.

"What the fuck are *you*?" I blurted.

A thin smile appeared on his thin lips. "Careful, daughter. Do not ask questions unless you are certain you want the answers." His voice was low and hollow sounding, the way a big dog's bark sounds from its barrel chest. Despite his earlier attempt to clobber me, he stood there unmoving, his hands drooping down by his sides.

"I'm not your daughter," I said automatically.

"Semantics. Your mother's egg was fertilized with my seed. You are my biological material."

His tone was so matter-of-fact that I didn't have it in me to doubt him. In that moment, somewhere in the back of my mind, something delicate and vital began to break down. I pushed it away. "Did you hurt my animals?"

Genuine confusion appeared on his broad face. I pointed toward the door. "My dogs. Did you . . ." I swallowed hard, unable to stomach the word on my lips. "Hurt them?"

Distaste twisted his features. "I see. No. I have not entered your abode."

Then why weren't the dogs barking? "What do you want?" I blurted.

The smile that twisted his lips was greedy, a child set loose in the candy aisle at the grocery store. "I want you, Allison Alexandra Luther. Revenge on an old foe is an attractive boon, but she hides like a cockroach from the light, and I grow tired of her games." He spread his hands wide, and I almost bolted at the small movement. "You are mine, and you have value to me."

He said it like I should be honored.

"No. This is . . . no," I sputtered. I began backing away slowly, because that's what you do with really super crazy people. The creature advanced at the same pace. I retreated to the wide area I'd left between my car and the garage door, but it wasn't far enough. I eyed the car door. Could I move fast enough to get in and get the car started before he stopped me?

He saw me looking and smiled indulgently. With an amused shake of his head, he leaned down and picked up the front bumper of my old Subaru with one hand, lifting it to his waist. His movements were graceful, easy, and so *human* . . . and so was his cruel little smile as he let go of the bumper, letting the car crash down. Both front tires gave out with a nervous pop.

I began to choke on the air I was breathing. I backed up a little farther, shaking my head in denial. I was going into some kind of shock. This couldn't be my father. This made no sense. Nothing made sense. "This can't be happening," I whispered.

He advanced again, his arms slowly beginning to rise toward me. "I see that my son has hurt you," he said disdainfully, eyeing the bruises on my face and neck. "That was not his place. You can be certain that I will have words with him when we get home."

"*Home?*" I squeaked.

"To your brothers and sisters. They have been waiting for one such as you."

My knees gave out then, and I collapsed into the grass on the other side of the driveway. Fear washed over me, and for the first time in my entire life, I didn't bother to even fight it. He began to bend toward me—to take me, I think, but I didn't care anymore. I was done.

And then Simon's little Chevy plowed into the creature's knees with enough force to send it exploding through my garage door.

The driver's door flew open right in front of me, and Lily's head popped out. "Get in the fucking car!" she screamed.

I stumbled to my feet and ran.

I don't remember fastening my seat belt, or any of the ride, for that matter. There was a buzzing that wouldn't stop, some bright lights, and my hands were clutched tight around my seat belt. I'd drawn my knees up to protect them, protect my insides. Eventually the car stopped, and my door was opened. There were voices, too, and they were raised, but I wasn't registering any of it.

"I swear, Simon, we are deep in *we need a bigger boat* territory here. I don't know what that thing was, but it was after her. And now she's catatonic, and I don't know what we're supposed to do."

"Did you look at the guy's aura?"

"Uh, no, Si. I was a little too busy getting us the hell out of there before it ate us!"

"I highly doubt he was going to *eat* you. Could he have been her father?"

"Um, does she *look* half-blue to you?" Lily's voice scoffed. "No way."

"He wasn't really blue, Lily. I told you, your eyes were playing tricks on you. You should have taken a picture."

"Taken a . . . Are you *kidding* me?"

I wished they would stop. I wished they would just go away and leave me here. Maybe I could pass out, and Sam would be there, and she could explain. Or maybe she could get our mother to explain.

But would it even matter?

The voices eventually faded, or maybe my brain finally figured out how to tune them out. I stared at the dashboard, and time stopped meaning anything to me. It wasn't meditation, and I'm not sure it was shock. I was just *done*. Time passed, and I was fine with that.

I started in my seat when a cool hand touched my cheek. I was still clutching the seat belt in front of my chest. I didn't let go.

"Lex," Quinn said quietly. He was kneeling awkwardly in the footwell of the passenger side. There was no sign of Simon or Lily. "What happened, honey?"

"That thing is my father," I whispered. "I'm half monster."

I let him reach across me and unclick the seat belt, then carefully thread it through the space between my arms and my body until it wound back into its spot. Gently, he grasped my ankles one at a time, sliding them off the seat. I didn't resist when he reached down for me, just allowed him to wrap my hands around his neck and pull me out of the car. I couldn't seem to find my footing, so I leaned against him, letting his arms keep me from crumpling.

He stroked my hair. "It's okay," he whispered.

"No. It's really not."

"Lex," he said again, his voice patient. "Look at me." But I couldn't. He reached down and tilted up my chin. "You're talking to a *vampire*," he said, with just a trace of humor on his lips. "I have to drink human blood in order to function. I can press any human to do anything I want. I've killed people, Lex. For no other reason than my boss said it was necessary. Who's the monster here?"

The first tear wobbled its way down my cheek. He reached up with a cool thumb and wiped it off my face. "I guess I'd just gotten used to the new world order," I mumbled. "Vampires, witches, werewolves. But that thing we saw wasn't any of them, and it wasn't human. And I'm its *daughter*." My body began to shudder. He held me tighter.

"And now that you know this, are you any different than you were yesterday?" he asked. Pragmatic, as usual. "Nothing has changed, Lex. *You* haven't changed. You just know something that you didn't know before, that's all."

I kissed him then, because how could I not? He returned the kiss with enthusiasm, being careful not to touch the bruise on my face, and heat flooded into my numb body, reminding me of everything I already had. Then I opened my eyes for a second and noticed a rack of shovels and rakes. They seemed oddly familiar. I pulled back and looked around us. Where the hell were we?

It was obviously someone's garage. And I'd been here before.

Then I finally put it together. Simon and Lily had needed to come up with a hiding place for Maven's body, and they couldn't take her anywhere that was connected to the witches. So they'd set up a new base of operations in a place Emil wouldn't know about. A house they knew would be empty.

John's house.

Chapter 31

I stormed into the house to find the Pellars. They were both in the living room. "I can't *believe* you broke into John's house!" I yelled.

"She's back!" Lily said gaily. She was sitting in the easy chair in John's living room, playing a game on her phone.

"The guy puts his spare key on top of the door frame!" Simon countered. "He deserves to get burgled, and look, we're just picking up a little."

That brought me up short. It was true—Simon was on his hands and knees on the floor, stacking toys into a pile. "What are you doing?"

"Just ignore him," Lily said, dismissive. "He gets a little OCD when he's stressed."

"Or he's stepped on five different Duplos and he's sick of it," Simon muttered.

"But he's gonna figure out that you were here!"

"No, he's gonna figure out *you* were here," Quinn said mildly, coming up behind me. "And because you love him and Charlie so much and feel bad about your fight, you cleaned the house up a little." I wheeled around to glare at him, but he just shrugged. "You have to admit, it's kind of brilliant. John's not Old World, and Charlie's just a baby. There's no reason for anyone to look for Maven here. And besides, your family's safe in Florida."

I wanted to argue that we were still putting them in danger, but I bit back my protest. We could move Maven right away, tonight—as soon as we figured out where to put her. But in the meantime I had more pressing concerns.

I checked my watch. It was a little after eight. I looked at Quinn. "Did they explain what's been happening?"

He nodded. "Crystals, telephone to the dead, scary blue guy. I'm caught up."

"I looked up the meaning of *milites mortis*," Simon broke in. "The rough translation is 'soldiers of death.' Or possibly 'knights of death.'"

"Fantastic," I said.

"Yeah, but what does that mean?" Lily asked.

Simon looked at me. "You said this group kidnapped boundary witches, right?"

I nodded. "But Nellie wasn't sure they were actually hurting them. There were rumors that you could make a lot of money if you joined them. Like it was a business."

"This is a leap," he said slowly, "but what if it was the business of making more boundary witches?"

We all stared at him. Simon held his hands up defensively. "I know, I'm just taking a shot in the dark. But if you were a boundary witch, and you were worried that there weren't enough boundary witches in the world, what would be the best way to make more?"

"Kidnap the witches and force them to . . . breed?" Lily said, wrinkling her nose in disgust. It was the same unsettling word Emil had used to grouse about boundary witches not having relationships with other witches.

Everyone fell silent, and I could feel all of them deliberately not looking at me. If Simon's theory was correct, there were people out there who wanted to force me to carry a baby.

"Even if you're right," I said, the rasp suddenly sharp in my voice, "what does the jolly blue giant have to do with this? Is he working for them?"

Quinn took a step forward, shaking his head. "It doesn't matter. We're not letting them take Lex. We're going to find Emil and Mr. Freeze, and we're going to shut this down. Tonight."

Everyone nodded. I didn't feel nearly as confident, but if it was an act, I hoped he'd keep it up for a while. "First thing, we have to go back to my place," I said, half-expecting them to protest. "I have to make sure the herd is all right."

"They're fine," Simon told me. "Between Lily's crazy story and you being so out of it, I drove back over there. There's a big-ass hole in your garage door, but nobody else was there." He paused to push his glasses up on his nose. "Anyway, I went into the house through the garage door to see if he'd gotten inside. Nothing was disturbed, as far as I could tell, but I didn't see the cats and dogs. I found them in the bedroom." He grimaced apologetically. "I'm sorry about just going into your bedroom like that."

I waved it off like I was blocking a punch. "Were they okay? Were they alive?"

"They're alive," he reported. "They were under your bed."

I stared. "What, *all* of them?"

Simon nodded. "I counted. They were terrified, but I didn't see any injuries. I thought it best to leave them where they were."

I let out a deep breath of relief. "We should still get them out of the house. That thing knows they're important to me."

Quinn, who had been leaning against a sideboard, straightened up. "So we'll go get them right now," he said reasonably.

I bit my lip. "You really think we can take the time?"

He shrugged. "Sure. It's a good idea to keep moving anyway, if Blue Man Group is looking for you." I tried really hard not to smile at that one, but I kind of failed. "And we all know you're not going to be able to think straight until you know they're safe," he added.

I was touched that Quinn wanted to help, but we both knew he was the wrong person to deal with the animals—they had an instinctive fear and hatred of vampires, and although a couple of them had eventually learned to tolerate Quinn, it wasn't the right time to push that, not when they were already scared.

Ordinarily I would have called Jake, made up a story, and asked him to take the animals to his vet clinic, where there was room for all of them for a couple of nights. But I couldn't risk that the thing—I really needed a better name for him, because "my father" made me nauseous—wouldn't come back while Jake was still there.

So after some discussion, we decided that Lily and I would go get the animals and drop them off with Jake, while Simon did some online research and Quinn went "to get something to eat."

As Lily and I walked into the cabin a little later, I was awed by the silence that had fallen over the house. It was *never* this still and quiet. Even when all the dogs were outside at the same time, there were always cats sneaking and skittering around, starting little squabbles with each other. The blue man may not have come inside, but it still felt like someone had broken my home.

I made straight for my bedroom, flipped the light switch, and crouched down to look under my bed. I very nearly burst into tears when I saw all four dogs huddled under there, staring at me with wide, anxious eyes. Chip and Cody came wiggling out right away, climbing over and over me, tongues lapping frantically until I had to laugh. "I'm sorry, guys," I murmured, petting them.

None of the others wanted to come out from hiding. I tried cajoling, treats, and a stern tone, but they were too panicked. I hated to force them when they were like this, but they were at risk if they stayed where Emil might come looking. So in the end Lily and I had to simply pull the bed away from the wall and scoop them up.

Quinn had lent me the Jeep, which had more room in the back than Simon's car or my busted Subaru, but it still took a while to get them all secured. It didn't help that I only had two carrying cases for all those cats. The cranky iguana was the only one seemingly unaffected by my father's appearance, which made me wonder if whatever the animals sensed about him had to do with proximity. Mushu lived in the back bedroom, far away from the front door where the blue man had been prowling.

When we finally closed the Jeep's back doors, everyone was very unhappy, and Lily and I both had scratches up and down our arms. She waited outside the passenger door—"so your dogs don't climb all over me, no offense"—while I went back into the house to pack up a few essentials. I wouldn't be able to come back here until this was over, one way or another.

I threw some clothes into a duffel bag, barely paying attention to what I grabbed, and then went into the now-empty back bedroom where I kept my weapons safe. I stood there for a few minutes examining my options. I had no idea what would hurt the giant blue guy, so I put a little of everything into the duffel: a couple of shredders (in addition to the new one strapped to my arm), my Ithaca shotgun in a soft case, extra ammunition, and a Gerber LHR combat knife in a sheath. After a few minutes of consideration, I also dug out an old Patagonia fanny pack—they weren't called that anymore, but that's what it was—and tucked in my Smith & Wesson revolver, which had the best stopping power of any of the sidearms I owned. I wouldn't be able to draw it from the fanny pack as quickly as I'd like, but none of the concealed carry holsters that fit me could hold a large sidearm. Much better to be a little slow on the draw than to be in a situation where I needed to leave my weapon in the car so no one would see the holster. Just to be on the safe side, I tossed my favorite quick-draw holster, a gift from Quinn, into the duffel. I also threw in the longest jacket I owned, a lightweight, knee-length number that was a little baggy on me and flared out at the waist, which made it the best thing I had for disguising weapons.

I went back out to the driveway, but before I could reach for the driver's door I heard a woman's voice from behind the Jeep.

"Allison Luther?"

Lily and I both jumped, and my hand went to the weapon in my unzipped hip pack. But the speaker was a small, unassuming woman standing at the end of my driveway. She was probably in her midthirties, with a white-blonde braid circling the top of her porcelain face, and she was dressed simply in loose black pants, a white tee, and a denim jacket. Even in the dim illumination from the house lights, I could see that the T-shirt was swelled out. I was just guessing, based on Sam's pregnancy, but I figured she was seven, maybe eight months along.

She stood there with her hands in her jacket pockets, radiating calm and something else. I couldn't put my finger on it until Lily stepped in front of me.

Her fingers were thrust out to her sides, and I could swear I saw actual light sparking off them. My jaw dropped. Obviously I wasn't the only one Lily was training with. She—and no doubt Simon—had been practicing apex magic. "Who the hell are you?" Lily demanded.

"Lily!" I hissed. I wasn't stupid enough to believe pregnant women were harmless, but this one looked like she was there to sell some kind of raffle tickets, or maybe see if I was registered to vote.

"She's a witch, Lex," Lily said over her shoulder. "With some *serious* juice."

The woman's smile was calm and unperturbed. "No need to worry, little witch. My name is Kirsten, and I'm here to help."

Chapter 32

"Help how?" I asked, at the same time as Lily said, "Kirsten who?"

The woman turned to Lily first. "Harms is the name you'd know. And I am here voluntarily, as a favor to Jesse Cruz."

Now it was Lily's turn to look shocked. I, on the other hand, felt like an idiot. I'd been so distracted by the meeting with the blue man, I'd completely forgotten about my call with Cruz. He'd probably been worried.

Before Lily could recover, I stepped forward. "I'm Allison Luther, but everyone calls me Lex. What do you mean, you're here to help?"

The woman—Kirsten—glanced between Lily and me. "I'm sorry, but I can't talk to you in front of a clan witch. I didn't go through our regular channels."

I opened my mouth to protest, but Lily took my arm. "Please give us a moment, ma'am," she said contritely. The woman gave her a regal nod, and Lily practically dragged me back toward the house.

"What's going on?" I hissed.

Lily positioned herself so her back was facing the woman. She took a deep breath. "You know how Si and I sometimes joke that my mom's a witch queen?"

"Yeah . . ."

"Well, that woman back there is the real deal. In Sweden, witches have actual royalty. She's from that family, though her mother moved them to America."

I stared at her. "How do you know all this?"

"Because she runs the witches in LA, the way my mother is the witch in charge of Colorado. Only in Los Angeles all three Old World factions have equal billing."

Cruz had said as much, but I hadn't really expected it to be true. "Okay, I get it, she's impressive. But can we trust her?"

Lily shrugged, but her expression was still a little rattled. "If you can trust this Cruz, I guess you can trust her. I don't like leaving you alone with her, but . . ." She winced. "Honestly, if she wanted to drop a house on you or something, I probably couldn't stop her. I've been using apex magic for six months. Kirsten Harms has probably never done anything else."

I squeezed her arm, feigning a confidence I didn't feel. "I'll be fine. Why don't you go ahead and drive the animals to Jake's clinic? I'll take a cab back to John's."

The whole time we were talking, Kirsten just waited patiently at the end of the driveway. When we walked back down to her, Lily said a cautious goodbye and headed for the Jeep.

Before I could think of anything to say, Kirsten turned to me and asked pleasantly, "Would you like to go for a walk? It's a lovely night."

"Um, sure."

We started along the road near my house. It should have been pitch black out here, but the clouds from earlier in the day had finally parted, revealing a nearly full moon and a dazzling number of stars. It was almost as light as it'd been that afternoon.

"How did you get here so quickly?" I asked after we'd walked for a few minutes. Well, I walked. Kirsten's stride was closer to a waddle.

A smile broke over her pale face. "The cardinal vampire in Los Angeles has a private plane, though it's not exactly something he advertises. But Jesse seemed to think you needed help right away. And when he explained the circumstances, I worked out that his concern was justified."

I checked her out of the corner of my eyes, but her expression was unreadable. "I don't follow."

"Jesse said you were having a problem related to boundary magic and people dying with no apparent injuries," she said. "I went online and found articles in your newspaper about the deaths, and eventually confirmed that there have been unusual animal attacks in Boulder recently. I probably would have come out here on a commercial flight for that alone, but Jesse said you were not answering your phone. He was very worried."

I had dropped the disposable phone in the driveway, and it had been crushed when Lily drove up to rescue me. My regular cell had buzzed in my pocket while I was sitting in Simon's car, but I hadn't had a spare moment to think about it, let alone check to see who'd called. "I'm sorry. I was on the phone with Cruz when I encountered . . . something. It kind of drove all other thoughts from my mind."

Kirsten stopped walking and turned to face me. "Was that something a large man with blue-toned skin?" she asked, perfectly calm.

The bubble of uncertainty in my chest popped, replaced by a flood of relief. "You know what he is?"

"I do." Her face and voice were suddenly sad. "And if he's here, you're going to need to know, too." She paused. "I'm sorry, I got tired more quickly than I expected. Is there somewhere we could sit down?"

I eyed her belly doubtfully. "I'd invite you into my house, but he knows where I live. We only came back to get my rescue animals away from the house."

The look she gave me was unmistakably sympathetic. "Then things are worse than I thought. But I can help with that, at least."

"How?"

She smiled, a look full of wry amusement. "Magic."

• • •

I hadn't seen a whole lot of magic performed, and nearly all of it had been what I now understood to be minor charms and hexes—spells that could clean a messy room or protect a person from immediate physical harm. But Kirsten operated on another level entirely. We walked back to the front of my house, where she pulled a few small supplies out of her bag—apothecary bottles, a small piece of carved wood, some sort of herb in a baggie—and asked me to help her crouch down near the ground. I did, holding her slender arm carefully. She seemed awfully fragile for someone so swollen with life.

Kirsten mumbled something under her breath, scratched a circle around herself in the dirt, and sprinkled the herbs. I wasn't sure what was happening until a sudden lack of light caught my attention. The stars were as bright as ever, but the lights I'd left on in the house had been extinguished. My busted car had vanished from the driveway, and even Kirsten's rental car seemed to have disappeared from the curb. The house looked completely deserted.

I gaped. "How did you do that?"

Kirsten gestured for me to help her stand, which I did. "It's tricky, finding a spell that more or less works on witches," she said cheerfully. "The magic in your blood would block most things I could throw at you directly, but this isn't a spell to affect you—it's a spell to bend light. You're just seeing the effect, like anyone else would. But it only works from a distance."

"So we can move around inside the house—"

"And it'll still look deserted, yes. Until first light."

Within a few minutes we were settled at my kitchen table with tea for me and hot chocolate for Kirsten. She wrapped both of her small hands around the mug, and I marveled at her. She may have dressed like Lily, but she reminded me so much of Maven: the same delicate looks that belied extreme strength and power.

I was dying for her to start explaining, but she sat there for a moment, and I realized she was trying to figure out where to begin.

"Jesse said you only learned about being a witch fairly recently," she said at last. "Is that true?"

I realized, then, that this woman either didn't know what I was or was taking the news better than any witch I'd met yet. I was hoping for the latter, but decided not to mention the whole "death in my blood" thing unless I had to. "Yes. But the witches here have been giving me lessons. I'm catching up."

"Have they explained what boundary witches did during the Inquisition in Europe?"

It seemed like an odd place to begin, even if she did know what I was, but I started to nod. Then I reconsidered what Simon and Lily actually said versus what I'd sort of pieced together from context. "I was told that boundary witches were particularly upset by the persecution of witches during the Inquisition. They wanted to raise the dead and send them after the Inquisitors. I got the impression that a few of them even did it. Then they were stopped." It occurred to me for the first time that I'd never actually asked what had stopped them. Suddenly that seemed like a pretty enormous oversight.

Kirsten just nodded again, taking a ladylike sip of her hot chocolate. "That's the cleaned-up version, yes."

"So what's the real version?"

"They did raise the dead and send it after the Inquisitors. That part is true." It should have sounded ridiculous, but her voice was so solemn it scared me. "But it wasn't an army of the dead, like something out of a horror movie. It was just one person. And he wasn't really a human."

"What was he, then?"

She put the mug down, squaring her shoulders. "The first boundary witch."

Chapter 33

"Technically," she corrected herself, "I suppose you'd say he was—is—a conduit."

I frowned. "I've heard that word before."

"I'm sure you have. Conduits are the common ancestors of vampires, werewolves, and witches. You could think of them as . . ." she paused, searching for a word, then gave a little smile. "Super-witches. They were so powerful that it scared even them. In fact, they were *too* powerful to survive, as a species, because they kept killing each other, or killing humans." Her smile turned wry. "Historically, humans do not care for being vastly overmatched. Anyway, eventually there was a speciation, and conduits became the three groups you know today."

"When did this happen?" I asked. "When did humans get magic?"

She gave a little shrug. "Best guess? Early Bronze Age. But that's more of a vampire question. Most of the witch records about ancient history have been lost over the years, in part thanks to the Inquisition. At any rate, just prior to the speciation, some conduits were born with certain strengths. Like how some modern witches specialize in a certain kind of magic."

I thought of Sashi. "I've met witches like that."

She nodded. "In this case, the conduit had a talent for interacting with the dead. He was born with it, just as he was born with blue-tinged skin. And a few other abilities that are particular to him."

Until that moment, I hadn't really believed we could be talking about the same person. Early Bronze Age? That would make him . . . what, like five thousand years old? If he'd been walking the earth for five thousand years, why wouldn't more modern witches know about him?

Kirsten must have read the doubts on my face, because she chuckled. "No, he's not immortal. He died after a few hundred years of life, just like the rest of the conduits. But his connection to death allowed him certain privileges. He can be . . . raised."

"From the dead. Raised from the *dead*," I repeated. I couldn't help it. It sounded so stupid out loud.

"Yes. But at great cost. One human sacrificed for each day he walks, that's the deal."

"The bodies in Boulder," I said, thinking aloud. "They were murders."

She nodded. "I understood when I read that there were no wounds. Lysander has no need for the bodies themselves. He takes his victims' spirits, leaving them with no visible injuries or marks."

So he'd been in Boulder for two days, just like Emil. "Lysander? That's his name?"

She put her hand out, flat, and then tilted it back and forth. "Last I heard, that was his preferred name, but he's had a lot of them. There have been stories and legends about him for thousands of years, with varying degrees of accuracy. Nergal in Mesopotamia, Horus in Egypt, Hades in Greece, and so on. Later, there were rumors about him that were nonspecific, and he was given names like ghoul, barrow-wight, and revenant," Kirsten said. Now she was reminding me of Simon, who was always interested in having *all the background*. "But where I'm from," she went on, her face darkening, "we call him the draugr."

I frowned. "Draugr?"

"You may have heard the word before. In Norse mythology a draugr is an undead creature, similar to a vampire in some ways. They live in barrows or graves, and animals or humans who come into regular contact with those locations lose their minds."

So the mysterious illness plaguing animals was connected to Elise's psych cases after all. If Lysander had been lurking around my regular haunts, no pun intended, it would make sense that some of the wildlife would be affected. I wanted to kick myself, but how could I have known it was a magical illness? "Why? Why do normal humans go crazy around this guy?"

"Because Lysander's power is like a toxin that seeps into the groundwater, or radiation that hangs around long after the bomb blast." She shook her head. "That's what happens when you put an ancient conduit in the modern world."

"How do you know so much about him?" I asked her. "My friends haven't been able to find any history or testimonies about boundary witches' actions during the Inquisition. Not even rumors on the internet."

Sadness crept into her eyes. "I know," she said, "because the Inquisition wasn't the first time the draugr was brought back from the dead. Thousands of years before that, he was raised briefly in Scandinavia. That's where our legends come from. Like all legends, they've changed and warped over time, but Lysander hasn't. That's also why we do not play with boundary magic."

My tea was gone, so I got up to put more hot water in my mug. I didn't really need more tea, but I did need time to absorb everything Kirsten had just said.

I was oddly relieved to hear that the man I'd encountered *was* a sort of man. Conduits were derived from humans, after all, or whatever the Bronze Age equivalent had been. I could accept that the thing I'd run into was a super-witch.

But I was still struggling to wrap my head around the idea of him being my father. Why would my mother . . . I winced, not wanting to let my thoughts go there. Maybe the draugr had spelled her somehow. Maybe he'd pressed her mind. I could have asked Kirsten what she thought, but I wasn't sure what she'd do if she knew that I was the draugr's daughter.

By the time I added milk and sugar to my tea and got back to the table, I had at least figured out what to ask. "Who raised him?"

Kirsten, who had just drained the last of her hot chocolate, set down the mug and pointed at me. "That's the right question. Raising the draugr is boundary magic of the highest order, and it can only be done by a coven of boundary witches performing a complex ritual. I don't know anyone who could do it."

An entire coven of boundary witches? I was the only boundary witch I knew of in the state, if you didn't count Nellie. Emil's mother was supposedly in Nova Scotia, but he hadn't made it sound like he had a lot of family there. Then again, Lysander had said something about my sisters and brothers.

No, I realized abruptly. It hadn't been them—Lysander had implied that they were all weaker than me. It had been the others, this "militis mortis."

I asked Kirsten if she had heard the term before, but she shook her head, frowning. "I haven't, but my people haven't practiced boundary magic in many centuries. I don't even know any boundary witches, other than yourself."

I almost choked on my tea. "You know?"

One side of her mouth turned up. "Of course I do."

"You haven't, like, spit in my face or tried to kill me or anything."

She laughed out loud. "Well, what good would that do? No, I understand what you are, but I trust Jesse Cruz. And he trusts you." Her eyes went distant for a moment. "Besides, even if you were an insane force for evil, right now the draugr wants to claim you, and you may be the only one who can stop him. That makes you worth defending."

I took another slow sip of tea, accepting that. And making a mental note to thank Jesse later. "Okay, well, what else can you tell me? You said Lysander has particular abilities. What can he do?"

"So many things," she said, with history now weighing on her face. "The draugr can command the wraiths. He can make his own size change. He can move through the ground as smoke. And on top of all that, he's still the most powerful witch alive. During the Inquisition, he would raise his arms and call the lives right out of people's bodies."

My gut tightened with fear. "By choice? Or did the people who raised him make him do it?"

"Both," she said matter-of-factly. "He killed the Inquisitors, just as the evocators wanted. But he also killed their families, and their neighbors, and *their* neighbors. Entire villages were slaughtered, and the Concilium had to blame it on a plague outbreak."

That word had been in my history lessons from Simon and Lily. The Concilium was a group of vampires who used to serve as a sort of head government for all the Old World in Europe. Apparently, it fell apart when the New World was discovered, and the US never had any kind of formal governing system for the supernatural. It was still the Wild West over here.

"How did the Concilium stop the draugr?" I said, leaning forward. Context was good, but what I really needed to know was how to destroy the thing. Biological father or not, he was killing people in my town. I couldn't allow that. And I couldn't let him kill Maven.

But Kirsten spread her hands. "I'm afraid I don't know. The Concilium fell shortly afterward, and I don't know of any records."

"Do you have a guess?" I rushed to say. "Or can you tell me anything else I can use to fight him? Weaken him?"

She frowned, thoughtful. "Possibly . . . I have books on Scandinavian history in my personal collection, so during the flight here I read up on the draugr legends. He can move around during the day, but he's weaker when the sun is up. He gains power at night, but he also needs to take a life every night to stay alive." She lifted a shoulder. "In theory, if you can keep him from killing anyone for a whole twenty-four hours, he may run out of magic and collapse. He wouldn't be permanently destroyed, mind you," she added, "but he would go back to an . . . inert state."

I chewed my lower lip for a few seconds. "What about a null?" I asked. "What would happen if one of them got near the draugr?"

Kirsten's eyes widened. "That . . . is interesting. I never even considered it. I don't know that nulls were around during the European Inquisition. If they were, there are no records of one of them going up against the draugr." She smoothed her hair, thinking it over. "I think a null might undo him," she said at last. "Or at least collapse him into remains once again. I can't be certain, of course, but the draugr is sustained by active boundary magic. That could work . . . if you had a null."

And that was the problem, wasn't it? If I tried to use a null against the draugr, it would involve putting one in close proximity to him. I couldn't exactly call John and ask him to bring Charlie back so I could put her in danger. She wasn't even two years old, for crying out loud.

But then again . . . she wasn't the only null I knew anymore. I *hated* the idea of asking Scarlett Bernard for help, but what choice did I have? "There's a null in LA, right?" I said to Kirsten. She didn't know I had come to the city the previous fall to investigate Sam's death. It was supposed to be a secret, since I wasn't supposed to invade other Old World territories without going through channels. "Scarlett something. Do you think she would help? I could, um, pay her." I didn't know *how* I would pay her, but I'd find a way.

But Kirsten shook her head. "Ordinarily, yes. But tomorrow night is a full moon. Scarlett has to stay in Los Angeles and care for her"—a slight hesitation—"dog."

"Shadow?" I asked, before I could stop myself. Shadow could be considered a dog like Captain America could be considered a kid from Brooklyn. She was a bargest, an indestructible creature spelled to fight werewolves.

Kirsten's eyes sparked with interest. "Jesse told you about her?"

Shit. Jesse wasn't supposed to share Old World secrets. I couldn't let him get in trouble. "No. Scarlett and I met once, briefly."

"Ah." She nodded. This was the moment where she could ask follow-up questions that would get me in trouble, but she just smiled. She'd decided to let it go. "At any rate, Shadow can't leave LA County, and if Scarlett isn't nearby, she'll go after the local were-wolves. But if you haven't found a way to defeat the draugr by the following night, perhaps she could help."

Which sounded like a great plan . . . except waiting two more nights would mean the draugr would murder two more people.

Quinn texted me a few minutes later, wanting to make sure I was all right. Lily would have returned to John's house by now and explained the situation. I sent him a quick message that all was well, then got up to walk Kirsten out.

When we were close to the house, I could see my broken car and her rental on the street, but as soon as we moved a few feet away, they disappeared. Kirsten paused and turned to me. "Here," she said, holding something out. I cupped my hand and she dropped car keys into it. "Take my rental. You're going to need to get back to your friends."

I protested—I couldn't leave a pregnant woman stranded in a strange city—but she assured me that she'd just call a cab.

"Kirsten, I can't let you do that. You're, um," I glanced at her pregnant belly. "Not from around here," I finished.

She shot me an impish smile. "Oh, I can still call a cab just fine, believe me. Besides, I'm rooting for you." She paused, and the smile faded away, replaced by some kind of regret. The whole time we'd been talking, Kirsten had seemed serene—worried, even troubled, but always very composed. For the first time, I saw that poise falter just a little. "A long time ago, my ancestors had an opportunity to stop the draugr, and they failed," she said quietly. "Even now, the witches of Sweden feel some responsibility toward this particular creature. Any other time I would stay and help you fight him"—she rested her free hand on her belly—"but I can't take the risk just now."

I nodded. "I wouldn't want you to."

Duffel bag in hand, I climbed into the rental, a Kia Sorento, and tried to pay attention to the unfamiliar knobs and dials while my head was spinning. I was too distracted to even worry about ghosts on the road. My birth father was a conduit. He was, in a way, the magical incarnation of death.

Then Quinn's voice echoed in my head. "*You* haven't changed. You just know something that you didn't before, that's all."

I set my teeth, and my insides settled for the first time in what felt like days. Damn right. Maven might have been out of commission, but that didn't mean I was helpless. Boulder was my town, and I wasn't going to let this asshole kill anyone else in it. Lysander could beat me in magic, but I had resources he didn't know about: friends, weapons, and knowledge. I wasn't going to lie down and die.

Not that it would do any good if I did, I thought ruefully.

My phone rang, and I checked the screen. Elise. I swallowed hard to clear my sore throat, hoping she wasn't going to tell me about another body. I hit "Talk" and said, "What's buzzin', cousin?"

"Allison," said a hollow, unpleasantly familiar voice. "We need to finish our conversation."

Chapter 34

I stomped on the brake, halting the Kia in the middle of a deserted street. *Lysander had Elise.* And in a split second, I knew how: someone *had* been following me on Pearl Street the other night. And I'd led him straight to someone I loved.

My foot stayed planted on the brake, and everything else inside me hardened at once. My muscles went tense, my fingers clutching at the phone. I felt my abdominal muscles contract, along with my lungs. I forgot everything around me. My focus was absolute. "Where's Elise?

"It is unfortunate that you have brought us to this precipice. Today could have gone very differently."

I pushed the words through clenched teeth. "Where. Is. Elise."

"She is with me. She is even still alive, although that will change very soon."

"What do you want?"

"I want what I came for," he said, and for the first time his voice took on an edge. "Maven dead, and you in my service."

"What does that mean, in your service?" For some reason I didn't think he wanted me to swear an oath of loyalty. He wanted me *for something.* I was just hoping it wasn't the thing with my uterus.

"Emil will collect you at the sculpture garden. Do not inform your friends. This is a family matter."

I opened my mouth to scream at him, to demand to talk to Elise, but of course he'd already hung up the phone.

I squeezed the cell until my knuckles ached, looking around at the darkened street. Quinn was expecting me back at John's any minute now. What was I going to do?

I could call Quinn and tell him everything. There was no question that he and Simon and Lily would help me take down Emil and Lysander. But how did I know Lysander didn't have someone watching me right now, or monitoring my phone? Hell, Emil could be doing that. Just because he was meeting me at the sculpture garden didn't mean he was there already.

I looked down at the phone in my hand. If Quinn didn't hear from me, he'd track my location. If he showed up at the sculpture garden, Lysander might kill Elise just to punish me. I couldn't risk it.

I drove farther into town until I reached one of Boulder's many coffee shops. It was closed now, but I set the phone on the concrete sidewalk next to the door, behind a little shrub. If Quinn tracked the phone to the coffee shop, he'd assume I was there, still talking to Kirsten. As long as he didn't Google the coffee shop's hours, it should buy me a little time.

I looked at the small duffel bag that lay in the footwell of the passenger side. *Be smart*, Sam's voice warned. But what was the smart move? At the moment, I could really only see *one* move.

Spring the trap.

I parked several blocks away from the sculpture garden and approached on foot. I'd changed into dark clothes from the duffel, and I crept along the row of hedges to circle the side. I got low to the ground and peeked between the bare branches. I was expecting to see Emil waiting there with a smug grin. If I could catch him by surprise, maybe I could get the drop on him. If Lysander would trade Emil for Elise—

But as I turned the last corner, my hopes were dashed into the spring grass. Emil was there, all right, standing in front of the bench near the *Crossing the Prairie* sculpture with a smug little grin. He wasn't alone. I had half-expected Lysander, but instead there were six vampires standing in a circle around Emil, obviously there to protect him. One of them bent her head and whispered something to him, and he nodded.

"Hello, little sister," he called. "You might as well come out—you've been spotted. Well, scented, anyway."

Crap. I stood up and strode around the corner. "How's it going, Emil?" I asked, as casually as I could. My eyes were fastened on the vampires. I recognized two of them from the photos Maven had shown us of the Denver vampires. Three of them I didn't know. And the last . . . I took a small step sideways so I could see the woman behind Emil's shoulder. Shock flashed through my chest. It was Opal. She was one of Maven's vampires, and I had thought she was loyal.

"You?" I blurted. "How could you?"

Opal didn't respond. In fact, I realized, none of them were responding to anything. "She can't hear you," Emil said, not unkindly. "None of them can. He's pressed them."

I swallowed hard. Of *course* Lysander could press vampires. Why hadn't I thought of that? "That's how he got Ford and the others to come after me," I said, mostly to myself. Emil wasn't working for Ford. Lysander had pressed the vampire to do what he wanted.

Emil frowned. "Yes. And if you'd just gone with them, you could have saved everyone a lot of trouble. We could have laid Lysander back to rest by now, and two fewer people would be dead." He didn't sound smug, or like a supervillain in a comic book movie. He just sounded . . . tired.

"Where's Elise?" I demanded.

He flicked on a heavy-duty flashlight, pointing it over his shoulder. I recognized the metal sculpture at the back of the garden, raised above the others with a few concrete steps. It was a cowboy on top of his horse, reining in a wild mustang as it reared on its back two legs. But the sculpture had always been a rusty brown color, not silver. I squinted at the flashlight beam and recognized the long silver bundle draped across the cowboy's lap. It was Elise, wrapped in duct tape from her ankles to her armpits. A rectangle of tape was plastered over her mouth as well.

"Elise!" I shouted, and began to run forward.

A vampire stepped in front of me, his expression completely blank. "No, you don't," Emil said. He nodded at one of the vampires in the back, who walked mechanically over to Elise, baring his teeth.

"How do I know she's alive?" I shouted.

Calmly, Emil dipped two fingers into his shirt pocket and pulled out a thin cigar, sticking it between his lips. He patted his pockets for a lighter and finally flicked open a silver Zippo to ignite the end. After taking a deep drag and exhaling, he finally spoke over his shoulder to the vampire near my cousin. "Hit her."

Before I could so much as open my mouth to protest, the vampire lifted Elise's head, ripped off the tape, and slapped her hard across the face. "No!" I shouted, but Elise moaned, shying away from the blow. The vampire let her head fall again. I screamed at the sound of her cheekbone striking the metal sculpture.

"There, see? Alive," Emil said.

"Walk away," I said through clenched teeth. "Leave now, and I won't kill you. *Brother*."

In response, Emil reached down and adjusted something on the bench. "Come on now, Lex," he said in a soft, soothing voice. "Let's get to the car. We'll leave Officer Luther here, where someone will find her in the morning." He held out an arm.

I stepped forward, ignoring the vampires who'd begun to close ranks around Emil. "Didn't you hear me, asshole? Get the fuck out of my town."

Emil paused, genuine shock on his face. "How are—why aren't you listening to me?" he sputtered. He touched his shirt near the collar, probably feeling for his necklace.

"You mean why am I not smiling and curtseying and following you into hell?" I snapped.

He glared. "That was a perfect grid, and I buried the stones this time."

I reached into my own neckline and pulled out the dangling cord, showing him the chunk of mahogany obsidian. I was expecting his face to fall, or maybe get angry, but the look he gave me was different. There was surprise there, and maybe even a bit of respect.

Then the look vanished, and he shook his head. "All right, fine. We could have done this the easy way, but you really are your mother's daughter. Lysander's not going to like that."

"Where is he?" I demanded. "Why didn't he come himself?"

"He finds it hard to control himself in public places," he said, his voice cool. "And his . . . mmm . . . supervisors have forbidden him from mass murder. That's why he has to travel with a keeper."

That surprised me—not what he'd said, but the fact that he'd answered so candidly. "What does he want with me?"

"Haven't you figured it out yet?" he said with a broad smile. "You're the new keeper. And if all your reproductive organs work correctly, the new surrogate. You'll bear his child."

I gaped at him, but he just gave a little shrug, unapologetic. I shook my head in disbelief, taking a step back. "No. *No.*"

"Is it the incest thing?" he said, putting on a sympathetic expression. "Don't worry. These days we use artificial insemination, so you won't actually need to sleep with him. It's all very modern. If it helps, we don't think his offspring are susceptible to the same genetic defects caused by interbreeding, say, Dalmatians."

"*Why?*" I practically screamed.

"Because," Emil said, as calm as I was upset, "he needs a minder, and he needs to reproduce. Otherwise the boundary line will fail."

"Let it," I spat. "And you're his minder."

"Not for much longer," he said casually. It brought me up short. He pointed to the cigar dangling between his lips. "I've got six months, maybe a year. He was going to find you eventually, of course, but it forced us to move up the timeline."

"Why me?"

"Because you're the best," he said. He was trying to keep his voice light, but there was an edge of resentment there. "The strongest. Like your mother. He was *pissed* when Valerya got away. You're like a second chance at her."

"I won't do it," I whispered, taking a step back.

"Your choice. But, of course, we'll kill the good officer. And I doubt Lysander will stop there. He's just dying to be let off the leash. So to speak." He smiled at his own joke. "He's had to be so careful since the Concilium fell. If you anger his sponsors, they'll let him have this city." He waved a hand dismissively. "They can always make up a story. Bird flu. Airborne Ebola. Zombie apocalypse. You know."

"Why are *you* doing this?" I asked him. "You're not a true believer. Do you even care about the bloodline?"

He paused at that, and the look that passed over his face was dark and complicated. "It's not that I don't care," he said after a moment. "It's that I care about other things more." His voice quieted. "My mother, for instance."

My anger stuttered to a pause. What had Sam said about Emil? That he was basically a good guy who'd done some bad things? "Lysander threatened her," I said, understanding. "You have to help him. What will they do to her if you don't?"

He was obviously trying to appear nonchalant, but the anger was showing through it. "They'll make her try again. She's too old, of course, but her body doesn't appear that way. They've made her try for the last five years, going through the process over and over. I need to find her replacement before I die."

"I'm sorry," I said, and I actually meant it. "Sorry for what they did to you both. But I am no one's fucking concubine. Leave my town now, and I won't come after you. I promise."

He studied me, and for about two seconds, I actually thought he was tempted to listen. But then he tossed the cigar on the ground, stepped on it, and pointed to me. "Take her," he told the vampires.

When they stepped forward, Opal was in the lead.

Chapter 35

One of the six stayed near Emil, making sure I couldn't harm him, but the other five slowly stalked forward, spreading out so they could surround me. I gritted my teeth. Now what? I made eye contact with Opal, who was closest. Lysander hadn't warned them to avoid my eyes, and unlike Ford, Maven didn't train her people to evade me. I'd never tried to undo a press before, but there was no time to think about it. If they got me into a car, I would never return.

I closed my eyes quickly, dropping into the mindset of my magic. The vampires appeared to me as glowing red embers, brighter and more vibrant than the blue of Emil and Elise's humanity. I darted forward and placed my tattoos on either side of Opal's face. More quickly than I'd ever done it, I opened a connection between the two of us and locked her into it. "I'm not your enemy," I said softly. "I'm your ally. Remember me."

She halted, and in her body's stillness I could feel the confusion. Instinctively, I realized that Lysander's press had gone deep, deeper than I ever could. It was like he'd rewired their brains. The other four vampires were closing in—I could feel them only inches from my back.

Well, I would just have to try harder. I poured everything I had into Opal, all the power I could summon. *"Remember me,"* I said fiercely. "Defend me."

Then the others were on me, and I lost my grip on the mindset as I was bodily pulled away from her. The two vampires who reached me first were the ones from Denver, and although I tried to catch their eyes to press them too, they carefully avoided my gaze. They grabbed at me, but they were clumsier than the vampires I had fought in the past. Maybe Lysander's press had dulled their reflexes. The one at my back grabbed me around the waist, and before anyone could seize my arms I snapped an elbow back fast, bursting his nose. He was surprised enough to loosen his grip, and I dropped low, ducking between their legs to dance back.

I felt pretty good about that for about two seconds, then one of the female vampires I didn't know was suddenly in front of me, wrapping one hand in my hair and pinning my left arm to my body with her other hand. I tried stomping on her instep, but she barely even flinched. A male vampire in front of me snatched my right wrist and began wrenching it backward, until I cried out in pain. A third vampire ducked down and grabbed both of my ankles, and no matter how much I struggled I couldn't kick free of his grasp as he began to lift me. Emil was saying something in front of us, but I didn't bother listening. "No!" I screamed, but the most I could do was wiggle. I twisted as violently as I could, but their grips were absolute.

Then there was a sickeningly loud crack as the head of the vampire bending back my arm seemed to snap to one side. His grasp abruptly loosened, and he crumpled to the ground. I twisted to peer down and saw that his neck was broken. My eyes went up, and I saw Opal standing there. She gave me one quick, meaningful nod, then punched the vampire holding my left arm so hard that her nose seemed to cave inward. It must have done something to her spine, because she dropped, too.

Two down.

Startled by this new threat, the vampire holding my legs shifted his grip, and I caught him off-guard by intentionally toppling myself backward onto the ground. I used that precious second of surprise to tug the shredder free from my forearm. I couldn't get an angle on him, but Opal recognized my intention and grabbed his shoulders, slamming his back against the ground. I regained my balance and struggled forward to plunge the shredder into his chest. His heart exploded soundlessly, and the light left his eyes as his body began to decay.

Three down. Two left.

Emil was shouting instructions to his vampire guard, but I tuned him out and focused on the remaining vampire near us. His teeth bared as he stepped toward me, single-minded, and I realized he couldn't adjust Lysander's press—I was his target, and he couldn't look away from me and focus on Opal even if it killed him. Which it did, a heartbeat later, when Opal snapped his neck. He would survive, as would the other two, but it would take them awhile to recover.

Opal reached down, offering me her hand. I took it and climbed to my feet. "Are you okay?" she asked, looking worried. "I'm sorry, I . . . I'm not really sure what's going on."

"Tell you later," I promised. "You're doing great." I turned to face Emil, my hand going to my back. "What do you think, *brother*? You want to send your bodyguard after us, too? I don't like his chances."

Emil's mouth dropped open, but he wasn't looking at me. He was staring at Opal, his eyes wide. "You broke his press," he whispered. He said it like I'd deciphered some famously unsolvable math theorem. He turned to me, shock still written on his face. "Come with me," he said, his voice weak.

"I thought we settled this. I'm not going anywhere with you."

He gestured with frustration. "That's not what I mean! Come back with me. You and me and my mother—maybe we could find a way to stand against them."

"Them?"

"Lysander and his other followers. The Knights of Death. Our family and a few others."

My eyes narrowed. "You are *not* my family. I have a family."

The look that he gave me was unmistakably puzzled. "But you don't belong with them."

"Of course I do," I said without thinking. *Dammit, Lex.* I shouldn't have taken the bait.

He took a pleading step forward. Opal tensed, but she watched me, waiting for a cue. "The Luthers aren't like us, Lex," he said urgently. "They age quickly, and live just as fast. Soon they'll leave you behind. Then, not so long from now, their lives will be finished, and where will you be?"

I didn't want to listen, but I couldn't help it. My thoughts leaped to how Dani was nearly a teenager, how Elise and Anna were both in serious relationships that might lead to marriage. Paul was moving to New York, my dad would be retiring in a few years, and Charlie would start preschool the following year. And where was I? Working at a convenience store by day and running around with vampires at night. I couldn't even bring my boyfriend to family dinners.

Sensing an opening, Emil took another step forward. I reacted instinctively, drawing the Smith & Wesson from the fanny pack I'd twisted backward. It had been pointless when there were so many vampires against me, but Emil I could shoot. I pointed it at his forehead, but he ignored me. "It's already happening, isn't it?" he said softly, his eyes probing. "Marriage, kids, careers. All those things you can't have. And they can't understand why not."

I tried to push the words out of my head, but he'd hit me in just the right spot. It *did* feel like a gap was opening up between me and my family. Would it really just get bigger? Would they all drift away from me?

Would I have to watch them die?

"Come with me," he pleaded, his eyes desperate. "Help Sophia and me stand against the rest of them. We're your flesh and blood. We understand what you're going through—the slow aging, the vampire relationship, all of it. Your vampire can come too, if he wants. You could learn from my mother, and together we could do more for boundary magic than the Knights ever did."

I looked at him for a long, frozen moment. "You choose your own family," I said quietly. "You came to my town, you tried to kill someone who's been good to me, and you allowed *that creature* to take innocent lives. Last chance to walk away."

His face hardened with fury, and I saw my error. In his eyes, he'd just offered me an olive branch, a true connection between equals, and I'd spat on it. "Kill them both," he growled.

The vampire shot forward, but I put two shots in his body mass. It wasn't anywhere near the heart, but it slowed him down enough for Opal to smash into him, snarling as she rode him to the ground. Seeing this, Emil pulled a knife out of his pocket, flipped the blade open, and turned to run—but not toward the parking lot and freedom. Toward Elise.

I raised the gun and put a bullet in the back of each of his thighs.

He crashed to the ground like a fallen tree. When I was positive he wasn't getting back up I ran forward, fumbling to undo my belt to make a tourniquet. I dropped to my knees next to him and saw that blood was spurting out of the wound on his right leg. I'd nicked the femoral artery. He was dying.

I yanked out the belt and tried to gingerly ease it under the leg, but Emil saw what I was doing and held up a hand. "Please," he begged. "Don't."

We locked eyes for a moment, and I understood. He wanted to go out like this, instead of in six or twelve months. More than that, he didn't want to be the draugr's daytime pet anymore. I nodded once.

Letting go of the belt, I fumbled at his pockets and came out with a cell phone. I tossed it to Opal. "Call Quinn," I ordered. "Get him here now."

Without watching to see if she did it, I turned back to Emil. He was looking at me with resignation. "You don't know what you've done," he said weakly. "If you don't surrender, he will level this town. I can't stop him now. Your niece . . ."

His eyes began to roll back, and I slapped him across the face. "What about my niece?"

"When I found you, I did my homework. Lysander wants Charlotte dead. All nulls dead."

The sudden fear stung me, but I had to push past it. "My mother, what really happened?" I demanded.

His eyes went distant. "I met her a few times . . . didn't know her well. My father and the other families, they took her from her home when she was nineteen." He coughed weakly. "She was never willing."

My hands balled into fists, and angry tears burned my eyes. They'd let the draugr rape her. I wanted to hit him, to shoot him again, to hurt him like they'd hurt Valerya, but then a hoarse whisper floated from his lips. "The same as they did to Sophia. And every other strong evocator they've found in the last five hundred years."

Through a blur of tears I could see that Emil was fading. I'd held enough dying men in my life to recognize it. "What was the plan?" I hissed. "Where were you going to take me?"

"He wouldn't say, in case," he mumbled. "I was supposed to call when I had you."

Shit. "Where has he been hiding out during the day?" It wasn't like a blue giant could check into the Holiday Inn.

"My dealer, she hooked him up with a spot." His eyes were already beginning to lose focus. "He wouldn't tell me. Didn't trust me. He just said it was somewhere where he'd feel at home. Lots of dead. Here . . ." His arm floated up to touch his chest. "Take it . . ."

I yanked down his collar to see the heavy crystal necklace he'd been wearing the night of his attack on Maven. Emil touched one stone in particular, tapping at it weakly. "It was Val's," he whispered. "Sophia made it for her. I'm sorry, Lex." His eyes drifted closed.

"The dealer!" I shouted, shaking him a little. "Who's your dealer?"

I bent my head down and managed to catch Emil's last, whispered word.

"Atwood."

Chapter 36

Ardie fucking Atwood. Just like that, I knew where to find Lysander.

I checked Emil's pulse more from habit than anything else but he was gone. Carefully, I pulled the leather cord over his head and tugged it free. The knot was big and clumsy, but not terribly difficult to pick apart. I slid off the crystal Emil had indicated, leaving the others with his body for now. I didn't want to mess around with gravitational magic any more than I had to, especially if I didn't know what it was supposed to do. I was just hoping whatever stone had worked for my mother would work for me, too.

The crystal that had belonged to Valerya was four inches long and cylindrical, only about as thick as my thumb. It was dark green, with tiny red flecks in it. For a moment I thought Emil's blood had dripped on it, but no, the spots were too tiny. I had seen this stone when I was thumbing through the little book from the New Age store. It was called bloodstone, precisely because of those red flecks.

It hummed softly in my hand, and I understood that this crystal had more power than the cassiterite I'd bought in Boulder, or even the mahogany obsidian around my neck. Emil had probably taken good care of it. I took off my own long necklace and hastily added the crystal to the cord. I wished I remembered what bloodstone did, but there was no time. I was going to have to trust that it was something good.

I was exhausted, and I still felt like hammered crap, but I had to go after the draugr. He was expecting Emil to cart me back to Nova Scotia for him, so I would have the element of surprise, along with my carload of weapons. This was the best shot I was going to get.

I left Emil's body on the ground and climbed to my feet, looking around the garden. Five lifeless vampire bodies were crumpled on the ground around me, with Opal sitting in the middle of them, her knees huddled to her chest. For the first time I registered that she wore a bloodstained white cocktail dress.

Making my way around the vampire bodies, I went over and crouched in front of her. "What happened to you?" I asked.

"I . . . I'm not sure," she confessed, looking miserable. If there was one thing I knew for sure, it was that vampires hated to be pressed. "The last thing I remember is getting a call to come in and see Maven. I went to Magic Beans, but . . ." She crinkled her face, unable to remember. "I think someone was waiting for me."

"It's going to be okay." I touched her shoulder, awkwardly. "Opal, I need you to wait here for Quinn. I'm going after the person responsible for all of this."

She gave me an uncomprehending look. "But don't you want Quinn to go with you? He always goes with you."

"If he did, Lysander would press him, just like he pressed you," I told her. "Quinn would never forgive himself if he hurt me. Just tell him . . . tell him I love him, okay?"

She nodded dully. I didn't know if the message would make it to Quinn or not, but it didn't really matter. He knew.

I took Emil's cell phone from her, stood, and ran for Kirsten's rental car. But when I got there, a familiar Jeep was parking behind it.

Quinn jumped from the seat with vampire grace and rushed over to me, hands touching my face, checking my neck. "Are you okay? What were you thinking?" he said in almost the same breath.

"How did you get here so fast?"

"I was already on my way. That witch, Kirsten, called Hazel to apologize for not going through the proper channels for coming into town. Hazel called Lily. When we realized you were no longer with Kirsten, I knew something must have happened. Or someone took you." He tilted his head at the rental car. "Rental cars have GPS now."

I threw my arms around him. He let me hold him for a moment, then pulled back, his hands clutching my upper arms. "I can't believe you came to meet Emil without me. What happened?"

His nostrils flared, and his pupils contracted. I nodded, realizing he was smelling Emil's blood. "Emil's dead. He had Elise, and he said I had to come alone, and I killed him." I could hear myself babbling, but I couldn't seem to slow the words. "Can you please press Elise and get her home?" I would feel guilty about brainwashing my cousin later. "I need to go."

I made it about a third of a step in the direction of the Kia before he stopped me. "*What*? Where?"

I hesitated, trying to think of a lie he'd believe, but the pause gave me away. "You're going after Lysander, aren't you?" he demanded. "I'm coming with you."

I reached up, wrapping my fingers around the back of his neck and pulling him down to meet me. "You can't, Quinn. Lysander can press vampires."

He only blanched for a moment. "I'll wear sunglasses. I won't look at his face."

I pressed my forehead against his. "No, baby," I said softly. "You know that's not good enough. He's too strong."

His face clouded over, and I saw what it cost him to say, "Then at least take Simon. Hell, take him and Lily both."

"I can't do that either. Even if I were willing to risk them, which I'm not, the only way this will work is a surprise offensive. You *know* that, Quinn."

He jerked his head away from me. "If you won't take Simon, then I'm coming with you," he said stubbornly.

I sighed. Quinn trusted me to handle so many situations by myself—Ford's vampires outside the Jeep, for example—but this was too much for him. "Look, you swore an oath of loyalty to Maven." I gestured over my shoulder. "Maybe Emil's blood could help her. Take it to her. I'll be fine."

It was a flimsy excuse—only last night, Emil's blood had been full of belladonna—and we both knew it. Quinn's eyes narrowed. "Don't you *dare* try to make this about me choosing her over you. You want to go alone because you're afraid to risk me." His eyes widened. "Or is it that you're planning to let him have you?"

I tried to keep my face neutral, but he was right. If I couldn't beat Lysander, I would have no choice but to go with him. Emil was right: he would keep coming at me, and more people would get hurt. I would be the new keeper, the new surrogate, whatever, if it meant he would leave my town and my friends alone.

"He took Elise, Quinn," I pleaded, my voice cracking. "He's not going to stop until I go with him or one of us is dead. And we can't die." Tears filled my eyes. "I have so much to lose. Charlie—"

"Don't make this about Charlie," he said angrily. "Your whole life is about Charlie. Everything you do is to protect that little girl."

That brought me up short for a moment, and I felt my temper rising. "So goddamned what? That sounds like a pretty great plan to me."

"But you're more than just a bulletproof vest," he contended. "Charlie might be your mission, soldier, but she's not your life."

"You're one to talk," I snapped. "When's the last time you did anything that Maven didn't explicitly order?"

He just looked at me. "When I fell in love with you."

My eyes filled. I tilted my head up to kiss him, but he recognized it as goodbye and pulled away from me. "No. Don't let him do this to you. To us."

The tears began to fall. Closing the small distance between us, I reached up to touch his face with both hands. I made sure the tips of my griffin tattoos touched his jawline.

Then I opened the connection between us.

I felt his mind fight it for one instant, felt the hurt and betrayal like a physical blow to my stomach. But I kept going anyway, and I had the connection locked into place before he could jerk away from me. His face went slack.

"Take charge of this scene," I instructed, hoping that the press would work in spite of my wobbly voice. "Take care of the vampires and the body, and make sure Elise gets home safely and doesn't remember what happened tonight. Forget that you saw me here. Do not worry about me until the next time you see me."

It worked. Quinn gave me an empty nod and shambled off to follow my orders. I took one quick, sobbing breath and fled for the car.

Chapter 37

I cried most of the way to Denver. I had violated Quinn's trust. Even if I survived this, I would have to live with that. And if I didn't survive, or if I was taken away to be a surrogate, he would have to live with the knowledge that he had failed to stop me. And that I'd betrayed him.

I cried for Quinn, for me, but a little bit for Emil, too. The look on his face when he wanted me to let him die . . . I wouldn't forget that anytime soon. He had been working against me, planning several moves ahead to keep me on the defensive. In fact, I'd been on the defensive since the moment that gray fox broke through my window. But looking at it now, I knew Emil wasn't evil. He'd been backed into a corner, surrounded by terrible decisions.

Only an hour earlier, I'd had a brother. And then I'd killed him.

The tears finally stopped, and a feeling of resolution crept over me. I was doing the right thing. Well, no, but I was doing the only thing I could.

I hadn't planned to talk to anyone else before confronting Lysander, but as I went over my plan of attack, I realized I'd overlooked something. Luckily, I knew Lily's number by heart. I punched it into the disposable phone.

"Hello?" Her voice was cautious and worried, expecting bad news.

"It's me."

"Lex! Oh my God, where are you?"

"Lily, listen to me," I said clearly. "Emil confessed that he got the belladonna from Ardie Atwood. She's in on this whole thing." As quickly as I could, I explained what I'd learned. Ardie had told Quinn and me about Billy's out-of-state network of magical degenerates, which she must have inherited after his death. Emil had bought belladonna from her and used it on the Denver vampires, knowing that it would draw Quinn and me out to investigate. He must have planned to capture me and then go after Maven, but Quinn and I had bested Ford and his associates. Emil then had no choice but to move ahead with his Plan B—attack Maven, forcing me into a position in which I needed his help. Lily listened quietly through the whole thing, uncharacteristically never interrupting.

"I don't know how much Ardie knew about Emil's intentions," I concluded, "But she was definitely the seller, and she lied to us about it. You can't ever trust her again, okay?"

There was a long pause, so long that I checked the phone screen to make sure the call hadn't dropped.

"Okay," she said finally, and then repeated it to herself. "Okay. I'm glad you told me." Another brief pause. "Wait, why are you telling me on the phone? Where are you?"

The tears choked in my still-sore throat. "I love you, Lily."

"No!" she shouted, surprising me. "Whatever stupid, suicidal plan you've got, don't do it."

"Lily . . . I have to."

I was about to hang up, but she blurted, "Then you have to promise me something."

I paused. "What?"

"*Be a witch*," she said fiercely. "Not just Lex, the ex-soldier, not just Maven's employee or Charlie's bodyguard. Simon and I, we've been trying to teach you that you're a witch first, and I don't think we've succeeded."

"I hear you."

"Boundary magic isn't a tool in your toolbox, Lex. You're it, and it's you. You're the channel. Don't ever forget it. And *please* be safe," she begged.

I smiled, even though she couldn't see it. "Lily, it's been an honor."

Then I hung up the phone.

As soon as Emil had said that Ardie was involved and Lysander was surrounded by the dead, I knew where he'd be.

I'd been to the Botanic Gardens in Denver as a child, and two years ago I'd chaperoned a field trip for my cousin Brie's son, Peter, when Brie came down with the flu. The volunteer working the ticket booth that day had mentioned an upcoming "haunted tour" event at the Gardens, and my face must have shown my skepticism. Lowering her voice so the children wouldn't hear, she'd informed me that the ground we were standing on had once been part of Denver's first cemetery. Although the cemetery had been moved, not all the bodies were successfully reburied.

"To this day," she'd said dramatically, "they'll sometimes dig for a new exhibit and hit *bones*."

At the time, I assumed the story was garbage, the type of crap that was cooked up every Halloween to milk the ever-growing haunted house industry. But it was just so *weird* that I looked it up later.

And it turned out I owed the ticket seller an apology. Sure enough, the land containing both the Botanic Gardens and the neighboring Cheesman Park, where Sam and I had gone to outdoor concerts as teenagers, had been designated as Mount Prospect Cemetery in 1859. It had eventually been divided into different sections for Catholic, Masonic, and Jewish burials, plus additional sections for paupers and Civil War veterans. Mount Prospect was badly organized, unattractive, and riddled with stories of corruption and controversy. Soon the grounds became less of an official cemetery and more of a sewer for the unwanted dead.

When a better site opened in 1876, the number of burials at Mount Prospect—now known as City Cemetery—began to decline. By 1893 the city got fed up and decided to turn the area into a public park instead. They gave notice to the relatives of those buried at City Cemetery that they had ninety days to move their loved ones.

Unfortunately, not everyone bothered.

Which left the town with a big problem. There were never complete records of who was buried at City Cemetery or where the graves were located, so the city had no way of knowing how many people were left after the relatives' ninety days were up. In an effort to clear up the whole mess, the city hired an undertaker named McGovern to dig for all the remaining bodies and move them to a new cemetery.

But McGovern, as it turned out, was the world's least ethical coroner. Since he was paid by the body, the undertaker would often split the remains of one person into two or even three coffins to collect more fees. Eventually the city leaders figured out what was happening and fired him, but they never got around to replacing him—or to figuring out exactly how many people he had really transferred. Thousands of bodies stayed buried beneath the grass. And every year, the night security guards at the Botanic Gardens reported strange noises, objects moving around by themselves, and all the other classic signs of hauntings.

When I'd first read the story, I'd been shocked that the city knew about thousands of unclaimed human bodies, and no one had done *anything* about it. The situation was disgraceful. I had said as much to Sam, who'd been the pragmatic one for a change. She pointed out that none of the deceased could have living family members left, and at least the bones were buried beneath a park and a garden. There were worse places to have your final resting place. She had a point, and I dropped the subject—but it had never sat well with me, especially given the way I'd seen bodies treated when I was overseas.

As I got off the highway in Denver and made my way south on York Street, I decided that the most unnerving part of the whole situation was that no one could say for certain how many bodies were still buried beneath the two tourist attractions. Some said four thousand; others estimated more like eight. All anyone could say for sure was that there were unclaimed dead beneath the public spaces. And this, I was certain, was where Lysander was holed up. Surrounded by bodies, at least some of which had to be remnants.

I shivered, and for the first time I wished I'd made an effort to understand ghosts better. I'd spent so many months trying to avoid seeing them that I had a very limited understanding of how they worked. What kind of ghosts would inhabit a former cemetery? What could they do to me?

Just stick to the plan, I told myself. Use modern weapons to blow Lysander to bits, scatter his remains before sunrise.

What could go wrong?

The Gardens were closed, of course, but there were several spotlights highlighting the big scrolled sign of the entrance building. When I finally arrived, I drove slowly past the Botanic Gardens, craning my head to look for . . . I don't know, a strobe light of the damned or something. But nothing looked disturbed, and there was no neon sign saying, "This way to the draugr."

So where was Lysander?

I drove straight past the property and turned right onto East Eighth Avenue, home of a number of stunning, unbelievably ritzy mansions, which bordered the south side of the Gardens. I parked illegally on one of the side streets, said a silent apology to Kirsten because the rental would probably be towed, and climbed out of the car to get ready.

First I buckled the quick-draw holster around my hips, abandoning the fanny pack in the backseat. Then I strapped on all of my weapons—the combat knife, the revolver, the Ithaca on its sling, extra ammunition. If the car was going to get towed, I didn't want to leave them inside. I also wanted all the firepower I could get.

When I was done, I actually felt relieved, like I'd put on appropriate-for-the-weather clothes and would now be prepared for rain. I tossed the long jacket on over everything, took a deep breath, and said a silent prayer to Sam or God or anyone else who might be listening. Then I took off for the Gardens.

I didn't know a lot about breaking and entering, but I wouldn't need to: the entrance to the Botanic Gardens was a brick building bracketed by fencing on either side. Presumably any valuables were locked up in the building, but nobody uses razor wire or electrified fencing to protect some plants. The fence itself was nothing but an eight-foot-high wall. I snapped the little leather strap that would secure the Smith & Wesson in my holster, took a running start, and grabbed the top of it. I did a pull-up, got my upper body onto the upper surface, and then it was a simple matter of swinging my legs over and dropping to the ground in a crouch. Something like cedar chips crunched under my feet as I landed and went still, looking around me.

Denver had more clouds than I'd seen during my walk with Kirsten, and I was immediately struck by the darkness, much more than I'd expected in the middle of a big city. Up ahead I could see tiny lights in a line, like little lanterns, but I was too far away for them to do me any good. I crept forward as quietly as possible, moving my feet whenever they bumped into plant life. The smell of mulch and pollen was heavy on the thin air, but the Gardens were nearly silent. No birds, no squirrels or rabbits rustling through the trees. Was that normal?

After several hesitant steps, I could make out the cobblestone path just ahead. There were small, solar-powered torches stuck into the ground every few feet along all the walkways, each one giving out just enough light to illuminate the space a few feet around it. I could see fairly well inside a fifteen-foot bubble around me, but everything outside it was completely opaque. Like walking into a heavy fog.

It also didn't help that there were wisps of actual fog scattered around the grounds, moving along the sidewalks. No, wait. I squinted, my eyes trying to pick out the details of what I was seeing. The wisps of fog were tall and defined and . . . people-shaped.

They were remnants.

Once I recognized them, it hit me that they were *everywhere*. Mostly they stuck to the paths, floating along between the lights, but every now and then I saw a wisp of light wandering around in the darkness like it was trying to find its friends. I realized that if I really focused on one of them I could make out more details: clothes, hair length, that kind of thing. Most of them were wretched-looking: visibly sick, frozen in fear, or obviously injured. A few even had nooses dangling from their necks. Some of them just seemed confused and lost, like they didn't realize they were dead, and that was even sadder than the others.

But why were they all here? If they were the remnants of the people who were buried beneath my feet, why were they here instead of where they'd actually died?

The draugr. I had the sudden feeling that Lysander was the answer to both questions. Hugh Mark, the first remnant I'd met at the Boulderado, had been drawn to me. As an active boundary witch, I represented the connection between life and death; how could he *not* want to talk to me? Wraiths, like the ones I'd encountered in the sculpture park, were stronger and meaner, which was why Lysander had needed Sophia to trap them in crystals. But remnants were just weak psychic imprints, and these fluttering, bewildered moths had finally found a flame.

I was a little relieved—without Emil and his crystals, I doubted Lysander would have any wraiths along tonight. But the number of remnants floating around the Gardens was still completely unnerving. I swallowed hard. I would just have to ignore them.

Stepping onto the path, I focused on choosing a direction to search. Where would Lysander be? My original plan had been to locate him by calling him from Emil's phone, which would have the added benefit of distracting him—hopefully enough for me to hit him with the shotgun. But now that I was standing here, threading my way through hundred-and-fifty-year-old ghosts, I understood just how big the property was. There were any number of buildings with their own basements and hidey-holes, not to mention twenty-some acres of foliage. The task of finding one person on such a huge property seemed ridiculous. I would only get one shot at calling him on Emil's phone before he got suspicious. I needed to narrow down the search area somehow. With no better ideas, I pulled the Smith & Wesson, picked a direction, and began inching along the path with the weapon at my side.

I tried to give the drifting remnants a wide berth, but as much as I tried to maneuver around them, it was like being stuck in a pool of jellyfish. You would avoid bumping into one, only to careen into two more. Each time one passed through me, I had a brief flash of an image: the blast of gunfire, hospital sheets, a crowd looking up at me from below. Then the remnant would reach the other side of me, and I'd be left feeling desolate, cold, and hollowed-out. Each time this happened I felt as if it were taking a piece away from me. Soon I was fighting against a rising panic at the thought of so many of them. How much more could I take before I curled up in a ball and gave up?

At last I spotted a small map stand just ahead, and I rushed toward it gratefully. The light from the solar torches wasn't bright enough for me to see the image, so I risked pulling out Emil's phone and turning on the screen. Bending so my face was as close to the stand as possible, I scanned the map carefully and determined that I was in something called the Crossroads Garden, which seemed as likely a place as any for the most powerful boundary witch in history. Since he wasn't here, though, I kept scanning. How would a super-witch kill a little time in a botanic garden? No pun intended. I ran a finger down the list of exhibit titles, hoping something would jump out at me.

And then something did. My eyes nearly skipped right over the words, and I had to go back and reread them to make sure. I smiled to myself. Yeah, if I were Lysander, I'd probably find it amusing to lurk near that particular exhibit. I looked up, oriented myself away from the remnants, and stole along the path toward one of the Botanic Gardens' most famous acquisitions.

Chapter 38

In August of 2015, the Denver Botanic Gardens made national news when a rare flower called *Amorphophallus titanum* bloomed for the first time. The name literally means "giant misshapen phallus," but as fun as that name is, the plant's nickname is even better: the corpse flower.

It takes fifteen years for one of these giants to bloom for the first time, and when it does, it emits a terrible odor that famously smells like dead bodies. The petals are also a dark purple, sort of like rotting body parts. The corpse flower evolved this way to attract carrion bugs, which pollinate it, but their rarity and the long gestation period make them something of a tourist attraction at gardens around the world.

As soon as I read the name, I remembered the news stories about the Denver corpse flower, which the Botanic Gardens had rather unimaginatively named "Stinky." It drew huge crowds to the Gardens, and several of my family members went to visit it, but I passed on their invitations. Even back then, I'd smelled enough corpses to last a lifetime.

Stinky was housed inside the greenhouse complex, which was a straight shot along the cobblestone path where I was standing.

In just a few minutes, I was close enough to see the nearest door to the greenhouse building—and it was standing wide open, allowing weak light to spill through. My heart thudded with adrenaline, and I was so focused on moving quickly and avoiding the remnants that I didn't see the long object lying across the cobblestones in front of me. I tripped, sprawling forward as the cell phone flew out of my hand and skittered away into the darkness.

I cursed under my breath, rubbing at my skinned palms. I wasn't usually that clumsy. Rising to all fours, I turned around and squinted down to see what I'd stumbled over. There was just enough light coming from the solar lanterns for me to make out a black jacket, black pants, and a badge hanging on a belt. I gasped and fell back onto my ass. It was the security guard.

After I got over the initial shock, I quickly reached forward to check the carotid pulse at the man's neck, hoping someone had just knocked him unconscious. Nothing. I held my hand in front of his nose, checking for a breath. But he was dead and, as far as I could tell from the little solar-powered lights, without a mark on him.

Fear turned my stomach into fluttery acid. I'd hoped that the draugr would wait to kill again until he learned whether or not Emil had succeeded in taking me. There was no way to know if he'd decided to "feed" out of boredom, or if he'd figured out that Emil was dead and I was still loose. I stood up on slightly shaky legs, trying to make a decision: keep going or go back and wait for help? But if I called Simon and Lily, Quinn would insist on coming too, and then the draugr could press him into doing anything.

The decision ended up being moot, anyway. Despite my efforts, finding the cell phone in the dark proved impossible. I had no idea where it had slid off the path, and it was one little object in an enormous cluster of plant life. I swore under my breath. So much for my plan to call Lysander when I got close.

Then I smelled it.

The stench wafting along the cool night breeze was almost comically bad. It did smell like a dead body, but also like Charlie's poopy diapers from when Sam had been breastfeeding, and a little bit like rotten eggs. In fact, if those three scents got together and had an olfactory baby from hell, that would be the smell of the corpse flower. What else could it be?

But the corpse flower supposedly only smelled when it was blooming, and as far as I knew, that wouldn't happen again for at least a few years . . . unless there was someone with power over life and death in there, manipulating it. I holstered the revolver and lifted the shotgun, stepping forward with my eyes trained on the open greenhouse door.

I crept through the open doorway into a short corridor with a cluster of drifting remnants. There was another open doorway just a few feet down the hall. He had turned on a bright light inside that room, and that's where the smell was originating. My eyes were watering, but I stepped forward resolutely, keeping my weapon raised and my footfalls soft. When I reached the doorway, I put my back against it and peeked around the side.

Lysander was there in all his mammoth-sized glory, standing in front of the greenhouse window in his big coat. He had his back to me, but I could see that his arms were raised and waving like a conductor. I looked beyond him and recognized the famous corpse flower in full bloom. As Lysander moved his hands, the plant's enormous single petal—it probably had a more scientific name, but I didn't know it—peeled down from its center stalk, displaying bruise-purple coloring on the inside. The stench worsened. Then Lysander waved a hand, and the petal closed back up again.

He was *playing* with it.

The flower weighed nearly a hundred and fifty pounds, and watching him manipulate it was fascinating, like watching a time-lapse video in reverse. But I tore my eyes off it and aimed the Ithaca at the back of Lysander's head. I let out a silent exhalation and began to squeeze the trigger—

"I don't really think it smells much like death. Do you?"

I froze, though he hadn't so much as craned his head to look at me. "A hint of it, certainly, but not enough to earn its name." He paused, and when it was clear that I wasn't going to answer, he finally lowered his arms and turned around, dry amusement on his face. "You don't really think that in my thousands of years of life no one's *ever* tried to shoot me in the head?"

Well, there went the element of surprise. I considered lowering the Ithaca—but then again, why take his word for it?

I pulled the trigger.

I had loaded the old 12-gauge with three-inch magnum shots, the heaviest ammunition I could handle, and just for the hell of it, I slam-fired all four shots in a row. It was literally the most damage I could do short of an actual grenade.

The shells should have blown at *least* part of his head off. Instead, his temple just looked a little dented.

While I was still gaping, Lysander turned back toward the corpse flower, raising one hand, and I felt something sort of brush past the part of me that was witch, like a breeze ruffling my hair. Then the corpse flower withered and collapsed, as did the pretty decorative plants surrounding it. Plants don't have souls—they don't even glow in my boundary mindset—but Lysander seemed to be drawing the very life out of them. As he did, the damage to his head repaired itself. He began turning around to face me. Was it my imagination, or had he shrunk a little?

"Neat trick," I said, my heart ricocheting around my ribs. "How fast can you do it?"

Quick as I could, I dropped the Ithaca on its sling, drew the big Smith & Wesson revolver, and fired bullet after bullet into Lysander's head. I'm an excellent shot, and I wasn't standing very far away, so every single .357 round impacted his skull.

But Lysander didn't fall. Instead, he stretched out both his arms, and there was a fleeting rush of power in the room. I instinctively closed my eyes, like you do for a gust of wind, and when I opened them, all of the plants in the greenhouse were dry husks on the floor, and Lysander was looking at me calmly, a terrible smile spreading over his face. I might be able to play with the essence of people, but Lysander could suck the life out of anything. And now his face was perfectly healed, although it was a few inches lower than it had been. At least that was something.

"Interesting," he said condescendingly, as though I had tried to eat peas using a knife instead of a spoon. "My turn."

He pointed toward me, his fingers flicking outward. I dove to the side and managed to avoid most of the raw force he sent careening toward me, like a souped-up version of the Pellars' catapult spell. The edge of it caught my shoulder, though, and I spun sideways, jarring my back against the door frame.

"Let's take this outside," Lysander declared. He raised his hand to flick at me again, and this time I was too off-balance to dodge. The energy hit me in the stomach and I shot backward, straight through the greenhouse window, and was airborne for what felt like an hour. I passed through several remnants as I flew, sending bursts of bleakness through my mind as I crashed down on the pavement outside.

It hurt. In a lot of places.

I groaned against the blazing pain and flexed my limbs to check for broken bones. That hurt even more, and a whimper escaped my lips before I heard Lysander's steady footsteps in the corridor. I couldn't take another hit like that, so I crawled forward to a short ledge and tipped my body over the edge. It was only about three feet to the ground, but landing hurt almost as much the second time. At least he couldn't see me from the greenhouse door.

I huddled back against the wall, digging ammunition out of my pocket and reloading the revolver as quickly as I could. The footsteps paused, and then I heard a low, hollow chuckle. "Hiding? Truly? All right, little deathling, I'll play." There was a long scrape as he sent giant potted plants flying off the ledge over my head. They crashed to the ground with enough force to shatter the enormous clay pots. I covered my face against the impact, but a few bits of broken pottery scraped against my hands. I gritted my teeth. Tossing stuff around, that was garden-variety witch magic. Where was he getting it?

Then I remembered the security guard. Right. He'd taken a life, which for a boundary witch was like the fuel to do regular spells. How long would the magical energy from a human death last? It wasn't something I'd ever cared to find out.

"I admit, I didn't expect you to fire," Lysander continued. "You have more courage than most of those who have challenged me. Unfortunately, no more intelligence." He'd moved in the opposite direction from my hiding spot, and I heard another crash as he threw something else. "You think you're safe because your magic doesn't want you to die," he called out, "but that only means I can cause you that much more pain before your body yields."

Think, Lex. Okay, first thing, I needed to disarm him. I couldn't take away his magic, but maybe I could force him to use up whatever he had left. There were no other people here he could rob of life, so he'd have no other way to get energy for trades magic. There were still the plants, but corpse flower aside, how much magic could you wring out of plant life?

I stood up and turned around. "If it's any consolation, you're a huge disappointment to me too, *Father.*"

He whirled around, irritation crossing his face. I could barely see him through the darkness and the always-moving wisps of ghost, but in this lighting his blue skin almost cast an eerie glow. Then he smiled, and his body seemed to suddenly sink into the cobblestones.

My mouth dropped open as he disappeared. The draugr could swim through earth. Kirsten had mentioned something about this ability, which explained how he could constantly rise and fall from the grave, but I'd forgotten. No wonder Lysander was hiding in the Botanic Gardens. It was nothing but natural earth and graves.

Before I could begin to contemplate a move, his body rose back up from the ground and resurfaced about three inches in front of my face. I took a few quick steps back, and registered that he'd changed again. Gone was the eight-foot-tall behemoth I'd first met, now replaced by a smallish man of about five-seven. So the more magic he used, the smaller he got. Good to know.

"Disappointment?" he sneered, as if all I'd wanted my whole life was a birth father who could melt into the ground. "You spend your life as a vampire's lackey, wishing you could be part of the family that pretends to accept you. Whereas *I* . . ." To finish his point, he thrust out an arm, like a dancer reaching for his partner, and I could feel the brush of magic again. It was as if some sort of force was being sucked into his arm. I was so focused on him that it took me a moment to realize that every single plant on that side of his body, for as far as I could see, had just shriveled up and died.

And the draugr grew in front of me. Theatrically, he thrust out his other arm and did the same thing on the other side. The power seemed to visibly rush up his skin and toward his face, which suddenly grew as his mass increased. I stumbled backward, needing to tilt my head up to look at him. He stepped forward, advancing on me. In no rush to kill me.

Okay, yeah. I was out of my league. I was not going to beat him with magic.

"All these tricks," I said, trying to keep my voice from shaking as I retreated, "and yet you're still basically a stud horse that the boundary witches trot out whenever they need to put some life back in the gene pool. No pun intended."

He paused, and I got the impression that for the first time since we'd met, I'd actually thrown him a little. Or just really, really pissed him off. I kept talking, as quickly as I could get the words out. "I mean, they wake you from the dead, update you on our world, and send you out on *errands*? 'Hey, Sandy, here's a cell phone and a combustion engine, now go get a new broodmare and kill all my enemies.' And you think *I'm* the lackey?"

His eyes narrowed into slits, and he raised a hand and flicked another powerful wave of energy at me. I was ready for it, though, and I darted sideways, doing a neat little roll that *really* hurt the bruises on my back. "You know nothing of me," he spat.

"So explain it," I challenged. I was backing up slowly again, but he followed. "You're the Knights of Death's secret weapon, sure, but do you ever make any decisions? Come to think of it, can you even make the call on killing me? I mean, here I am with my grade-A uterus and plenty of boundary magic." I gave him a derisive look. "Don't you need to run this by someone in charge?"

He shot energy at me again, and again I managed to duck it, but not quite as easily this time. My body was slowing down from all the abuse, and it didn't help that I'd walked through at least three remnants since I'd come out from hiding. But at least he'd shrunk down a little. He stepped toward me again. I didn't want to keep backing up—he'd killed all the plants in this area, so moving to a new section with more plant life was not optimal—but I needed to buy a little more time to recover before I could fight him. I took another step back.

"You said Maven was an old enemy," I tried. "Did she actually do something to you, or were you just kind of *ordered* to hate her?"

I didn't actually see steam coming out of his blue ears, but the look on his face pretty much implied it. "She is the last of them," he hissed, and thankfully he stopped advancing. He wanted to be heard, just like every Bond villain ever. "The last of those who opposed our people, who stood by and allowed evocators to be slaughtered like lambs."

My brow furrowed, and I didn't have to fake my confusion. "The last member of what?"

His head tilted, as if to say *she didn't tell you?* But he answered me. "The last of the Concilium."

Chapter 39

I stared, shocked. Maven had once been part of the ruling body for the entire Old World.

My tired, battered brain began to scrape together all the snippets of information that had been right in front of me. I flashed back to a moment six months ago, when Maven was rambling after she defeated Clara. *I did not want to lead, you know. The last time . . . ended badly.* At the time, I hadn't really analyzed the statement, but now I realized she had been referring to the Concilium.

This certainly explained why Lysander wanted to kill Maven, but the way he'd said "the last of them" rang a bell in my mind. "The Concilium didn't fall because of the colonization into North America, did it?" I asked him.

His blue lips twisted in a sardonic smile. "Of course not. It fell because I killed them. All but the youngest member."

"How?" I asked. I was so intent on the story that for a moment I forgot to be afraid of him. "How could you kill the strongest vampires in the world? Surely you didn't press all of them. Eventually they must have caught on."

He nodded, obviously pleased with himself. "I pressed the first two and poisoned the rest."

"Belladonna," I whispered. Maven's aversion to belladonna. No wonder.

"Yes. After it took effect, I tore their heads off." His lips pressed together in a thin line. "But one of them escaped me. For five hundred years, I hoped to finish what I started. Imagine my surprise when I found her hiding with one of my own deathlings."

His face brightened into a sudden crooked smile. It didn't look right on him. "But you're mistaken about one thing. I have no intention of killing you, not tonight. With your—what did you call it? Your grade-A uterus?" He stepped closer, his voice dropping to a whisper. "You need to learn manners, little girl. I can put your body through unimaginable horrors. I will kill you, break you, and teach you to obey me. I have broken so many before. Your mother, for instance."

"My mother escaped you," I said through gritted teeth. "She gave up her life for me, in every way possible. And I bet you don't even remember her name."

He snarled and started forward again. I stepped backward. "Which is fine," I went on, "because you don't deserve to say it out loud."

That was when I stumbled.

It was my own fault—I'd forgotten to pay attention to where I was going as I retreated. In the back of my mind, I'd figured I had acres and acres to run from him, and as long as I led him deeper into the Gardens rather than toward the exit, I would be able to keep him away from people. Sure, there were foot-deep ponds here and there across the property, but I could survive wet feet.

But the topography of the park included more than just ponds and buildings. My foot slipped over the edge of the walkway and onto soft grass. I regained my balance and glanced over my shoulder, but there were no lights behind me, not even the little solar torches. I stared into the darkness, and after only a few seconds my eyes adjusted. I realized we were at the brink of the Garden's grass amphitheater: four slopes leading down to a big tiled base in the center, where they held outdoor concerts in the summer.

In the seconds it took me to recognize where I was, however, Lysander saw his opportunity. He blasted me with another wave of energy, sending me flying. And even as I was in the air, I knew how much the landing was going to hurt.

I was right. I hit the grass a quarter of the way down, but my body kept tumbling, rolling with a momentum I was helpless to stop. My right wrist snapped as I instinctively tried to catch myself, but at that point it was just one more pain added to many.

I fell forever, losing both firearms in the process, and when I finally caught my body on the hard tiles at the bottom, it wasn't fast enough for me to keep my head from thunking on the ground.

I don't think I blacked out, but I was too stunned to do anything but collapse on my stomach, the tiles cool on my cheek.

My mind lazily drifted to the scene in *Raiders of the Lost Ark* when Indiana Jones is trying to find a spot that doesn't hurt. Everything hurt. Even my elbows and lips. My wrist and the bump on my head screamed the loudest, but I was too dazed to really register it. So much pain. I was in awe of it.

But he's coming for you, Sam's voice insisted. Groaning and keeping my bad wrist in the air, I managed to roll onto my back, giving me a view of the top of the embankment. It was too dark to see anything but the stars, drifting down toward me. Wait, no, that wasn't right. Stars don't all fall at once. I squeezed my eyes shut and opened them again, trying to jump-start my sluggish thoughts.

"You want to resist? To be a hero?" Lysander called down to me. He was in the same position at the top of the amphitheater. "Fine. Resist them."

The glowing figures descending on me were not, in fact, stars. They were remnants. Hundreds of them. Thousands.

On a whim—and because it was the only thing I could do that didn't involve movement—I dropped into my boundary mindset, where I saw life as sparks inside of people. To my surprise, the remnants looked more or less the same in the boundary mindset: smoky wisps of people. But when I was viewing them through a lens of magic, I saw them in greater detail. Each of them was swirling with black, just like the gray fox, and they were being driven toward me like cattle.

The leaders of the crowds descending on me had reached the tiles now, and were creeping closer. Before they completely surrounded me, blotting out the stars, I caught one brief glimpse of Lysander. If Maven glowed in my mindset like the sun, Lysander was a supernova of swirling, oily black. The figure threw back his head and laughed as the remnants fell upon me like I was the last spark of warmth in an eternal winter.

Chapter 40

A tattered woman with a black eye thrust a revolver in my face and squeezed the trigger. I fell out of a boat and my limbs wouldn't move right, didn't know how to swim. I lay wasting away in a bed with white sheets, coughing blood into the pillowcase because I was too weak to lift my head. An enormous steer knocked me down, and I could feel its hooves begin to slice into my back.

Death after death pounded into me as the remnants attacked. Although none of my physical wounds were fatal, I felt like I was finally drifting toward my own death. I curled into myself, shivering as each ghost took a bite from my aura, at everything that made me me. I was so cold. I was so lost. The barrage of ghosts continued, and I drifted further from myself. *I'm sorry, Sam,* I thought. *I don't know how to fight.*

Yes you do, cried a voice in my head, but it wasn't Sam's voice, not unless Sam had developed a Russian accent after death. This confused me enough to bring me back to myself for a moment. The voice spoke again, *You have everything you need, baby girl. Do not let this perversion take you, too.*

Valerya.

I couldn't begin to process the fact that my dead birth mother had just communicated with me telepathically. I just couldn't.

The deaths were still coming, but I tried to focus my thoughts, just for a second. She said I had what I needed, but what did I have? The shotgun and the revolver were around here somewhere, but they were useless against remnants. I still had the knife in its sheath. And—

I lifted my uninjured hand and clutched the cord around my neck. The necklace had fallen out of my shirt and was lying on the ground inches from my skin. I groped along the cord until I could wrap my hand around the obsidian.

Nothing happened.

It was an effort not to panic, not to allow my thoughts to fizzle out and images of death to claim me. I tried to remember how to even think about magic. What was the first thing Simon had taught me?

Extend your senses.

I blocked out everything that was coming at me and focused on the skin of my hand, the way the smooth stone felt as it warmed to my touch. I concentrated on the idea of vibrations, the beautiful chunk of mahogany obsidian tuning to my body. And then I listened for the stone, the same way I'd listen to my own body.

The images of death vanished.

I still hurt, and I still felt cold, but now that the psychic attack had ended I could at least think again. The relief was immediate, like jumping into a cool pond on a steamy day. But the remnants continued to mill around me, passing straight through me, making it impossible for me to see beyond them.

On the other hand, I realized, the remnants would also make it impossible for Lysander to see *me* from his perch at the top of the amphitheater. He was letting the ghosts take all the fight out of me so he could swoop in, pick me up, and ferry me off to concubine camp. But now I had bought myself a few seconds before he'd realize I was no longer suffering.

Think, Lex, think. I listened for Valerya or Sam, but I heard nothing, and I realized that just as the obsidian was protecting me from psychic attack, it was probably keeping me from psychic help.

You have everything you need. That implied more than one thing, didn't it?

Valerya's stone. I lifted my hand with the broken wrist and gingerly touched the large chunk of bloodstone, wrapping my skin around it. I concentrated on it just as I had with the obsidian.

I suddenly felt . . . better. Grounded. Clear. Strong.

And I knew what to do.

I needed my hands free, so I used my good hand to unceremoniously stuff both of the stones into my sports bra, just over my heart. It was weird and awkward, but I didn't care. I wasn't going to risk losing contact with them again. I stood up, ignoring the remnants that continued to swarm around and through me, drew the knife from the sheath on my back, and swiftly made a shallow cut on my right forearm, well above the broken part.

As the blood beaded on my arm, I felt the frenzied remnants go still, attracted to the death magic in my blood. Ignoring them as best I could, I knelt down on the tiles, dipped my fingers in the blood, and drew a dark red circle. It was clumsy and a little lopsided, but it closed tight, and that was all that mattered.

It seemed like there should be words—an incantation, a spell, something—but Simon had told me that the stronger the witch, the less necessary rituals became. So I just stepped outside the circle, looked down on it, and concentrated on a single word, a single idea. And when I was ready, I said it out loud.

"Door."

There was no puff of light, no smoke, no glitter of any kind. But the brown tile at the bottom of the amphitheater faded away, replaced by a dark, swirling smoke. It was neither ominous nor celestial; it was just an exit. A bridge.

I felt the attention of the remnants and raised both my arms. "Go," I commanded them, in the same tone I used when I pressed vampires. "Be at rest. Be at peace. It's time."

One by one, the remnants drifted toward the circle I'd drawn—the bridge to the other side. They crossed over the line of blood, some hesitant, some greedy, and each one sank into the tile and vanished, not unlike the way the draugr moved through the earth.

My body, which had been in such pain only a few minutes earlier, thrilled with the magic. The pain was still there in the background, but it had been replaced, however temporarily, by something else. A radiance I had never expected.

I assumed Lysander was still at the top of the amphitheater, but as long as he didn't come down here, I didn't bother looking for him. My attention was on the remnants making their way across the line. Many of them passed through me on the way, but I felt nothing except a brief gust of cold. After a few minutes I closed my eyes and dropped into my boundary mindset, where I could see more detail.

They were smiling at me. Every single one of them. Smiles of gratitude, of relief, of incredible peace. I smiled back, tears running down my cheeks.

One of the remnants seemed just a little brighter and more alert than the others. He held back a little, and after all the others had gone through, he turned to me and extended a hand, palm up. Hesitantly, I moved my good hand to hover over his. He bent down and pressed his lips to my hand, the briefest kiss of cold. *Thank you*, he mouthed as he looked up at me. I nodded, and he took a step backward, his grateful eyes still on me. He vanished through the circle.

I released the mindset and crouched down, my broken wrist cradled to my chest. I licked a finger on my good hand and carefully wiped away a line of blood, breaking the circle.

Lysander floated up through the ground a few feet to the side, making me topple over in surprise. He had shrunk down to my own height—apparently directing the remnants was magically taxing.

But his smile was cruel as he raised his hands to applaud. How had a thousands-year-old conduit learned about sarcastic applause?

"Very impressive," he said, not sounding particularly impressed. "Someone has been teaching you." He closed his eyes and seemed to take a deep breath, but I recognized the expression. He was feeling around with his magic too. Extending his senses, as Simon would say.

His eyes opened. "Perhaps the dead boundary witch here in Denver has taught you a few tricks? I must remember to pay her a visit later. Thank her for helping my daughter." His smile said that he would be doing anything but thanking Nellie.

"Fuck you," I managed to say, still clutching my broken wrist. "Get out of my state. Go crawl back into your hole."

He laughed. "You still don't understand, do you?" He gestured to the tiles, which still held the broken circle of blood. "None of this matters. You killed Emil, you laid the remnants to rest, but you still cannot beat *me*. You will *never* beat me. I said I won't kill you, but I can come after your friends, your little niece. That vampire you're fucking." He extended his hand. "Or you can take my hand and walk out of here with me, right now."

I didn't move, didn't answer. His expression softened. "You've shown me you are a worthy prize, deathling. Come with me willingly, and I will treat you well. And all the people who love you will be safe."

We were frozen for a moment, his hand extended in peace, a respectful smile on his face. I would be well treated. My family and friends wouldn't be harmed.

You're more than just a bulletproof vest, Lex.

Be a witch.

You have everything you need, baby girl.

I pushed the voices out of my head and reached up to Lysander, offering him my injured forearm. I knew my expression was defeated, conflicted, remorseful. That was fine. He took my forearm gently, helping me to my feet with a broad smile on his face. Maybe it was because he'd shrunk down to nearly my height, but this close, and in the dim lighting, he seemed utterly human. That made what I had to do even harder.

Where did Lysander's magic come from, what was the *one thing* that we both had?

Blood.

As fast as I have ever moved in my life, I lifted the combat knife I'd pulled from its back holster and slashed it across Lysander's throat, digging in as deeply as I could. While his eyes were still widening in pain, I bent and jabbed the knife into the meat of his thigh, digging for the femoral artery.

He was thrown off-balance by the two sources of pain, and it took him a full second to stretch out his arms toward the grass, trying to suck in more life that he could sacrifice to heal his wounds.

But my idea was working. Lysander couldn't make new blood any faster than anyone else, not without boosting his body with magic. And there were no more lives for him to suck up and turn into witch magic—he couldn't take mine, as a fellow witch.

He tried to fend me off, but I only attacked harder. I reversed the knife grip and stabbed for the carotid artery, the brachial artery in his arm, all of the major organs I could remember. I did it quickly, *fwip-fwip-fwip*, going for speed over accuracy. He bellowed with pain and rage, but the blood was pouring out of him now, and though he squeezed enough magic out of the Gardens to heal a couple of wounds, he couldn't heal them all. I kept going, darting around him in a circle as he began to slow down. The amphitheater grass all around us had turned as brown and dry as old pine needles. Now there was nothing left for him to kill.

Except for me. He couldn't use my spirit, but I could see him deciding that revenge would be a nice consolation prize. He took one step toward me, but the blood was flowing now, the tiles getting slippery, and I thought, *more*. I plunged the knife again and again, reopening the few wounds he'd healed, carving new ones. I stopped aiming at arteries and just stabbed and sliced anywhere that wasn't already bleeding. He fought me, getting in a few blows to my face and arm, but the more strikes I made, the more feeble he became. At last, with a widening pool of blood spreading over the tiles around us, Lysander dropped to his knees. I made one final cut, to the draugr's jugular, and he collapsed with a splash of blood.

Chapter 41

I froze after he fell, not sure what to do. I knew next to nothing about the draugr's physiology. Boundary magic had sustained him, but if my own experiences were any indication, he wasn't exactly dead—more like in stasis, waiting for the medical intervention or passing of time that would allow his biology to restart.

I wasn't going to let that happen.

My knife was sharp, but I only had one good hand. Cradling my injured arm, I scooted painfully across the tiles, slogging through the blood until I reached the shotgun, which lay at the far end of the tiles. I dug in my coat pocket for more rounds, and managed to reload using mostly just one hand. I couldn't slam-fire one-handed, so I had to painstakingly pump the shotgun, hold it in the exact position I wanted it on Lysander's neck, and squeeze the trigger with my left hand. Then I propped the shotgun against my body, pumped it again, and repeated.

On the third shot, Lysander's spinal cord blew apart.

Only then did I let myself fall.

Lysander had a disposable phone on him, so I was able to call Lily. I knew Quinn's number by heart too, but I didn't have the guts to call him myself. Lily promised that she and Simon were on the way to help, and I eyed Lysander's body and asked her to bring clothes, some baggies, and an ax. The last request clearly bewildered her, but she seemed too relieved to hear from me to ask questions. I asked her to get Quinn to send the Denver cleanup crew to the Botanic Gardens right away to begin covering our tracks. I had no idea how they were going to explain the dead guard, the withered plants, or the damaged buildings, but I didn't actually give a shit. I was done.

As soon as I hung up the phone, I lowered myself onto the sloping dead grass and let my eyes drift shut.

An hour later, everyone had arrived. The Denver cleanup crew, a man and a woman I'd seen a couple of times before, immediately got to work on dismembering Lysander's body. It sounded grisly, but dismemberment wouldn't actually kill him—not that I would have been sorry if it did. While they chopped—looking alarmingly well-practiced—Simon got to work bagging up some of Lysander's blood. Thanks to the tiles and a small Wet Vac he was able to collect quite a bit of it, and he also took some samples for his own experiments. I only watched him for a second, but he had a dopey grin on his face as he labeled sample bags. For Simon, I'd essentially declared an extra Christmas this year. Lysander was an actual conduit, and studying his samples would completely reenergize all the studies Simon had been doing for the last six months.

Quinn hadn't come with them, but I hadn't really expected him to. Someone had to stay with Maven's body and keep it safe in case Lysander had other deputies.

And I'd pressed him not to worry about me.

Lily, on the other hand, came straight over to me, took one look at my wrist and my various bruises, and ordered me to go to the hospital immediately. Since I was covered in Lysander's blood and there was nowhere we could quickly shower, she dragged me to a garden hose and helped me out of my clothes, casting looks around us to see if anyone else was watching. I didn't give a damn, myself. Anyone who really wanted to see me naked could have at it.

It was a warm spring night, but I shivered a little in the night air as Lily picked up the spray nozzle. "Are you sure?" she asked nervously. "This water has to be pretty cold."

"Just get it over with."

When the icy water had sloughed off all the blood and I was dressed in a set of Lily's yoga clothes, I went over to Simon, who crouched next to Lysander's remains, scribbling notes in a small Moleskine. He looked up as I approached and, without a word between us, took off his canvas jacket and wrapped it around my shoulders. I smiled my thanks, and he volunteered to personally clean off my weapons and get them back to me. He *was* excited.

I stepped closer, hoping no one from the Denver team would overhear. "Si, I need you to take possession of *every single one* of those body parts," I said in a low voice. "Get them to your skin beetles, okay?" He gave me a curious look, but I just shook my head, my expression suggesting we'd talk later. "If anyone challenges you, use Maven's name," I whispered. "I'll take the heat."

His expression grew serious, but he just nodded. "Are you going to be okay?" he called as I struggled back toward an impatient Lily.

"Eventually."

Lily drove me to one of the biggest hospitals in Denver, where she told the hospital staff that I had been in a tractor accident on my farm. A car accident would have been more plausible, but in that case I would have arrived by ambulance, with the police in tow. A kind nurse did ask specifically about the bruises on my neck and around my eye, which were clearly older than the others. I explained that I had been mugged a couple of days ago, and it was a completely separate incident. That raised skeptical eyebrows, but no one challenged me directly.

After I was admitted, Lily had quite a few suggestions for the intake nurses. I smiled and let my attention wander as she bustled me around to X-ray and CT technicians, never leaving my side. When the final count was tallied in the early morning hours, I had three broken ribs, a bruised kidney, a broken wrist that would eventually require surgery, and a concussion.

I had gotten off easy.

They made me stay in the hospital overnight to monitor the kidney problem, and I was hurting too much to protest. Then I was on too much morphine to protest. And then I was too asleep to protest.

I heard snatches of conversation as I slept, and voices that seemed so familiar, but I tuned it all out. When I opened my eyes again, sunlight was streaming in through hospital curtains, and the clock on the wall said 4:00. I'd been out for more than twelve hours.

There was something in my hand. Lifting it seemed like too much work, so my eyes wandered to my left. And met the warm brown eyes of John Wheaton.

Even through the morphine haze, my mouth dropped open with shock.

"We have to stop meeting like this," he said frankly.

I was so surprised that I laughed, a choking noise that probably sounded a lot more like asphyxiation than humor. John winced and apologized, but I shook my head a little. "S'okay," I mumbled. Then I finally realized why he was here. My parents were my emergency contacts. Oh, crap. They knew. I groaned. "How much trouble am I in?"

John held his hands about three feet apart. "Your folks were pretty freaked out. Your dad couldn't fly because his back is acting up again, so he and Christy are driving back. Charlie and I caught a flight this morning. She's with Cara right now."

"Surprised my mom didn't come instead," I mumbled.

John gave me the half-smile I knew as well as my own face in the mirror. "I insisted."

Joy blossomed inside me, but then his face turned stony and he added, "I figured you probably wouldn't be able to tell them whatever really happened, and might not have had time to cook up a story yet."

"John . . ."

He sighed, pulling back from me. He stood up and paced a few feet away. "I know. It's not your fault. It's never your fault." The words were harsh, but he didn't sound angry. He sounded heartsick.

"John . . ." I said again. "She's going to be okay. I won't let anything happen to her, I swear."

He spun around, looking incredulous. "You . . . you think *that's* why I'm upset? That I'm worried about Charlie?"

My brow furrowed, which somehow managed to hurt a little. "Why else would you be upset?"

"For the love of . . . Lex! I'm worried about *you*, you idiot!" He dropped back into the chair, giving me a completely exasperated look. "I know Charlie's going to be okay. Of *course* Charlie's going to be okay, because you would die before you let anything happen to her. And you told me you can't die." He gestured to the tubes in my good arm, and the taping and heavy neon cast holding together my broken wrist. "But look at what you're putting yourself through! Look at how broken you are, all in service to Charlie! How can I live with that? How can I let that go on, while I sit around doing nothing?"

I stared at him, openmouthed. *That* was what was bothering him this whole time? Then why had he stopped having me babysit on Fridays?

Because he didn't want to be any more indebted to you than he already felt, I answered myself. We were both idiots.

"You're not doing nothing," I said when I could manage it. "You're raising a toddler by yourself, holding down a demanding job, and putting up with two different nutty families. I'd rather have my gig than yours."

It was his turn to laugh then, and I saw him brush away tears with the back of his hand. But he shook his head. "It's not enough. You're risking everything, and I can't even . . . it's not enough."

I didn't need Sam's voice in the back of my head to know what to say this time. "But Charlie needs her father more than anything I could ever do for her. She needs you home every day, changing diapers and singing songs and stepping on Legos. Having an aunt is great. Having a parent is imperative."

His face softened as he finally relented. He reached out and squeezed my good fingers. "I love you," he said softly.

"I love you, too. And I love Charlie."

"I know you do, Allie. She's as much yours as she is mine." He gave my fingers a final squeeze and stood up. "I should let you rest now."

I snagged his hand. "Hang on. Can I borrow your phone for a minute?"

He raised an eyebrow, not unlike Quinn, but handed it over. I opened a new text message and addressed it to all the members of my family, including my parents. By the time I got all the names in I was sick of typing with one hand, so I gave it back to John to take dictation. "FYI, Lex was in a minor car accident last night, getting checked out at BCH. She's fine, just a broken wrist." It didn't hurt that my actual car was in the shop by now, thanks to Simon's arrangements.

Before he could hit "Send," I asked John, "What do you think for emoticons?" I pretended to give the matter serious thought. "Is there one with like a tiny ambulance? Maybe an exploding car?"

"I do *not* emoticon," he said airily as he sent the text. He pocketed the phone and kissed my forehead. "I'll come visit in the morning with Charlie, okay?"

"That would be nice."

As he walked away, a thought sprang to life in my brain, out of nowhere, and I heard myself blurt, "Hey, John? What made you decide to go to Disney World?"

He paused on his way to the door. For a moment he looked bewildered. "I . . . I don't know. I wasn't planning on it or anything. I was just going to do a dinner for Charlie's birthday, keep things low-key, but then . . . I don't know."

I waved him on. "Never mind. I'm just glad you guys had fun."

When he had disappeared down the hall, I let the smile fade from my face, feeling a sudden ache of grief. Emil. He must have gotten one of the Denver vampires to press John into taking Charlie and my parents out of town. I was sure it hadn't been Lysander—he would have just killed anyone in his path. Hell, he'd probably told Emil to kill John, Charlie, and my parents to pave the way for Emil to swoop in and pose as my long-lost family member. But my brother had chosen to spare them. Charlie was, after all, his niece, too.

Maybe Sam had been right about Emil after all.

Chapter 42

After John left, I called Elise to check in. I had to spend a little time reassuring her that I was okay and she didn't need to visit me in the hospital. As much as I loved my cousin, if anyone would recognize that my injuries didn't line up with my cover story, it would be her.

"Oh, hey," I said after convincing her not to rush over. "My friend Lily thought she saw you at her yoga class last night. Any chance it was actually you?" Elise had exactly as much patience for yoga as I did.

There was a pause, and then Elise said, "Nah, I don't think so."

"Don't think so?"

"I, um, drank most of a bottle of wine last night," she admitted. "I passed out on the couch at like eight-thirty, woke up with weird bruises. I don't *think* I got up and made my way to drunken yoga, but if asked to testify under oath . . ."

I laughed. We talked a little bit about her recent pressures at work and how the police were starting to think the two dead bodies were just a bizarre coincidence. Maybe Quinn could nudge that theory along a bit. She didn't mention any weirdness at the Botanic Gardens, which just meant that the cleanup crew in Denver had done its job. If the poor security guard's body was ever found, they would make sure there was an obvious cause of death.

• • •

I checked myself out of the hospital a few hours later, ignoring the protests of two doctors and several nurses. They really just wanted me to rest in bed for the next few days, though, and I could do that at the house. As a concession to their efforts, I did call my cousin Anna to drive me home. I bought a scarf in the hospital gift shop to cover the bruises on my neck, and after exclaiming over my cast and variety of bruises for a few minutes, she didn't press me with more questions about my "accident." Which was part of why I'd called Anna instead of Elise.

I'd put on Simon's oversized canvas jacket over the yoga top, and when I reached out to push the elevator button I automatically tugged up one sleeve. "Ooh!" Anna said, seizing my good arm. "New tat?"

"Oh. Um. Not super new," I said, instinctively tugging down the sleeve. Then I remembered myself. "Here, check it out." I slipped off that side of the jacket, showing off the intricate swirls of ink on my left forearm.

"A griffin!" Anna squealed. "That is so cool! Am I the inspiration?"

"Definitely," I told her. "I've got one on the other arm, too." I waved the cast.

She threw her arms around me, then reared back when I grunted in pain. "Oh! Sorry! But seriously, that is just . . . wow. What a fantastic design!"

While Anna drove toward the cabin I borrowed her phone—I really needed to go find mine at some point—and called Jake. He insisted on keeping all my animals at his clinic for one more night so I could rest. He promised to deliver them to the cabin in several trips the following day.

Anna wanted to sleep over and keep an eye on me, but I insisted I was just going to take some painkillers and go to sleep again, so there was no point in her hanging around.

The cabin was strangely silent after she left. It was a bit relaxing not to have animals prowling around fighting over the cat food, but mostly I missed the company of Dopey and Pongo, and the joyful energy of Chase and Cody. I even missed the cats, though they generally regarded me as an employee who occasionally moonlighted as furniture.

I took the painkillers, as promised, but I couldn't seem to fall asleep. At eight-thirty, I was lying in my bed, scratching at the edges of my cast.

I wanted to call him. I *really* wanted to call him. But what would I even say? *Sorry I brainwashed you? Look, honey, it was for your own good? Everything turned out okay, so let's just move on?* It all sounded condescending, insulting, and just generally terrible.

But I missed him.

At nine-thirty, I couldn't stand it any longer. I unfolded the covers, carefully climbed out of bed, and stepped into some old Toms. I was still wearing Lily's yoga clothes—they were too tight for me to take off by myself with the cast on, and I'd forgotten to ask Anna for help before she left—but I managed to thread my cast through the sleeve of Simon's jacket again, and drape a scarf around my neck. Then I called a cab.

I didn't know where they had moved Maven, so I asked the cab driver to take me to Magic Beans, figuring Quinn might be there tying up loose ends or dealing with the business stuff. Or at least someone there would know where he was. The cabdriver eyed me in the rearview mirror the whole time, although I couldn't really blame him, all things considered.

The ride into downtown Boulder cost more than I made in half a shift at the Depot. When I finally walked into the coffee shop, the same kid at the front counter had his nose stuffed in a textbook, and I remembered that finals were happening this week. It felt like Maven had summoned Quinn and me here to tell us about the belladonna at least a year ago, but it had only been a few days.

Shaking my head, I walked straight past the student and back to Maven's office door, which was ajar. "Quinn?" I said, pushing it open.

He wasn't in there. Instead, Maven was sitting behind her desk, dressed in a shapeless lime-green top that wouldn't flatter anyone. She had about fifteen necklaces heaped around her neck, and her thick glasses were pushed up high on her nose. In other words, she looked completely normal. For Maven.

"Uh . . . hi . . ." I said stupidly.

She smiled, but looked nearly as surprised to see me as I was to see her. "Hello, Lex. Would you close the door, please?"

I did as she asked, then made my way toward her desk, sort of hovering in front of it. "I'm glad you're okay," I said. I would have hugged Elise or Lily in this situation, but I felt too awkward with Maven. "You look like . . . nothing happened."

She gave me a wry smile. "Mostly thanks to you, I'm told." She picked up her cell phone off the desk and sent a brief text. "Conduit blood is quite extraordinary."

"I had no idea it would work so fast."

She nodded. "Last night Quinn filled me in on most of what happened while I was . . . out," she continued. "I wanted you to know I will personally be making sure Ardie Atwood is held responsible for her role."

"Thank you," I said, meaning it. I hadn't been sure what to do about Ardie. I could have asked Maven what she planned to do to the duplicitous witch, but I decided I didn't actually care. Whatever happened to Ardie, she deserved. "Um, do you know where Quinn is?" I asked instead.

"I believe he's on his way to St. Luke's in Denver, trying to visit you," she said mildly. She gestured to her phone. "I just texted to let him know you're here."

"Oh." My face fell as I realized the implications. I'd been so afraid to talk to Quinn that I hadn't mentioned I was leaving the hospital. Stupid.

"Sit down, Lex. We have a lot to talk about."

It was almost easier to stand than to jostle my ribs and kidney, but I did as she asked, gingerly settling into one of her visitor chairs. She offered to get me something to drink or eat, but I just shook my head. There was too much I wanted to know.

"You knew who my father was the first time we met, didn't you?"

She nodded, unperturbed. "Your bloodline was too strong for you to be anything but Lysander's child."

"A deathling," I said distastefully. That had been Lysander's word for it. "So when you hired me, it was for . . . what? Bait? Insurance?"

Her face softened. "Lex . . ."

"Just tell me the truth, please," I said, trying to sound professional. "I know I'm your employee, but I do believe I have earned it."

Maven sat up in her chair, folding her hands neatly in front of her. "You're right. But you have to remember that when we first met, I was trying *not* to take an active role in running the state. My intention was always to stay in the wings and let Itachi keep things going." Vampires don't usually fidget, but her small hand rose to tuck her orange hair behind her ears. "Then you walked in here, and I couldn't believe it. I'd never heard of one of Lysander's concubines escaping from his little harem."

"But why hire me?"

"It was an impulsive decision, but not a bad one. I knew right away that someday Lysander would come for you. You wouldn't be able to stand against him on your own, but together, I thought you and I had a chance. Me for revenge, and you for independence from your family ties."

"Why not just *tell me* that?"

She arched an eyebrow. "First, because Itachi had no knowledge of my past, and I had no intention of telling him. But would you have believed me? You'd just been told about the Old World, that your niece was in danger, that you were a witch. If I had added that your father was a conduit and you yourself could raise the dead, what would you have done?"

I considered. "At the time? I probably would have laughed all the way to the mental hospital. But there have been plenty of opportunities since Itachi died."

"You're right," she said, and her tone surprised me. I'd been expecting a fight, I guess, or at least an admonishment for challenging her. But Maven wasn't like that. She didn't need to flaunt her power or use it to put me in my place. She understood what she could do, and wasn't threatened by me. How many vampires could I say that about? Two?

"But I guess I just . . . didn't want to. Everything was so unstable, and you were just beginning to understand what you were. I wanted to give you a chance to trust me, to see that I wasn't your enemy, before explaining."

I sighed, but nodded. Would I have done things any differently, in her place? "Besides," she added, "I wanted to give myself a chance to get control of this state before we challenged Lysander." Her smile was rueful. "It's only now beginning to happen, thanks to you and Quinn. If you hadn't saved me . . ."

"And Simon and Lily," I reminded her. "They were also instrumental."

"Of course." Maven studied me. "What will you do now?"

For a moment I thought she meant from an occupational standpoint, which seemed silly—I wouldn't have gone through all of this if I weren't planning to keep my job with Maven. But I saw her steady gaze, and I understood what she meant. I thought of the remnants at the Boulderado, and the poor ghosts in this very building.

"I'm going to spend a week or two in town getting better, and taking care of a few things," I said evenly. "Then I'm going to take Lysander's bones and scatter them around the world." She nodded, knowing I wasn't finished. "And after *that*," I continued, "I'm going to find the Knights of Death and burn down their fucking clubhouse." Five hundred years of kidnapping and raping boundary witches was five hundred years too many. I wasn't about to let them have even one more.

Maven just smiled, as if that was exactly what she'd expected. "You'll need some vacation time, then," she said thoughtfully. "And a raise."

"A raise?"

She nodded. "You've saved my life three times in the last year, Lex. I'm funding your trip to disperse the draugr's bones, and when you get back, there will be a raise waiting for you." Her smile widened. "It will be substantial."

I opened my mouth to protest that I hadn't earned it, but . . . the truth was, I had. So I snapped my mouth shut and gave her a short nod. "Thank you." I would need to figure out what to do about my half-assed position at the Flatiron Depot, but I had a couple of weeks to think about it.

"You're welcome. I'd offer for you to take Quinn along, but—"

"You need him here," I finished. "I understand."

"I was going to say that you'll have an easier time traveling without a vampire, but yes. That too."

I stayed for a few more minutes while we worked out a few details for my trip, including a cover story for the humans in my life. When I finally left Maven's office, I saw Quinn leaning against the wall in the big room, giving me the crooked smile that made it impossible not to smile back. He was wearing jeans and an old leather jacket, and I wanted to run to him so badly it sent a fresh ache through my body. But I held myself back.

Quinn raised his hand, showing me a small object. My cell phone.

"You found it," I said, relieved.

I went over to take it from him, but he bent his elbow, holding it out of my reach. "You hid it from me."

I couldn't read his expression. "I was trying to protect you," I said.

"By pressing me?"

I winced, but stood my ground. "Yes."

He shook his head. "I understand why you did it. But a relationship where one person uses mind control on the other is not one I want to be in."

I bit my lip. Was he breaking up with me? Could I blame him if he was?

But he handed me the cell phone, crowding into my personal space. He leaned down and touched his forehead to mine. "Don't let it happen again, okay?" he said huskily.

"I promise," I whispered. And I kissed him.

When I finally pulled away, I brushed a couple of fresh tears off my cheeks and tucked the cell phone into my pocket. "Um, can you give me a ride home? I took a cab here."

"Of course. But you should know—you got a text from Elise about an hour ago," he said. We were moving toward the exit now. "I didn't mean to read it, but it came up on the screen. She and Natalie are playing Settlers of Catan with Paul and Jake tonight. They wanted you to come over. She said she could pick you up if you weren't able to drive."

"Okay, thanks," I said dismissively. I had no intention of going anywhere except bed.

But Quinn added, "I thought we could both go."

I stopped walking and cocked an eyebrow at him, trying not to let my heartbeat rise. "Everyone will be eating and drinking," I pointed out. "Alcohol. And human food."

He gave me an innocent look. "I'm actually allergic to alcohol," he said solemnly. "And nuts, and strawberries, and gluten . . . it's tragic, really, all my allergies. I have to be very careful."

I just barely managed to suppress a grin. "What happened to 'we can't tell your family we're serious'?"

"Allison Alexandra Luther," he said, taking my hand. "Some things are worth the risk."

Acknowledgments

Thank you for reading *Boundary Born*, and following Lex on this three-book journey. (And a special thank-you to those of you who turned up for the reader event in Boulder—Ardie, I borrowed your name!) Although I'm not done with this character, I'll be letting her do her thing in Boulder while I go back to Scarlett Bernard's adventures in Los Angeles for a bit.

Before that happens, however, I need to thank a number of people who helped me tell this story. I always thank my cousin and Boulder local Brieta Bejin for her assistance with this series, but she really went above and beyond for this book. In addition to putting me up for two different research trips and reading the book for Boulder accuracy, Briet accompanied me on a ghost tour over a lost cemetery, which is serious family loyalty. Thank you so much, cousin. Without your help and hospitality these books would be depressingly flat.

Thank you also to my husband Tyler, who put up with months of me babbling about crystals, and to my sister and beta reader Elizabeth, who once again answered the phone every time I got stuck and called her to complain. My deepest gratitude also goes to Paul Rickert, who took a turn looking over Lex's military authenticity, and to Jayme Haynes, who read through the novel for medical accuracy. Any further mistakes or liberties are mine alone.

An extremely large thank-you to Erin Bird and the Denver Botanic Gardens for all the help and information, not to mention a kick-ass ghost tour. (I apologize for killing one of your guards, who all seemed very nice.) The information about the lost cemetery is accurate to the best of my knowledge and research. If you find yourself in the Denver area, I highly recommend checking out this beautiful place and its plants. Just try not to think too hard about what else is buried there.

The Leanin' Tree Museum and Sculpture Garden is also a lovely real-life attraction (though I took a few liberties with the lighting and hours), as are the cookie-dough balls at Naked Lunch and the burritos at Illegal Pete's. Basically, Boulder is amazing and you should go there. I'm going to miss writing about this kooky, gluten-obsessed town, and I'll definitely miss having a regular excuse to visit. Well, besides you, Brieta.

About the Author

Photo © 2013 Elizabeth Kraft

Melissa F. Olson was raised in Chippewa Falls, Wisconsin, and studied film and literature at the University of Southern California in Los Angeles. After a brief stint in the Hollywood studio system, Melissa moved to Madison, Wisconsin, where she eventually acquired a master's degree from the University of Wisconsin–Milwaukee, a husband, a mortgage, two kids, and two comically oversize dogs—not at all in that order. Learn more about Melissa, her work, and her dogs at www.MelissaFOlson.com.